The Last Will and Testament of Ernie Politics

Vagrant Mystery Book 1

Brad Grusnick

Strange Scribe

This is a work of fiction. Names, characters, businesses, places, events and incidents are either the products of the author's imagination or used in a fictitious manner. Any resemblance to actual persons, living or dead, or actual events is purely coincidental.

Book Cover Design by Melissa Williams Design

Copyright © 2012 Brad Grusnick

KDP PRINT ISBN-13: 978-0615792200
INGRAM ISBN-13: 978-1511436984

For my favorite storytellers,
Richard Grusnick and Harry Kanikula.

1

The stale stink of piss snatched Ray away from the comfort of sleep. It was sweating from the walls, coupled with the stench of body odor and old cigarettes. His damp pants clung to his legs, stiffened by the holding cell's air conditioning. At first he thought he'd pissed himself, adding to the aroma of the room, but then he remembered how he'd gotten arrested. And why.

The ice machine was as good a place as any to fall asleep. Los Angeles' thick summer air drove most transient folks to the shore; cool Pacific winds and the dampness of the piers the only respite from the heat, but Ray didn't care much for the beach. Sand snuck into every pocket and crevice, buried for months in his only change of clothes. He preferred to suffer through the heat rather than find sand in his skivvies come January.

He remembered the sting of the sunbaked concrete. It seared his feet through the soles of his worn shoes as he walked the cracked sidewalk of the 101 overpass. A strip of seedy hotels on Sunset Boulevard, vacant in the daylight and popular only by the hour, offered small pockets of shade in their outdoor hallways. Ray could easily loiter there as he dug through the treasure troves of discarded soda cans next to the vending machines.

Huddled behind a wall of crumbling stucco, stewing in his own filthy juices, Ray watched a resident of the StayInn fill a towel with ice. The man, exhausted and hungover from the friendly exchange of venereal disease, let the cold air of the ice machine pour over his protruding belly before belching and stumbling away.

Making sure he wasn't being watched, Ray stuck his head inside the machine, the refrigeration cooling the dust-streaked sweat on his forehead. Frost soothed the ache building in his body and the world went away as he basked in the sterile smell of stainless steel and filtered water.

A door opening down the hall pulled him out of his daze and he closed the ice machine's lid. Beads of sweat immediately set up camp on his exposed skin. The frigid case beckoned to him, and opening the door again, he climbed in. The cold was sharp, but the dull bites of false winter were welcome after the beating he had taken from the sun pulsing in the cloudless sky.

He knew it was smart to get drunk before he tried his little experiment. A sober body couldn't have taken the constant cold and the mixture of bourbon in his veins and ice on his skin produced a comforting tingle that lulled him to sleep.

As his eyes slipped closed, he knew he'd made the right decision. When it came to the amount of paperwork a cop was willing to do for arresting a trespassing vagrant, liquored up was much easier to process than crazy. Ray also wasn't the kind of guy who got off on assaulting tourists at Hollywood and Highland.

A meth addict peered down into his field of vision, reminding him he'd accomplished his mission.

"You holdin'?" the gaunt man slurred, noxious gas billowing from behind his rotting teeth.

Ray sat up, his temples exploding as his eyes opened to the light in the room.

"Sorry, pal," Ray said.

Drugs and weapons were at the top of the list of things that didn't make it through processing, but those in need of a fix don't necessarily thrive on long-term memory or common sense.

"Ask him," Ray pointed to the bloated man with running sores on his face and neck. If the fuzz chose to not do an extensive sweep on anyone, it was the dude who might have given them leprosy. Meth Man didn't care either way. He would have licked the tubby guy's pustules dry if someone told him the juice was lined with buzzard dust. He shuffled across the room, leaving Ray to take in the rest of his roommates.

It had been a slow night for the Los Angeles Police Department. Two other drunks remained dead to the world, one wrapped around the steel communal in the corner. Decades of filth clung to his mouth as he drooled into the bowl, his lower lip stuck to the diarrhea-sprayed rim. A group of gang members had taken over the far corner of the cell. They'd managed to hang onto a deck of cards and were playing an odd variation of blackjack.

Ray stood up, bracing himself for the stiffness in his joints and swelling of his brain. He made his way over to the toilet and unzipped his fly. Doing his best to avoid splashing the bowl's current occupant, Ray stared hard into the reflective piece of metal bolted to the wall. If he was in the wrong cell or was given the wrong information, all the bullshit had been for nothing.

As his bladder finished evacuating, the final drops spattering the drunk's cheek, Ray's eye caught the small curl of paper from underneath the mirror. Tucking himself back into his ragged pants, he glanced over his shoulder. The poker game had become more heated and Chunky Sores had obviously been holding, because he and Meth Man were engaged in figuring out the best way to ingest said substance without arousing suspicion.

Ray turned his attention back to the mirror, standing as though he was still urinating, though the familiar ping was not reverberating off the bowl. He leaned forward with one hand held straight out to brace himself, like he was trying to pass a kidney stone, and began to finger the edge of the paper, prying it out from its hiding place.

He crumpled it into his palm and bent down to flush the toilet. The loud rush of water didn't awaken the sleeping drunk, he merely clutched the metal toilet tighter and darted his tongue out to lick the drops of Ray's piss off his cheek. Ray's stomach turned and he whipped around, a tattooed chest blocking his way.

"What you got there?"

He brought his eyes up from the dirty floor. Towering a good foot taller than him, one of the gang members breathed halitosis into Ray's face. His beard was shaved into a thin line at the sideburns, but gave away to a scruff of hair at the chin. One of his eyes was lazy and Ray couldn't figure out how to make eye contact with him.

"Bacon Cream!" Ray screamed.

"What muthafucka?"

"Happenstance would bequeath frosty bacon cream onto your majesty's jowls!"

A fist as large as Ray's head realigned his jaw, sending him to the ground. The impact caused his hangover to burst and the vomit burned his throat, stomach acid stinging the hole where one of his back molars had come loose. Crazy talk usually worked with the tough types, but Lazy Eye didn't care how crazy he was, his curiosity was already piqued by what Ray held in his hand.

"You puke on my kicks muthafuck?" Lazy Eye wrapped his hand around the back of Ray's neck and lifted him to his feet.

"You gonna lick that shit off them 'til theys clean, crazy muthafucka."

One eye bore into him as the other drifted off to some unknown focal point.

Ray's tooth slipped loose and dark iron began to fill his mouth. He spit the molar out and it bounced off of Lazy Eye's forehead, leaving a pink streak of blood and saliva between his caterpillar eyebrows.

"Cobb!"

Lazy Eye's rage was halted as all heads turned toward the voice beyond the bars. Ray raised his hand ever so slightly to indicate he was the one they wanted, and felt Lazy Eye's fingernails dig deep into the flesh of his neck before letting him go. By some miracle, he'd had enough sense to give the attending officer his name the night before. If he had been a John Doe, he might not have made it to the end of the day.

Raymond Cobb staggered out of the holding cell and down the hallway of the county jail to be released back into the world. In one hand, he held his swelling jaw, and in the other, the last will and testament of the man Ray knew as Ernie Politics.

2

Nick Archer was on his fourth Foster's, a final swig lingering in the rounded basin of the large can. He wondered if it would be worth the story later to approach the strange woman winking at him behind too much blue eye shadow at the other end of the bar. There was just enough alcohol flowing through his bloodstream to give it serious thought, but he figured it would be an embarrassment to tell people he'd caught syphilis from its Patient Zero. He sucked down the final drops of warm beer before shoving off the barstool and into the street.

The air hit him hard as he stepped onto the sidewalk. He passed by a dirty man in a goose down coat rifling through a garbage can.

"Gotta quarter?"

Nick waved him off and kept walking.

"She should be asleep by now," he said to himself, looking at his watch.

He had taken to leaving his cell phone at home just so his mother wouldn't be able to reach him. It was an awful thing to do considering the state of her health, but his moments of solitude were scarce and precious.

The doctors said it was a combination of asbestos and cigarettes that caused his mother's emphysema and eventual cancer. Early retirement from the world of textile manufacturing left her with a healthy pension, but an unhealthy dose of mesothelioma.

When the state went smoke-free she stopped leaving the house. It was the only place she could smoke while doing all the things she loved, but eventually everyone but Nick stopped coming to her. Her friends refused to leave the beautiful comfort of their new senior center to aggravate their angina in the less desirable part of Mid-City.

Sweat emerged from his receding hairline and rolled down his forehead as he ascended the steps of the house he grew up in. The atmosphere changed as he opened the front door, not necessarily for the better. The cold breeze of central air and cigarette smoke produced a haze thicker than the smog on the 405 and Nick was beginning to wonder if he wouldn't get emphysema himself just from living in the house. He tried to make the best of his situation and he loved his mother, but his tolerance deteriorated every time someone commented on how much his clothes stank.

Janice Archer was in front of the television, passed out in her easy chair. In one hand, she held an unfinished crossword puzzle from Parade magazine, and in the other, an uncapped ballpoint pen. There were tiny black lines written on the arm of the chair from the times she had stirred. A cigarette with a long ash hung from her lips, pieces of charred tobacco and menthol dusting the paper in her lap.

Trying not to disturb her, he pinched his thumb and fore-finger together to pluck the cigarette from between her lips. He pulled it free, a dark ring of lipstick around the filter. Nick found it amusing that she took the time to make herself up every morning, though she knew he would be the only one to see her. She joked that if he spent every day looking at her "without her face on," he would be dead long before her. Janice Archer had a self-deprecating sense of humor that Nick had inherited and appreciated. It kept them both from taking life too seriously.

The removal of the cigarette brought her back to life and she sprang awake, hacking with a low and familiar cough. The expulsion of air from her lungs blew the long ash from the cigarette onto Nick. He wiped it off his shirt before grinding the remains of the butt into a nearby ashtray.

"Ma, you gotta watch the falling asleep while lit up."

"Ah, I ain't dead yet. The Good Lord will take me with my lungs burning from the inside or outside."

"Yeah, but then I'll have no place to live."

"Sorry. Next time I get sleepy, I'll be sure to ponder the current state of the housing market and put out my butt. You happy?"

"Thank you. C'mon, let's get you to bed."

"You forgot your phone again. The department called while you were out."

"Ma, I told you not to answer my phone."

"Well, maybe if you weren't such a Mr. Forgetful, I wouldn't fret that you were missing something important."

"Even if I were, there would be no way for you to call me to pass on the message, so who cares? Just let it go to voicemail."

"Like I want to be your secretary anyway, big shot Detective Archer."

"You gonna start with that again?"

She shrugged.

"What'd they want?"

"They said you should come in an hour early tomorrow. Something about a backlog of cold cases. I don't even know what that means, just what he told me to tell you. Made me repeat it back to him. That Jenkins you work with is a condescending prick, you know that?"

"You don't have to tell me. I know. Thanks for getting me the message, Ma, I appreciate it."

"There you go, that wasn't so hard, offering a little thanks to your mother who you leave all alone to go drink swill and not come home with a girl."

He hated when his mother baited him into talking about anything remotely resembling his love life. He was glad she cared, but the last thing he wanted to talk to his mother about was picking up some chick at a bar and bringing her home to hump in his boyhood bedroom.

"I had one, but she was about twice your age and half as good looking."

"Hey, take what you can get. Maybe she has a brother for me."

"All right, enough banter with you, it's late. You need any help getting up the stairs?"

"You gonna put me on your shoulders and piggy back me up there? I'm fine. Go watch some TV. But not too late, remember, early to rise in the morning."

"G'night, Ma."

Nick watched his mother cough thick phlegm into a handkerchief as she steadied herself on the wooden banister. He waited for her to disappear into the bathroom before he went to the refrigerator to grab a beer, hoping to ride his buzz into dreamless sleep.

Flipping the bottle cap into the ashtray on the coffee table he stretched himself out on the couch and stared up at the tar-stained ceiling, wondering what kind of horse shit Jenkins was going to throw at him in the morning.

3

...the government is using race relations to keep the common man from uniting and bringing down the imperialist pyramid system. The racial tensions have been eased with the civil rights movement, but branched out into the Arab peoples, who in turn oppress their women. The establishment fuels the fires of negative racial and gender relationships by publicly condemning the oppression of women, while privately encouraging proper gender roles with the sales of things like Barbie Dolls. This association of women with the perfect body image and infinite sweetness, causes internal struggle for both men and women as they try to grow into the modern world, while trying to hold onto the All-American tradition of the nuclear family. This constant tension keeps society focused inward on their own problems and not on the outward problems of big government committing crimes against humanity. John Q. Public trying to be sensitive and well rounded, while still being the breadwinner and Jane Q. Public trying to make her way in the modern world establishing an able minded identity while still being able to take care of the family and bake them goods like strawberry shortcake....

The splash of cold, rusty water couldn't wash away the images of Ernie Politics ranting on the corner of Franklin and Vermont, throwing doll heads at passing cars. Ray stared back at his weary reflection in the gas station bathroom mirror, remembering the last time he saw his friend alive, but couldn't shake the crime scene photos his imagination had constructed.

He could see Ernie's thin arms, the pink translucent skin sawed off at the wrists where his attacker had removed the hands. His face was contorted into permanent shock. Streams of dark crimson flowed down his cheeks, a hot spring bursting forth from the pits where his electric red eyes once lived.

After the police interviewed Ernie's known acquaintances, the file went into a pile of unsolved transient murders, the "to do" stack of a retiring detective in the Robbery-Homicide division. In the movies, it's always one last case that draws the old, grizzled officer back into the fold, tying up all the loose ends. In reality, it's like any other job. On their last day, they're ready to get the hell out, spend some time with their grandkids and enjoy midday naps, leaving that pile of cases for the next guy.

The case did have some interesting particulars. An albino with missing appendages caused a bit of a stir. But with no motive, no real background, and no known enemies, curiosity quickly deteriorated into a theory that the murder was part of a gang hazing. Ernie was singled out because of his big mouth and unusual appearance. Now the ashes of Ernie "Politics" Gaffney sat on a shelf in a plastic bag, waiting the requisite four years before the Los Angeles County coroner's office tossed it into a mass grave along with the remains of a thousand other unclaimed bodies.

The gas station owner banging on the restroom door pulled Ray from his memories. He dried his hands and face with a wad of paper towels and unlocked the door.

"Get outta here before I call the cops."

Ray stopped and stared at the gray-faced man just long enough to make him uncomfortable, then tossed the used paper towels at his feet before walking past him.

He stopped at the outer pumps, pulling a stick of gum out of the pack he'd pocketed while asking for the bathroom key, and looked at the prick across the street. With Ernie gone, he figured he'd never have to talk to that son of a bitch ever again, but there he was, enlisting the asshole's help for the second time in forty-eight hours. It only seemed logical to go to the man who knew Ernie Politics best, but Ray hated Benny 7-11.

Benny always made a point of his appearance. He didn't wear the same ragged clothes day after day. He would go to the Goodwill donation bin on Hollywood Boulevard at dawn, just before the place opened, and would pick out the most original ensemble. Then he would give himself a hobo shower in a public restroom, even taking the time to shave his cheeks and chin, but he never touched his disgusting mustache.

It began to take on a life of its own, growing well over his lips and beyond the creases of his hustler's sneer. The ingrown and dead hairs acted as a filter for all of his meals, preventing the wettest remnants of his food from reaching his mouth. The effort he placed in making himself look somewhat respectable was always undercut by the pride he took in neglecting the hideous creature on his face.

Benny made his living soliciting change from people who frequented convenience stores. He would greet the patrons politely, opening the door for them, asking that they not forget the doorman on the way out. As he opened the door for them again when they left, he would hold his paw out for a polite donation. Sometimes the ploy worked, sometimes it didn't, but Benny 7-11 always had a smile on his face. Regular customers at the handful of stores Benny had in his rotation were amazed at how upbeat Benny was when he opened the door, no matter how many people decided his service wasn't worth their spare change. It was because Benny had a special secret.

When business was slow, Benny 7-11 would go into the store. The shopkeepers tolerated his presence because what-ever money he could finagle out of their patrons, he usually reinvested in their merchandise. He was good-natured, never obstructed the entrance, and never hindered their business. He would slowly wander the aisles, plucking a Grandma's Cookie or pack of sunflower seeds from the shelves. He'd spent time building up the clerks' trust, so they figured they didn't have to watch him too closely, knowing he would never shoplift. But when their eyes were turned away, or focused on other customers, Benny 7-11 would make his way over to the coffee station and grab a handful of to-go coffee lids. Those lids made their way into the waistband of Benny's pants and eventually came to rest on his sweaty, never washed, hairy as his upper lip, balls.

He usually did one more lap of the store before returning to the coffee station and pulling the lids out of his drawers, checking them for stray pubes, and putting them back into the stack at random intervals. He'd pay for his item and resume his post back outside the door, grinning from ear-to-ear every time he was ignored by a person holding a coffee cup, right before they took a nice big gulp of mocha java laced with his rancid nut juice.

Benny 7-11 had sent Ray into lockup after he'd started poking around for information. A few weeks earlier, Ernie Politics had been arrested for aggravated assault and ended up in the same cell Ray had recently occupied. Like most of L.A.'s homeless, Ernie had a few previous arrests, most of them misdemeanors: trespassing, public intoxication, disturbing the peace. Usually he did nothing more than putter his 99-cent store shopping cart up and down the streets of the City of Angels. After he was found dead, Ray went looking for Benny to find out what had really happened. And, of course, Benny had a long-winded story to tell.

"So, Ernie attacks this spic kid, don't know who, probably just some asshole in the wrong place and was real quickly taken into custody, right, and shoved in the clink to cool off. Now, you and me and everybody else knows, you spend a day in holding then you's done. Released. Finito. Maybe they send him up to Gateways for some antipsych meds. But he don't move. Ernie was in holdin' seven whole days. They didn't process him to be moved to general population to await trial, didn't do nothing with him. About day three at the L.A. County Bed and Breakfast, he starts to get real paranoid, like they're never coming for him and are gonna let him rot. So, he starts beggin' around the room for a paper and pen like they're hookers and blow, finally getting a ballpoint out of some dude covered in shit and a stack of Post-it notes out of the pocket of some corporate dude with a double limit DUI blow. And then, they finally come for him."

"He starts rantin' to me about how they only let him out 'cuz they were followin' him and wanted to keep tallies on all his known associates before finally doin' away with him, and that all his secrets and final thoughts on the matter were, and I quote, 'In his will.' You want some answers? Get yourself arrested and look behind that metal slab they call a mirror in holdin' number two, hopin' you get yourself lucky enough to be placed in holdin' number two. All I know is, he tells me this whole tale and three days later they find him without his hands or eyeballs. He may have been crazy paranoid, but that shit is worth a look. Now, I'd go myself, naturally, but I have a livelihood to protect here. I'd hate to have mom and pop towelhead in there see me get dragged into a squad and then find themselves tellin' me to move along. You get my drift, Cobbsy?"

As much as Ray hated to admit it, Benny 7-11's intelligence had checked out, even if he was one tooth poorer for it. Now, perhaps Benny could be of more assistance.

Ray found him in West Hollywood at his usual perch on Santa Monica Boulevard, wearing a bright pink windbreaker and some loud golf pants.

"Looks like you had some jaw trouble there, Cobbsy," Benny called to him as he nodded politely to the old Asian man entering the store.

"The bulls didn't take too well to you sleepin' in an ice machine? Nice choice, by the way. You couldn't have gotten pinched for anything more pussy, like disrupting a feather convention or givin' out too many free hugs?"

Benny laughed at his own joke. Ray wasn't in the mood.

"You wanna put your bullshit slinging aside for a minute and see if you can make heads or tails of this nonsense?" Ray asked, holding the crumpled piece of paper out to Benny.

He snatched the paper out of Ray's hand, trying to appear tough. Benny 7-11 saw the burning hate in Ray Cobb's eyes and realized that with Ernie gone, he was definitely down a few friends and up a few enemies.

"Well?" Ray asked with an impatient tone. Benny unconsciously looked up at every person entering the store without him there to dutifully open the door.

"What're those, phone numbers or somethin'? Addresses? I dunno," Benny shrugged.

"Those numbers, that pattern. You've never seen it before?"

"You knew Ernie, man, he was always writing some crazy shit you could never make heads or tails of. There was always some theory about somethin' or another. Maybe it was the last year's average lotto numbers, like he was looking for a pattern, or maybe he was countin' how many people were in that cell with him from day to day. I sure as hell wish he was 'round right now so I could ask him, but far as I know, it was a dude who was hallucinatin' with paranoia, wrote some crazy shit on a scrap of paper and stuck it behind a mirror. Probably don't mean nothin'."

"If you thought Ernie was just talking nonsense, why the hell'd you send me in there?"

"You mean to say you didn't enjoy the air conditionin' none?" Benny joked. The throaty laugh scraped at Ray's ears.

"Turn it over," Ray stared through him, trying not to grit his teeth and irritate the hole where his molar used to be.

"Sometimes I wondered how that see-through bastard ever got to writin' so small. Can't make it out too good, my eyes ain't what they used to be, pretty sure I'm getting a cataract or somethin' in the left one, but that ain't no English. Looks like Russian or Spanish or somethin'. Only word I can make out is here at the top. Looks like," he squinted at the paper, "Manifesto. Jesus, that little bastard had a one-track mind."

"Do you have a copy of Ernie's manifesto?"

Ray never took the time to read the entire 1300-page rant on everything from how Black Friday was a communist conspiracy to how public buildings and bookstores use the cheapest brand of toilet paper to irritate the bowels of the lowest common denominator. The manifesto was Ernie's life.

"Naw, man. You know he changed that shit every few days, scribblin' stuff out, addin' notes in the margins, writin' extra pages. Last version I read was like two years ago, after that I'd just take 'em from him and throw 'em away. With Ernie, man, if he brought up some new thought on the proletariat or whatever, and explained it in that book of his, I'd just nod and smile at him right through it, repeating somethin' he said earlier in the conversation so it sounded like I was listenin'."

"Glad to know you were such good friends."

"Now don't you put that shit on me," Benny started to get upset, "Ernie was a good dude, always good for a talk and a laugh, but you couldn't take him all the time neither, so don't play mister innocent over here."

"I didn't come here to play the 'who was a better friend' game. I could give a shit. I'm just trying to get some answers and you are apparently the dumbest fuck in L.A. County."

"Would you care to repeat that, Cobbsy?" Benny asked, his anger swelling.

Ray got as close to Benny's face as he could, navigating past his mustache.

"You heard me."

The bell on the door rang over Benny's shoulder, neither of them taking notice.

"Get out of here," a heavy accent said from behind them, "I will call the police for you hanging out at my store!"

They broke their gaze and both turned to face the dark-skinned clerk who stood quivering on the sidewalk, brandishing a broom handle. Ray had taken one good whack to the jaw in the last twenty-four hours; he wasn't looking forward to another one. Benny just waved his hand at the man before hurrying around the corner with Ray behind him.

Once out of sight of the storefront, Benny changed his tone.

"Listen, Cobbsy, I don't wanna fight you on this. We both wanna know what happened to Ernie, right? So why don't we work together to figure out what this shit says? Find one of Ernie's latest manifestos. Fuck this big ego bullshit."

Ray looked down at the creased and stained paper in his hand.

"Seems to me, if you really wanted to know what this was, you would've gone after it yourself."

"What you want, Ray? You want me to admit I'm a chickenshit for lettin' you do the dirty work? Fine, I'm a chickenshit. Now gimme another look," Benny reached out for the paper as Ray shoved it into his pocket.

"I think I'm about done with you," Ray spoke softly, letting all the rage he felt toward Benny throb at the base of his spine.

"You wouldn't even have that shit if it weren't for me. You'd still be cryin' over that cardboard box Ernie called home, wiping your tears with the shit stains on his underpants."

"Time to walk away, Benny," Ray's hands remained in the pockets of his coat, but he could feel the electricity running down the tendons of his forearms, his fingers starting to shake as he held tight to the worn lining.

Benny stepped back and reached into his own pocket, pulling out a battered hunting knife. Ray remembered the day Ernie gave Benny the weapon, after Benny was mugged on Skid Row. Ernie slipped it into the cast where Benny's wrist had been broken and merely said, "For protection," before going back to handing out handwritten pamphlets. Ray looked down at the knife and back up at Benny. Sweat ran down Benny's face and spackled wisps of hair to his forehead.

"Really?" Ray asked without moving.

"Just give it here. Didn't wanna hafta do this, but you had to be stubborn."

Ray had seen people stabbed, beaten, shot, raped, and killed over stupid arguments and items of little importance, but Benny was a different brand of scumbag; he didn't pull out the knife unless he had to protect himself and his cash flow. Ray knew the note was more than just a piece of paper.

He looked at the dull blade, shaking in Benny's unsteady hand.

"Now's about the time I'm gonna make you admit you're a chickenshit. Chickenshit."

Benny flinched as he realized Ray wasn't going to relent to his empty threat. The thrust at Ray's gut was predictable and sloppy. The telegraphed movements gave Ray plenty of time to dodge the blow as he grabbed Benny by the greasy hair and slammed his skull into the cement wall.

"Listen up, you coffee-lid-dick-wiping motherfucker. I'm sick of your fucking face!"

Ray spit on Benny as he spoke, spittle catching on his mustache like rain droplets on a canopy of banyan trees. His fingernails dug deep into the tendons of Benny's wrists, causing the knife to drop to the concrete.

"If you didn't think this note meant anything before, you sure do now."

Ray kicked the knife out of Benny's reach and let go of him.

"I don't know shit!"

Benny was holding one hand to the gash above his left eyebrow, while the other was clumsily trying to gather the change that flew out of his coffee cup after being kicked in the struggle.

"Where'd you toss those manifestos?" Ray asked through clenched teeth.

"What?"

Ray kicked him in the guts hard and he doubled over on the cracked sidewalk, coughing.

"Ernie's papers, you dim shit! When you didn't read them, where'd you toss them?"

"In the garbage, fuckstick," Benny gasped in, trying to regain his breath.

Ray stamped down hard on the hand Benny was using to gather change and heard a snap as his shoe sandwiched Benny's middle finger with the cement. Ray silenced his shriek by giving him another sock to the midsection. Grabbing the scruff of his shirt, Ray raised Benny up to meet him face to face.

"I know you're dumb, but you're not stupid enough to deposit those papers where you knew Ernie would find them. You and I know that Ernie was about all you had."

His breath was fire on Benny's cheek.

"This little beating I gave you doesn't compare to what could come your way if you don't give me some answers. So, unless you wanna lose the use of both of your hands, I suggest you quit fucking around, or you'll spend the rest of your days masturbating with your feet."

"Lindberg," Benny rasped out between coughs and tears.

"You've seen what I can do to you, Benny. What're you feeding me?"

"Lindberg, I swear. Use my name. You'll get access."

Ray dropped the sobbing mess that was once Benny 7-11 to the ground.

"You know what happens if you're lying, right?"

Benny nodded, trying to keep himself in a little ball, not knowing where the next blow would come from.

"I'm going to need some insurance."

Benny looked up at him with glossy, shocked eyes, no idea what "insurance" meant and scared out of his mind to find out. Ray reached down, grabbed Benny's mustache, and yanked hard, pulling a huge section of it out by the roots, leaving a bloody gap. Ray shoved the hunk of hair into his pocket.

"Just a little collateral. If Lindberg pans out, you'll get it back."

Ray looked around to see if anyone bothered to take notice of his little battle. His hands were shaking as he grabbed the knife from the ground and tossed it into a storm sewer. Taking one last look at the damage he'd done, his mind unable to process what caused him to snap, Ray tried his best to control his breathing. The accelerated beating of his heart started an engine in his legs and he disappeared into the neighborhood.

Benny slumped against the wall, his middle finger broken and askew. He wiped the blood from his eyes and cried heavily to himself, cursing Ray Cobb under his breath.

4

Penny's eyes flicked back and forth over the computer screen, her finger lingering over the mouse, waiting for her brain to send the go-codes. All she had to do was click one little button and she would strike a blow for abused executive assistants everywhere.

Gabriel stepped into her cubicle and she clicked off the page, revealing the quarterly costs spreadsheet open on her desktop.

"O.M.G. Have you seen what Margie is wearing today?" Gabriel whispered between his cosmetically altered teeth.

"I try not to notice anything about Margie," Penny joked in her tiny voice. She swallowed her words and the quip came out flat, causing Gabe to ignore it and burst into his diatribe.

"Seriously? It's as though she spent the morning finding a vintage furniture store, digging in the dumpster for a discarded couch, and cutting herself a blouse out of the upholstery."

"I'm doing my best to avoid her today, probably a good thing I did," Penny said.

"Thank the Lord above, because, honey you would lose your lunch over that wonderful little scarf you've chosen to accessorize with today. Where ever did you get that little piece?"

"Oh, I found it on sale at Bloomingdale's," she lied. There was a discoloration hidden by the knot at her neck, an irregularity that landed it in the clearance bin at Marshall's.

"Matches the low-cut blouse you have on there to a tee. Way to show off the goods today, Pen."

She blushed. Penny supposed she had a good figure, despite the time she spent scrutinizing herself in the mirror, pinching a bit of fat here, sucking in to flatten her tummy there. She'd spent a lot of time at the gym lately. Not because she had some fitness obsession, it was more to avoid spending her entire life stuck on her couch reading magazines and eating peanut butter from the jar with a spoon. She had trouble hiding her glee that Gabriel would take notice of her. That anyone would notice her, really.

"All right, enough of the gabbity gabbing gorgeous, we've got a budget meeting in forty minutes and I've got a few expenditures I have to reconcile. What's the best way to get a reimbursement for going to Bardot and getting silly on Grey Goose martinis?"

"You could call it celebutantertaining."

"My stars and garters, I'm stealing that. I knew you'd have an answer. Peace."

"Bye, Gabriel," Penny smiled, giving him a little wave.

Penny turned back to her computer, but before she could return to what she was doing, a gargoyle's voice approached from behind her.

"Penelope?"

Margie and her mother were the only people on Earth who called her Penelope. As a child, she didn't mind the name; she actually reveled in its relative rarity. But when she was in junior high, Penelope came up in her Greek Mythology unit of English class. Delighted that she'd received her namesake from the wife of the great Odysseus, she couldn't wait to get home and ask her mother about it. She never regretted a question more in her life.

"Mythology? Honey, you were named that because you were conceived in the parking lot of Penelope's World Famous Chicken Fried Steak in Colorado Springs. Me and your dickhole daddy were on a road trip to see ELO in concert in Denver. I don't know about World Famous, but they gave me the runs somethin' awful for 'bout a week."

She never wanted to be called Penelope again.

Margie, however, when she hired Penny, saw her full name on her Social Security card. She determined that the name Penelope was much more pleasant sounding than plain Penny, no matter how many times Penny tried to correct her. She actually took pleasure in thinking she knew the best thing for Penny, down to what she should be called on a daily basis.

Penny swung her chair around and looked up at Margie, trying to hide her disdain for the rotund banshee.

"What can I do for you Margie?"

"Well, Penelope," Penny ground her teeth at the sound of her name, "When I asked you to put together this presentation for our new corporate branding proposal, I specifically asked that the previous brand logos be collated by color and not chronologically."

"You told me to place them in order of where we've been and where we're going."

"And in what way does that imply chronology?"

Fireworks burst beneath the surface as Penny's exterior revealed nothing but a sudden flush in her cheeks.

"I'm sorry I misunderstood you. Next time I'll ask you to be more specific," Penny said, swallowing her words in veiled hatred.

"It never hurts to ask. There are no stupid questions, but the ones that go unasked," Margie's nostrils flared, her condescending tone punctuated with a self-satisfied smirk.

"Now you've created twice the work for yourself. Please rearrange these. Standard rainbow spectrum from Red to Violet. I don't think I can get more specific than that. Oh, and Penelope, we do have a dress code here, let's try to keep the twins in check, shall we," she smiled through her over-applied lipstick, waving her finger at Penny's chest.

"Sorry, I'll get right on it," Penny said, lowering her eyes. Her fingernails dug deep into the upholstery of her ergonomic desk chair, all of her rage channeled into the plush fabric. Margie flashed her coffee-stained, crooked teeth at Penny before turning like a soldier and huffing back into her office.

Penny looked down at her barely showing cleavage, unbuttoned the top button of her blouse, and opened the web page back up, hitting the "Order" button with no reservation. Soon Marjorie Wells would be receiving a rather disturbing package and Penny would have her revenge.

5

Nightfall began to cover the sky in soot before Ray made his trek down to Lindberg Park, but he didn't dare start his journey without consulting Crispy Morgan first. Even on the streets there was a hierarchy, a protocol for achieving certain gains, much like the gang system in a prison. Beating an answer out of a scumbag solicitor worked on occasion, but sometimes going through the proper channels was the way to get things done. Ray had heard too many stories and knew he couldn't go down to Lindberg blindly. He had to play by the rules.

Where Beverly Hills swoops around to the underside of West Hollywood, Peter "Crispy" Morgan held court at the far end of a Mobil station, monopolizing one of the few remaining public pay phones in Los Angeles. Crispy was a barterer; reveling in the philosophy that one man's trash is another man's treasure. He knew when you had nothing, everything was worth everything, nothing was worth nothing, and everything was worth nothing. He was a good person to know.

Crispy was using a penknife to empty the contents of several discarded butts into a napkin to make one good cigarette. He was so focused on the task he didn't notice Ray until he was almost on top of him.

"How's it going, Crisp?"

Crispy looked up, pulled out of his trance. It took him a second to register the face of Ray Cobb with the swollen jaw and the speech impediment to accompany it.

"Well, shiiit. If it ain't Ray Cobb. Sit on down, you weary lookin' mu'fucka."

Ray did as he was told, sitting opposite Crispy's current project.

"Put 'er there, pal," Crispy offered, extending his pink, scared claw.

When Peter Morgan was part of the real world, he was a fry jockey at a popular fast food establishment. His whole life hinged on that useless job. At the time, it seemed like his only goal was to finish high school and get out of the house. The men in his family followed a vicious cycle; working minimum wage to barely pay the bills, then deciding to disappear or take drastic measures, like his father replacing the whiskey in his Coke with Drano. He wanted to make sure it wasn't going to be his fate, too. He got his high school diploma––his diploma, not his equivalency. He did it right, with his name announced and his momma crying in the auditorium and everything.

Peter Morgan was going to get out, maybe even apply at Los Angeles City College and get a degree in appliance mainte-nance or carpentry, considering how much he liked working with his hands. But then his momma was hit by some asshole in a '92 Chevy Cavalier as she crossed the street with her gro-ceries. Bastard ran a red light at one-thirty in the afternoon, so drunk he could have been chugging embalming fluid. The accident broke twenty-seven bones in her body and put her into a coma. They couldn't afford name-brand macaroni and cheese, let alone health insurance, and Peter had to stay at his job just to meet the minimum payment on the medical bills.

One day, after working a double shift, Peter got an idea. Federal disability and worker's compensation insurance were removed from his paycheck weekly. It was money he knew was going to nothing, so he figured he should do something about it.

An extra-large order of fries came over the computer, and instead of dumping in the bag of prepackaged fries, he thrust his right hand into the boiling hot vegetable oil, all the way up to the elbow. Tortured screams escaped his throat as he held his hand underneath as long as he could, smelling the sizzle of his flesh under the steaming oil bath. To this day, if he uses what's left of his right hand to wipe his nose, he swears he smells pork rinds.

Of course, he never got his worker's compensation or his disability. The corporate investigation's official ruling was that his injury was self-inflicted and in no way the company's fault. Several witnesses testified to seeing Peter shove his hand into the oil and hold it there, despite his protestation that he went in after a rogue chicken tender and got his finger caught on the vent at the bottom of the basin. While he was waiting for the settlement that never materialized, his mother died in her bed. Now he was paying her old medical bills along with the ones that began to arrive for the treatment of his crispy hand.

He started to sell things to keep up and soon he was in an empty rental, three months behind on the lease. With the clothes on his back, he left the apartment full of unpaid bills and bad memories and said goodbye to his old life. Peter was amused at how much stock he'd once put into the things he'd owned. In the end, they were all the same, just goods to be exchanged for other worthless things. From that point on, everything he had the privilege of owning, for however short a time, was both precious and worthless.

Ray took the burned shell of Crispy's hand and shook it hard, with no resignation, just as Crispy Morgan wanted it. Crispy went back to his task, knowing that everybody coming to him was looking for something. He had long ago rid himself of the pretense of small talk and would wait patiently until his visitors got around to flat out asking for an exchange, but Ray was one of his best customers.

"I've gotta go down to Lindberg tonight," Ray said, staring across the street.

"Shit, Ray, what you wanna go do that for?"

"Trying to figure out this thing with Ernie."

"That there was a buncha crazy bullshit, Ray. I could use a brand-new hand my own self, but I ain't gonna go 'round takin' somebody's hand that's already usin' it, let alone both of 'em. I ain't greedy."

"Maybe if I find one of them, I'll let you have it on loan."

"You think *She* has somethin' to do with it?"

"No. But I think Benny does."

"Dick Scrape ain't smart enough. You know where he rests his head, why you gotta go down to Lindberg?"

"Already been to see him. Benny's been depositing updates of the manifesto down at Lindberg."

"I hear tell *She* strains all garbage comin' and goin'," Crispy said, affirming what little information Ray had about the goings-on of Lindberg Park.

"I need the latest copy for some answers."

"You don't got one?"

"Thought I did, but there was no copy on his cart, no copy in his camp."

"Sounds like Ernie was ready for this," Crispy said.

"I would've said it was just a symptom of his paranoia, but anyone who wanted him out of the way would have had instant access to the manifesto had he not taken precautions."

"Had me a draft 'bout eight months ago, but I traded it to Kenny Flak Jacket for a vinyl copy of the Bugsy Malone soundtrack. I can find out where Flak Jacket's at for you if you want."

"I might have to see him anyway before this is through, but an eight-month-old copy isn't going to do me any good. I need the draft from the day before he was put away."

Crispy was struggling to twist his cigarette closed, but Ray didn't dare ask if he needed any help. He knew better. He waited patiently until Crispy got the makeshift blunt situated in just the right way, then offered a hand to cup the flame as he struck a wooden match on the pavement. Crispy took a deep breath in, let out a cough from the burning napkin paper, and let the long floppy cigarette hang from the corner of his mouth. He got up and went to an abandoned phone box, pulling out the coffee cups and bottles one at a time. His left hand reached in and felt around for his hidden treasure, finally pulling out something wrapped in a dirty white piece of linen.

"You lucky I like you, Ray. I was gonna mount this particular item right here on top of the phone, make it sorta regal like, at least for a while 'til someone come along and snatch it up. Don't get too many things passin' as a Lindberg offerin'."

"Somehow I knew you'd have something for me."

"Funny story," Crispy said, returning to the curb, "So you know Frankie Pink Slip, right?"

Ray nodded. Frankie Pink Slip was the founder of the ice machine catnap.

"Frankie Pink Slip was sleepin' in that tube slide in the park behind the Glendale Library when mu'fucka feels this sharp pain on the bottom of his foot. He wakes up straight hard, son, bumpin' his head on that orange plastic shit, slidin' down to the wood chips on the ground. This group of upscale asshole high school kids was pokin' at him with this sword, like this fuckin' skinny stickpin lookin' thing they picked up at this weapon store in that mall, the what's it? Glendale Galleria. Goddamn thing went through the bottom of his shoe and stabbed the sole of his foot, wakin' him up with one hell of a pain. So, dude does what anybody woulda, he takes a swing at one of the kids, managin' to clomp him on the back of the head. The little shit wit' the sword decides to defend his friend's honor or some shit, and charges at Frankie, sword straight out, ready to gut his ass.

"Lucky for Frankie, as Frankie tells it, the dumb mu'fuckin' kid trips over his own two feet and goes down hard, eatin' gravel. Damn kid was lucky he didn't run himself through. As a show of strength, as Frankie tells it, Frankie grabs the hilt of the sword, stickin' up out of the dirt like a cross marking a grave, and steps down hard on the blade. Cheap piece of shit was enough to go through his shoe once, but not twice. He snaps the thing easy, the hilt left in his hands, the punk kids runnin' scared, 'fraid this crazy homeless guy is gonna kill 'em. So Frankie Pink Slip has to make his broke-ass way to the free clinic, get a real painful tetanus shot from some pissin'-in-her-pants-scared volunteer, the whole time holdin' tight this glitterin' sword hilt. He tries to return it, sayin' it's all defective an' shit, you know, try to get some cash for his trouble, but the guy at the store wasn't hearin' none of it. So, he comes limpin' to me, gives me that hilt and in exchange I give him a pair of them, whatchacall'em, Halloween vampire teeth. He thinks it'll help scare off any other mu'fucka who wants to mess with him while he's sleepin'. I think he'd have been better off with a broken sword hilt, but I ain't no one to judge."

Ray reached out for the package when it seemed that Crispy was done telling his tale, but Crispy pulled it back from him.

"Ray, you know you don't gotta do this," he pleaded, trying to protect his friend.

"Yeah, Crisp. Yeah, I do."

"You do this, Ray, you gotta do it right, son. Folks come back from Lindberg sayin' they can't imagine hell bein' much worse."

"And yet they came back, Crispy. I've heard the stories. I know what I'm up against. What've I got to lose?"

"My sword," Crispy tried to joke, "and your life."

"Not much of a life to lose. If I remember correctly, I trade you straight up, the sword will be mine to lose anyway, not yours," the corner of Ray's mouth went up in a mocking smirk.

Crispy placed the package into Ray's hands. The metal of the blade was indeed cheap, but the hilt was in the shape of two golden dragons with a blue bead for each of their eyes. The gold of the handle was woven in Celtic style and it definitely had some weight to it.

"And now, what you got for me?"

Lost in the glitter of the hilt, Ray almost forgot that he couldn't have one thing without giving up another and reached into his pants pocket. Shaking out the clump of hair into Crispy's palm, Ray just smiled. Crispy looked down at the hair and then back up at Ray. From the look on his face, Ray could see he wasn't having it.

"Funny joke," Crispy said, his eyes telling Ray he didn't get the punch line, "You wanna trade me some nappy-ass pubes for that beautiful piece? What the fuck?"

Ray shrugged with his eyebrows.

"Pubic hair this is not, my friend. That's a chunk of the rat stain currently renting space in the area between Benny 7-11's nose and his upper lip."

"Wait. Hold up. This here's Benny's mustache?"

"Part of it. Harvested it myself."

Crispy Morgan let out one long hard laugh. He looked down at the clump of hair in his hand, pushed it around a little, and then brought his eyes back up to Ray.

"I'm gonna have to braid it together or some shit, but this'll make a fine trophy for someone out there. I know plenty'a folks that hate that prick, myself included, even more now that Ernie ain't 'round no more. One of the best exchanges I ever had. Thanks, my friend."

"Thank you."

Crispy transferred the contents of his right hand into his left and held it out to Ray, who took it and shook it hard.

"Be careful down there. *She's* supposed to be mad dog unpredictable."

"So I've heard."

"Make your way up to Robertson Boulevard, be sure and catch the 9:28 bus. Mention me to the driver and you'll get on free. Beats walkin' down to Culver City."

"Word is *She* doesn't hold court until after 2 a.m."

"*She* don't. But when you get down to The Dark Territory and have trouble gettin' in to see *Her*, you gonna need all your strength."

Ray nodded to him and started west, wondering what he had gotten himself into.

6

Nick had been staring at the files for three days straight.

8/4/89 - Hannah Theobaud, kidnapped from her family home, no leads, no witnesses, body found eight days later, strangled, no sign of sexual assault.

7/18/76 - Adam Bevan, murdered in his recently remodeled family room basement, case pending due to evidence tampering.

1/3/00 - Uki Huraka, raped in an alley in Little Tokyo, bled to death internally, no DNA evidence.

The list went on and on. He was flooded with a sea of unsolved crimes in no particular order and still wasn't sure if he was supposed to be organizing them chronologically, alphabetically, or by offense.

Nick started making a series of piles around his desk, trying not to become completely exasperated by the process, knowing each one of the folders he put on its respective pile was another life destroyed, with no prospect of resolution. There was a family out there somewhere for each victim, awaiting new evidence or a witness that would probably never appear. He hated himself for hoping a new, interesting crime would be committed to pull him off paperwork duty, but at least a new case with fresh evidence had the potential of getting solved. The black tags on the cold case files represented the death of hope.

"Archer!"

Nick blinked himself out of a partial fingerprint photo from a carjacking gone wrong in 1984.

"You think you can pull yourself away from that long enough to question a suspect?" Jim Jenkins barked at him.

"I don't know, I think I may be making progress with this case from 1991. Woman was choked to death with a dog leash. I think the dog might've done it," Nick said without smiling.

"Listen, smart ass, I'm just trying to give you a break so you don't lose what's left of that tiny brain of yours, but if you prefer, I'm sure I could find someone else willing to get involved in a case that happened in this decade."

"Where?"

"Interview two," Jenkins coughed into his palm, throwing the case file in his direction. Nick had to grab for it and in the process kicked out his foot, knocking over the "Blunt Trauma/1975-1981/A-C" pile of papers. He just let them slide down onto the tile floor without picking them up. It wasn't like they were going to get any more disorganized.

Flipping through the new file in his hands, he took his time walking down the hallway to the interview rooms. He had to stop himself for a minute and go back to read the details of the case. His brain had become so accustomed to skimming over paperwork with random, seemingly useless details, he had to re-acclimate to doing some real police work.

These were the days he wished he were better at minding his own business. Little over year ago he was just a uniform, crowd controlling a crime scene. He happened to spot someone in the crowd taking pictures with a wide-angle lens, someone without a press pass. For a few days, he was given shit from his crew, increasingly tall tales of his action sequence, chasing down this dude with a camera, leaving his post on a hunch and never catching him. He might have been suspended––if the same guy hadn't turned up with the same photo equipment a few days later at a similar scene. This time the detectives took notice. They managed to nab Kyle Vargas, The Barbed Wire Strangler. Son of a bitch would go home and jerk off to the crime scene photos in his darkroom before they were done processing. The semen scan of the room matched that taken from each victim.

Nick's buddies shut up real quick and it got him a pre-liminary meeting with the Robbery-Homicide Division. The police commissioner was doing his best to look good in front of the mayor and decided to make Nick his poster boy. He did a short six months as an officer in RHD before his new friend the PC pushed him to upgrade his shield. A barrage of tests and a psych evaluation landed him a promotion, a desk, and a plainclothes allowance. Officers who had been riding desks for years without an offer to take the exams hated Nick for the preferential treatment and the bosses thought he was a snot-nosed punk, even though he had the years on the force to back up his progress.

Soon after getting his detective shield, the PC found a new pet on a bigger case and left Nick alone to fend off the wolves. It didn't help that he was never the suit wearing type and did his best to avoid doing so, which immediately put him on Jenkins' shit list. Narco cops got away with dressing down, Homicide didn't. He was an outsider on both ends, resented by the uniforms on patrol and thought of as a fluke by the detectives. Most days he wished he had just done his job and kept his mouth shut, but that was never really Nick's style.

Lucky for him, Hank Drees was the uniform stationed outside the interview room. Hank was the only guy who sincerely congratulated him when he got the call up to the majors. He and Nick shared a slight head nod when they caught sight of each other.

"What's up, Hank?"

"Detective," Hank said.

"If I had known a promotion involved me being a file clerk, I would have stayed on the beat, waiting patiently to get shot at."

"I could shoot you, if that would help?"

"Two more days of cold cases and I might take you up on that offer. How's Kelly?"

"She's doing good, been playing softball and is gonna to try to get on the JV field hockey team in the fall."

"Your ex-wife trying to turn her gay on you?"

"Whatever, man. At this point, I'm just glad she talks to me. I don't know what happens on the other side of town in that house during the week. If I don't have to worry about some 15-year-old horny shithead skateboard punk trying to get in her panties, then she can rename herself Sappho for all I care."

Nick laughed with his friend. Since being moved into RHD, he hadn't seen much of his old crew in the department. His busy life was likely interpreted as conceited snubbing.

"How's your mom? She still smoking?"

"Still smoking? I think she's actually upped her dosage. The oxygen tank has increased her lung capacity. I'm surprised she hasn't started taking 'em two at a time."

"At least I don't have your second-hand stink reeking up my squad anymore."

"Still no partner?"

"I asked Renner not to give me any punk-ass rookie, I've been doing this too long to put up with another Nick Archer," he said, smiling, "He's doing me a favor giving me these daytime shifts, lets me see my girl more. Least he could do, considering my partner up and disappeared like a fart in the wind."

"I know... I'm bad about keeping in touch. The job, Mom, the whole unicorn figurine addiction."

Hank snorted at the bad joke.

"Anyway, good to see you, man. We need to catch a beer pretty soon."

"Venue never changes, big shot. Thursdays at the Rusty Kilt."

"You sure the boys are willing to have me? I have this image in my mind of me stepping through the doors, the needle scratching off the jukebox and everyone beating the shit out of me."

"You're always welcome, as long as you buy the first round. That'll stave off the wild dogs for as long as it takes to chug a cheap beer."

"I'll take your word for it."

Nick gave Hank a friendly swat with the file folder.

"Oh, one more thing. Watch it in there."

"Why? We got a violent one?" Nick paused with his hand on the door.

Hank busted out laughing and clapped Nick on the shoulder.

"Violent? Lady won't stop crying. Good luck getting her to answer questions."

"That slippery fuck," Nick said half to himself, wishing he'd asked why Jenkins was so willing to pass this particular interview onto him.

"Thanks for the heads up, Hank."

"My pleasure."

He could already hear the muffled sobs as he opened the door. The low light in the room revealed a tiny woman with her face buried in a damp handkerchief. He rolled his eyes at what he was about to deal with and found himself pining for the comforting consistency of a stack of unsolved murders.

The water flowed from her eyes like a cracked fire hydrant on a hot New York street. She didn't acknowledge him as he entered the room, sat down across from her, and opened the file on the tabletop. Before he spoke to her, he took one look up at the camera mounted in the corner, his eyes letting the guys huddled around the video feed know that they could fuck right off.

"Miss," he paused to look down at the folder, "Miss Searle?"

She was wailing like a banshee belting Wagner, but managed to nod a yes at him.

"Miss Searle, I just need to ask you a few questions."

She blew her nose and clutched the dripping rag to her face. The weeping hampered her lungs' ability to take in air, shortening her breath to staccato gasps. This wasn't how he imagined life as a detective.

"Listen, lady, could you stop with the--," he stopped himself, his hands going to his temples, trying to think of the best way to slip a laxative into Jenkins' coffee.

"Miss," his voice strained to get softer, "the sooner you answer me, the sooner I can get you out of here. You don't want to be cooped up in this dark little room anymore, right?"

Eyes peeked from underneath the wet veil, still held hard to her nose. Her waterlogged eyelashes clung to each other like they'd been lathered with 1920s mascara, framing her big blue eyes.

"Okay," she squeaked out at him in a soft voice, blowing her nose once more and lowering the handkerchief to reveal the rest of her face. She looked awful, but Nick noticed she was probably rather pretty on a good day. Her large eyes flanked a crooked nose that on another woman might be unsightly, but somehow it fit the composition of her face. At the moment, she was red and puffy, but something in him stirred as she softly moved a wisp of chestnut hair away from her face and over her ear.

"Thank you," he said to her, forcing a sincere smile. She was trying her best to return the kind gesture, but he could see most of her strength was focused on holding back the constant well of tears.

"You're an executive assistant at Keller & Hoff Real Estate, correct?"

"Mmm-hmm," she nodded, her lip quivering.

"And your boss was Marjorie Wells?"

"Yessss."

The dam broke once more and the waterworks flooded her cheeks, her face seeking the hankie to levy the deluge.

"Jesus Christ," he growled under his breath, but loud enough for her to hear.

"Miss Searle. Miss Searle? Penelope?"

"Pennyeeee," she corrected him through the sobs.

"Penny."

Nick's patience reserves were low. Mr. Sensitive didn't come easy to him. Add on that he wasn't exactly a Casanova when it came to talking to women and Nick Archer found himself in the middle of a shit tsunami.

"I know this must be tough for you," he softened, trying to remember his Witness Advocacy course from the academy, "but we're trying to get as much information as possible, so we can close the case on Miss Wells' death."

"I know, I'm sorry," Penny apologized. Fear and apprehension kept changing her face from deep red to pale and Nick knew it was touch and go with the weeping time bomb sitting in front of him.

"Let's see if I can make this a little easier on both of us."

Adjusting his position in the uncomfortable metal chair, he hoped that logic disguised as kindness might do the trick.

"I'm just going to go through the facts here and see if you want to give me any more helpful information, okay?"

"Uh-huh."

"Now, re-living some of this might be a bit upsetting, but this is for the good of everyone, all right? So, please try your hardest not to get too upset and I'll do my best not to ask you too many upsetting questions. Okay?"

"Thanks. You're much nicer than that other guy. Are you doing a good cop, bad cop on me?"

"He's not a bad cop, he's just a dick."

Penny laughed through her tears, doing her best to wipe the snot running from her nose.

"Was that a laugh? I'm breaking through, let's roll with it. According to this report, Marjorie Wells collapsed in a board meeting this past Tuesday, correct?"

He paused, waiting for the next wave of sobs. They didn't come.

"Yes."

"She had a seizure, lost consciousness, and stopped breathing. A co-worker of yours, Gabriel Byhn, tried to perform mouth-to-mouth resuscitation until the paramedics arrived. Miss Wells was declared DOA when she arrived at the hospital."

Penny took a deep breath and placed her palms flat on the table, like a drunk trying to keep the room from spinning.

"It just happened so fast. One minute she was getting upset about how the branding templates looked wrong and the next minute she was on the floor. We all thought she had a heart attack."

"Was Miss Wells what you would consider an overweight woman?"

Penny tightened her lips together and shifted in her chair. Her eyes went to the ceiling, as though she was searching the white panels for the appropriate words. Nick sensed she was trying to hide her hatred for Marjorie Wells. He would have reacted similarly if asked to politely describe Lt. Jim Jenkins.

"She was bulky, but I wouldn't really classify her as huge."

"Bulky? I wouldn't describe my boss as bulky. More of an overbearing fat pig."

She laughed at him again. He could see the fragile fortress around her crumbling.

"She definitely had those qualities."

"Were you aware that Miss Wells had hypoglycemia?"

"Not at all. Nobody did."

Nick was surprised he'd made it through so many questions without an outburst. He thought he might jinx it by acknowledging it, but he wanted to keep her endeared to him as long as possible.

"You're doing a good job keeping calm, Penny, thank you."

"You're welcome. Thanks for taking it easy on me. All of my friends, or people I thought were my friends, think I am this horrible murderous person."

"Speaking of that, would you mind if we get down to why you're here?"

Nick could see the strain in her neck as she gathered the willpower to hold back her emotions. She nodded ever so slightly to him, indicating he could continue.

"On Wednesday, the day after Miss Wells' passing, a package was delivered to her. The secretary sorting the mail, Nancy Uhl, forwarded that package to Miss Wells' next of kin, who in turn contacted us. Were you aware of the contents of that package, Miss——Penny?"

The salt water already started to pool in the corner of her eyes, but she nodded, yes, she did know.

"Apparently, the package contained some sort of threatening," he checked the folder, "green M&M's?"

Nick paused for a moment, making sure he had read the report right.

"M&M's? The candy?"

She nodded, "Mmmm-hmm."

"Threatening... M&M's?"

"I didn't know she was diabetic and besides she didn't eat any of them before she died and I wouldn't even know how to poison M&M's anyway and plus they came right from the manufacturer so I wouldn't have touched them and I did hate her, I'll admit it, but I never would kill her oh my God I'm going to jail," Penny's words came in a long vomit of syllables.

Nick stared at her, his mouth hanging open, taking it all in. And then, he couldn't help it. He burst into heavy laughter that made him sound like a braying madman.

Penny stopped sobbing once the wall of sound hit her. She was horrified that he would be making such light of her current situation, but soon it infected her and she found herself laughing just as hard as him.

"So you," he chortled, gasping between snorts, "you sent her, um, you sent her a box of personalized green M&M's that said

'Fuck off and die' and then she died. Of sugar shock." Saying it out loud incited another burst of laughter until it petered out naturally.

"Well, Penny, I have to say, I'm so sorry you've been put through all of this cloak and dagger police questioning, which obviously upset you, but there's no law against wishing ill will on someone, otherwise the whole world would be in prison."

He got up and walked over to her side of the table.

"Now, of course, we're still going to wait for the toxicology report to come back on this one, so don't make any plans to go out of town, but I don't think you have anything to worry about."

Her eyes went wide and she leapt up into his arms, hugging him tightly before he knew what was happening. He returned the hug awkwardly, remembering the conversation was being recorded for posterity. He pushed her away gently and gave her a smile.

"Thank you, oh God, thank you so much."

"Miss Searle, as far as we know you're guilty of nothing but having a very creative way of trying to quit your job and, let's be honest, terrible timing. You'll be contacted when we have our final reports on the case. And, if I were you, unless you count your intercepted package as your official notice, I'd take a few days off work, let things cool down a bit."

"Thank you, Detective... you know I never got your name."

"Archer. Nick Archer."

"Thank you, Detective Archer."

"You're welcome," he said to her, opening the door to let her out. She walked down the hallway and happened to catch him looking after her as she glanced over her shoulder. Penny gave him a fluttered wave that he returned, trying not to seem too eager.

"How the hell did you get her to talk?" Hank's deep voice whispered from behind him.

"Detective secret," Nick said back to him.

"Sorry I asked, dickhead."

"Catch you later, Hank."

Once Penny was out of sight, he took a deep breath and wandered back to his desk, returning to the mound of cases that couldn't be solved by a hilarious case of misunderstanding.

7

"I want him dead!"

"Have a little trouble with the razor this morning, Benny?"

Benny's hand went instinctively to the patch where his mustache used to be. He'd let the blood dry without cleaning it, resulting in the beginnings of a dirty scab, the surrounding hair a mess of dry, encrusted red flecks.

"I ain't here to play no games, Nestor. He made a fool outta me and now I wanna show him who's boss."

"I didn't realize that mustache was so important to you."

Benny could see the sides of Nestor's cheeks go up, giving him crow's feet at the edges of his dark eyes. The bastard was smiling at him from under that surgical mask.

"Will you come down here and talk? You're givin' me the creeps up there."

Nestor Tyre resided in the park area surrounding the entrance to Bronson Canyon. He was never without a suit of full camouflage, accentuated by a surgical mask, making him look like a first response Ebola doctor. If Ernie Politics represented the new regime of political activists, Nestor would have been his defense secretary. He rarely walked among the masses in the daylight, but when he did, it was to report information to Ernie. It was always a whisper or note passed with gloved hands, and then he would disappear back into the woods until he acquired the next piece of relevant intelligence.

Nestor made his way down to Benny 7-11's level, doing his best to keep to the shadows of the trees. He never acknowledged that his mask was bright blue and would give his position away to anyone who didn't happen to be colorblind.

"And what do you suggest I do?" Nestor asked him, cocking his head in curiosity like a dog responding to a strange noise.

"I *suggest* you go to your little weapons stockpile in your mythical undisclosed location, find Ray Cobb and blow his fuckin' head off."

"But you see, Benny, I'm saving that particular stockpile for when the revolution begins, which I'm certain could be any day now. Those weapons aren't meant for me. The neo-proletariat was meant to handle those elements of destruction, while I prefer the elegance of the sickle, held high at the head of a people's army, marching with a solidarity and singular purpose the Bolsheviks only dreamed of. Just because Ernie failed in his charge, doesn't mean we should be any less vigilant."

His intricately practiced speech affectation was pissing Benny off. Nestor had worked for years to perfect the linguistic eloquence of Karl Marx and Che Guevara, all part of his freakish cleanliness right down to his manner of speaking. Benny thought it made him sound like a pompous piece of shit.

"The fuckin' revolution? The revolution done already started, man! Look what they did to Ernie."

"There are so many 'theys' I have begun to lose track," Nestor mused, "We still haven't determined who was at fault for our fallen comrade's untimely demise."

"You think that's a coincidence? You think that just happened outta nowhere?"

"If I'm not mistaken, Benny, you were supposed to recover a certain document from Ernie before his untimely passing and failed to do so. A document that is now infinitely more important and may help to flush our game from its den."

"Cobb jumped me, Nestor! I had it in my hand and the son of a bitch sucker punched me and tore the hair outta my face."

"You didn't get a good look at it?"

"Some numbers and Spanish-Russian gibberish, man. I didn't exactly have time to memorize it while my head was being bashed into a concrete wall."

"And you didn't send him to me, instead you sent him to *Her*."

"I panicked, all right. And besides, you know Cobb. He's smarter than that. No offense, but he thinks you're one big package of Juniper Loony Bars."

"Benny, you forget the words of the illustrious Sun-Tzu, *Hold out baits to entice the enemy. Feign disorder, then crush him.*"

"Baits? What the fuck're you talkin' about? I knew he wouldn't come to you."

"So instead you counted on *Her* discretion? We still don't know where *Her* loyalties lie. Perhaps *She* was involved. Perhaps the lioness has positioned *Herself*, lying in wait for the coalition of males to devour each other so *She* can lead the pride."

"Man, what the fuck? This is why I never know what the fuck you're sayin'. You talk in fuckin' circles and riddles and shit. What was I supposed to do? He broke my fucking finger," Benny whined, holding up the crooked and loosely splinted appendage in front of Nestor's face.

"Would you like me to reset that properly for you?"

He backed away from Nestor, knowing that his version of first aid would give Benny something to truly fear. Nestor stepped out from behind the lengthening shadow of the tree he was using for cover and watched the sun descend behind the mountains, leaving a trail of orange and pink in the small handful of clouds.

"We'll wait and see what happens at Lindberg tonight. If *She* gives him the manuscript, then I'll pay him a visit and we'll get both documents. If he gets assimilated, then we... *you* will personally have to visit *Her* to recover the manuscript and the key. For your sake, Benny, I hope that Ray is as clever as you give him credit. I wouldn't want to know what a slimy tripe like you would have to offer *Her* in exchange for such treasures. You may not walk right for a while." He let his smug insult take hold, the indications of a smile emerging again.

Benny looked at Nestor's back as he kept his gaze steady on the setting sun. His rage had subsided for the moment, but every throb of pain in his finger reignited it again. He left Nestor staring off into the distance and headed down the hill, hoping he could scrounge enough change together to pick up a sandwich at the supermarket by the Scientology Celebrity Centre, waiting the night out to see just how smart Ray Cobb really was.

8

The bus crossed into Culver City and Ray pulled the cord to request his stop. He thanked the driver for the free fare and let his eyes adjust from the fluorescent lights of the bus to the darkness of the unfamiliar neighborhood.

The wide sprawl of the Los Angeles Metro Area offered plenty of stomping grounds and living on the streets gave him plenty of time to explore. Ray didn't tend to spend his days sleeping or talking to himself, so he kept busy getting to know his town. He prided himself on finding the safest places, the least patrolled, and the best food and shelter options. Venturing down to The Dark Territory in Culver City, according to the stories, was akin to wandering the streets of South Central launching racial slurs at anyone who would listen.

Lindberg Park was a place of legend in most circles. People spoke of The Dark Territory in whispers, an eerie shake to their voice––relaying a ghost story they're doing their best not to believe, denying their mind's descent into nightmares. All of the stories followed the same pattern; *Mary went down to Lindberg Park and was never heard from again, or ever since Dave came back from Lindberg Park, he hasn't been the same.* But Ray didn't believe the stories, or at least he told himself he didn't believe them. If Benny 7-11 could make Lindberg Park one of his favorite haunts, The Dark Territory couldn't be anywhere near as bad as the stories made it out to be. But the long bus ride gave his mind a chance to imagine the worst and it solidified his sense of caution. He'd arrived early just to be safe, giving him a chance to scope out what he was dealing with until the witching hour arrived.

Lumbering down Ocean Boulevard, Ray followed the sterile outline of the Los Angeles River. The concrete walls of the trickling waterway had choked all of the nature out of it, swallowing it like the city had swallowed so many people's hopes and dreams.

The residents of the area were out late, taking their dogs for one last walk before they returned to their feather-down comforters and soft pillows. Half asleep, some already in their pajamas, all of them had trusty plastic bags in hand to keep their community clean of dog droppings. The looks he got made his skin crawl, like he'd gotten lice from a blanket found behind an elementary school. He could feel several sets of eyes on him, memorizing his movements, as though they knew they'd have to recount them later.

A frumpy woman with dirty blonde hair stared at Ray bit too long, her vision still blurry from taking out her contacts for the night. The beagle she was walking yanked her out of her trance as it investigated a new smell. In her eyes, he didn't recognize fear. Instead it was curiosity, almost awe. Not because she had never seen him before, but because she wasn't used to seeing anyone like him in her neighborhood.

The residential area surrounding Lindberg Park was just as pleasant as most of the communities in Los Angeles. Crime was relatively controlled and the mean income of the residents was ample. But, in most communities, there were still the occasional resident bums. Most people resolved to live with the homeless epidemic, seeing the occasional vagrant rummaging through a garbage can for a stray bottle, or someone huddled in an abandoned doorway to grab twenty minutes of sleep before they are told to get moving. But there was none of that here. Bars were conspicuously absent from the windows of the homes surrounding the green of the park and any sounds of the city were drowned by the sound of the wind as it fluttered through the leaves of the trees.

The closer Ray got to the park, the emptier the streets became, until he stood on the edge of the grassy knoll. Staring at the park department's activities building, he finally realized he was alone. His logic and common sense began to give way to a vision of a barbaric band of marauders descending from the trees, tearing him limb from limb. He envisioned his head stuck on a pike in the playground, his body being devoured by cannibal savages before the darkness consumed him.

Ray blinked the image away and was back in the quiet neighborhood, his heart rate constant and keeping time in his throat. There was no kingdom of massacre, nor was there a small transient camp set up behind the playground equipment, folks with bindles cooking beans in the can over an open flame. It was just a park. It was desolate. Sterile.

Midnight came and went as he walked the small area of the park, wondering if he had been taken in by a whole lot of legend and fear. The space was open and in full view of the houses surrounding it. The only fencing enclosed the tennis court and the two park buildings were padlocked and empty. All he could do now was wait.

Those who survived venturing into The Dark Territory told tales of making a peace offering. It always had to be something regal, something of royal status. A good gift was rewarded and a bad gift was punished. He felt the sword hilt in his jacket pocket. It thumped against his chest every time he took a step, reminding him of why he was there. But there was no one to make an offering to. There was nothing.

He was starting to fade. Ray hadn't really slept at all since he'd passed out in the ice machine and that wasn't exactly what he'd call rest. His recent attempts at sleep were haunted by dreams of Ernie, his bloody stumps reaching out for him as the vacant black sockets stained his white face with ooze, wailing in the anguish of Purgatory.

Climbing the wooden playground equipment, he found himself at the top of a structure shaped like an old tugboat, surveying the whole park. There was no movement, save the slight rustle of leaves and swings catching the wind. The chains, smoothed by the touch of a hundred tiny fingers, creaked melodically in the night air. Sand, puckered by the footprints of children, created a pattern of chaos and led his eyes to a familiar sight. In the middle of the sandbox was a gigantic red locomotive.

There were portholes and handholds, a miniature version of the great iron horse that first brought the country together. Ray climbed into the bottom of the train and lay down in the sand. Peering through the porthole in the roof of the miniature locomotive, he looked up at the stars still bright enough to shine through the haze of light pollution and wondered what it had been like all those years ago, when being a tramp was to be part of a lifestyle, part of a community. A group of men, their world destroyed by war and depression, trying to make the best out of the husk of their former lives. An entire generation of hobos riding the rails, looking for whatever work they could find, their lives as inconstant as the wind.

Ray tried to imagine being a part of a Great Tramp Army instead of being a man alone against the world. It was hard to believe once there was even something as honorable as the Hobo Code. Imagining a set of rules for the existence he shared with so many others was laughable, now that the only rule of the land was "Survival of the Fittest." Everyone had allies and enemies, but no matter what, they always took care of Number One. These were the thoughts carrying him off to sleep when metal covers quickly slid over all of the portholes, encasing him in darkness.

9

"How was your day buried in paper?" his mother screamed at him from the living room.

"It was fine, Ma," Nick yelled back at her, throwing his bag onto the fainting couch in the foyer.

"Don't leave that there, I'm not here to pick up after you," she managed to scream out before she lapsed into an uncontrollable coughing fit. He picked the bag back up and put it over his shoulder, laughing, seeing their relationship hadn't changed since he was a child, but recognizing the irony that nowadays he spent more time cleaning up after her.

"You do anything fun today?" he asked her, wandering into the kitchen.

"There's a plate for you in the fridge. I didn't know how late you were going to be."

"You can likely expect me home early these days, Ma. As soon as the shift changes I'm glad to get the hell out of there. I have a whole new respect for file clerks. Surprised the suicide rate among them isn't higher," he called to her, his head stuck in the refrigerator, not really wanting the crusty looking pork chop with the side of green beans she'd made for him, but he knew it would hurt her feelings if he didn't pop it in the microwave and eat it like a good son. He pulled the Saran Wrap off the top of the plate and grabbed the pork chop by the bone, leaving the beans in the kitchen as he joined his mother in front of the TV.

"I put that on a plate for a reason, you know. To remind you that you're a man, not a dog," she coughed at him while lighting up another cigarette.

"I spent the day in the office being as white collar as humanly possible. I want to tear something apart with my teeth and bare hands to remind me that I'm a man and not some automaton," he said to her, tearing the meat from the bone with a growl and grinning at her as he chewed, wiping cold grease from his chin. She shook her head at him and went back to her program.

"So, what're we watching?"

"This new show on the Discovery Channel. This guy from Seattle thought God was talking to him, so he decides to go on a killing spree throughout––"

"And that's my cue to exit stage right."

"What? It's an interesting show. It wouldn't hurt you to sit down and learn a little something."

"Learn a little something? Ma, this kind of crap is what I've been looking at for eight hours a day for a week straight. You want me to save you an hour? He kills a bunch of people, each more brutal than the next and then makes some little mistake leading to the end of his reign of terror. I think I'll just go and read a book."

"Suit yourself. I'll let you know how it turns out," she shrugged at him, not taking her eyes off of the television.

"If I'm wrong, I'll owe you a Coke."

"Do you want to remind me when you became the grumpy old woman living in this house?"

"Enjoy your show, Ma."

Nick made his way back into the kitchen and tore some more meat off the bone. It was tough and cold, but he didn't really want to put in the effort of cooking anything, even if it meant punching in a few numbers on the microwave. He tossed the bone into the garbage can and scraped the untouched members of the plate in after it. The remnants of that day's newspaper went down on top of the food scraps and he pushed it down with his foot. The last thing he needed right now was a lecture from his mother about wasting food. And he was still hungry.

Nick washed the plate and put it in the drying rack before heading upstairs. Once in his room, he closed the door for secrecy, knowing his mother wouldn't be able to hear him if he left the door wide open and spoke into a loud speaker, but he wasn't taking any chances on her eavesdropping. She was a lonely woman and her favorite new way to entertain herself was by living vicariously through her son's interactions with the outside world. He tossed his messenger bag onto his unmade bed and sat down at his desk, pulling a scrap of paper out of his pocket.

He'd received the toxicology report that afternoon, but hadn't taken the opportunity to call Penny Searle as soon as he'd told her he would. If he'd made the call from his desk, that would have been it. She'd be absolved and he'd go back to his stack of paperwork, but ever since that interview, he couldn't stop thinking about her. Through the tears, she had this nervous, cute quality about her. Something he might never have noticed under different circumstances.

She appeared to be one of those pretty girls who hasn't been pretty her entire life, so had to develop a personality to compensate. She carried herself differently than someone who knows how gorgeous they are, having lived in the world of the unattractive and not forgotten the humility that goes along with it. He didn't know how he deduced this in the very short time he'd spent with her, most of it with her as a blubbering mess, but he just knew. It was his job to read people. Professional hazard.

Nick took a long look at the phone number he had scribbled on the piece of scrap paper from his desk. Holding the phone out at arms-length, calming his breath, he dialed her number.

"Just calling a witness... just calling a witness... just calling a witness," he mumbled to himself, a mantra to screw his courage to the sticking place.

The phone rang three times before it clicked over and he heard her voice.

"Hello?"

He didn't know why he was so nervous. His voice disappeared.

"Um, hello?" she asked the silence.

"Hello, Hi, is this Miss Searle... er... Penny?"

He knew it was her. He knew she lived alone. He just didn't know what else to say.

"I'm on a do-not-call list, how did you get this number?"

"No, um, Penny, this is Nick... I mean, Detective Archer, from the police."

From the police? Like the band? God, you sound like an idiot. Nick scolded himself, slapping his forehead.

"Oh, Detective Archer, hello. I'm sorry about that. I really can't stand telemarketers and that sounded like one of their opening lines."

"It's all right, I can't stand telemarketers either. I usually try to mess with them, tell them I'm a cop, threaten to arrest them or find out where they work."

She let out a small laugh. "I wish I had the guts to do that, but I always remember they're people, too, just trying to make a day's pay."

Great, now you sound like a dick, he thought, feeling unable to say anything right.

"I guess I never thought of it that way. The reason I'm calling is..."

"Oh God, what did they find? Am I going to prison?" He could hear the waterworks welling up in her throat and had to jump in quickly to halt the process.

"No! No, you aren't. We actually got the toxicology report back and Miss Wells died of natural causes. Diabetic shock before she even got wind of your M&M's."

"Oh, thank God," Penny blurted, starting to cry over the phone.

"Penny, are you all right?" Nick asked, wondering if this was the best time for him to call.

"Oh, yeah, I'm sorry. You must think I'm an emotional mess all the time. I'm just so happy. I haven't been able to sleep or eat. For a while there I thought I was going to die of nervous tension."

"I'm sorry we kept you hanging for so long, we just had to be sure for everyone's sake."

"Well, thank you for taking the time to personally call me. You must have stayed at the office late tonight waiting for the results, that was very sweet of you."

Nick looked around his dirty bedroom in guilt. "Yep, just wanted to get those to you as soon as I got them. Well, that or arrest you as soon as possible."

She laughed at him over the phone. He was glad she had a sense of humor about it, because, in retrospect, that statement could have been interpreted all wrong.

"Actually, I haven't had the opportunity to leave the office," he segued with a little white lie, "I was wondering if you've had dinner yet."

"Um, no," she said, her tone changing to slight suspicion, "do you have more questions for me?"

"No, no, not at all. You're in the clear. I just thought... well... if maybe you'd let me buy you a burger... you know... as an apology for all the heartache we may have caused you."

If Hank knew what he was doing, he'd have put a bullet in his foot.

"Yeah, that actually sounds really good. Like I said, I haven't been eating lately and when you mentioned that burger, I'll have to admit, my mouth watered a little."

"Great," he replied, with a little too much enthusiasm, doing his best to recover without sounding too eager, "Uh, do you know where Lucky Devils is? In Hollywood?"

"I think I've passed it a few times."

"Okay, uh, why don't we meet there at say," he looked at his watch, "like, eight-fifteen? Does that give you enough time?"

"Sure, eight-fifteen."

"Good. Great. So, I'll see you there."

"Thanks. This is so sweet of you. See you there."

"Great. Okay. Bye."

"Bye."

Nick clicked off his phone and threw it down onto his desk. Spinning around in his chair, he did a little dance, pounding his feet on the floor.

"WHAT'S GOING ON UP THERE?" his mother called, her voice muffled from beneath the floorboards. He opened up his bedroom door and called down to her.

"NOTHIN', MA!"

Her complaining jolted him back to reality and he slipped into the bathroom to floss the pork chop out from between his teeth. As he wrapped the long string of dental floss around his forefingers, he tried to think of the best strategy to segue this little meeting from a business thank you into a full-on date.

10

Ray stared into the darkness, time disappearing, giving away to the void of endless thoughts. He was frustrated for letting his guard down, allowing himself to be trapped so easily, but panicking would get him nowhere. The sides of the porthole covers provided no lip to slip a finger in and push them out. They had been crafted with great skill, the seams almost disappearing, enclosing him in a hermetically sealed coffin. He felt around his person until he came across a cheap Bic lighter, found in the gutter on his way to visit Benny 7-11. A few frantic flicks finally yielded flame. Looking down at the bed of playground sand beneath him, he tried not to think about what would happen if one of the portholes suddenly opened and flooded with sand. His coffin would quickly become his tomb.

Above his head he could make out some markings etched into the metal, lines he had seen in the moonlight. He'd initially attributed the scratches to some teenagers putting their initials into the playground equipment. Bringing the light closer, he recognized them immediately.

The Hobo Code may have been dead, but everyone on the street was still familiar with the old Hobo Symbols. Most learned them after they had been to a place giving out free food or where a person was kind and noticed the symbol on the wall or embankment. These he recognized immediately: a circle with two arrows through it and a spearhead. The message was plain as day, like primitive cave drawings. A previous occupant of this tube had something to tell future travelers: *Leave Quickly and Prepare to Defend Yourself.*

The flame began to burn his thumb and he let go of the button. Darkness reclaimed the space. Moonlight flashed in on him as the porthole above his head was removed and something was thrown down onto him.

"Put it on," a muffled voice said.

Ray felt around. Grasping the heavy fabric, he soon learned its purpose, despite his blindness. It was a hood, like the ones people were given in spy movies to wear when they were being taken to secret locations. Or the kind of hood terrorists made their hostages wear just before they decapitated them. Neither of those options sounded particularly pleasant to Ray, but he did what he was told. There was no turning back.

"It's on," he said, his voice muffled by the canvas. His words came back at him, mixed with the remnants of the sour breath of the previous wearers. If he got out of this anytime soon, he was going to find himself a toothbrush, or at the very least, a mint.

The portholes and the entrance to the locomotive opened around him. A hand grabbed the back of his jacket and guided him out of the playground equipment.

"You got a choice," the muffled voice said. It sounded like his captor was also masked because he could barely make out the words, though it sounded vaguely female.

"You can follow directions and let us take you to *Her*. Without struggle, without us havin' to tie your ass up. Or you can be a problem. You gonna be a problem?"

Ray didn't take kindly to the idea of being led blindly to his fate, but they held all the cards. If things were going to go bad, they wouldn't go bad until he arrived at the next destination. If he kept his hands free, he could get an advantage over whoever was leading him if the situation turned south.

"I'm not gonna be a problem. Lead the way," he said.

"Hold this," the voice ordered. A thick rope with a large knot at the end was given to him. The tether pulled tight and he was jolted forward, doing his best to keep pace.

"Where're we going?" Ray asked, trying his best to sound like he was just making conversation.

"Shut the fuck up. You don't get to ask nothin' 'til you give us some answers."

"Fair enough."

"Who sent you?"

"Benny 7-11."

The rope went loose and a hand to his chest stopped him cold.

"He ain't allowed to see *Her*. He don't have the right."

"I'm not him."

"You're his friend."

"Actually, I beat the ever-loving shit out of him about twelve hours ago. If there was anyone in the world I'd like to not be associated with more, it would be Benny, but he told me he gave *Her* some documents I need. As I'm sure you know, no one comes to *Her* without a reason."

"I know the documents you're talkin' 'bout. But if you be misrepresentin' yourself to get to *Her*, you'll regret your choices. You feel me?"

"Duly noted."

Short-tempered, but reasonable. Latin accent. Definitely female.

In a few short sentences, his captor had given him plenty to work with.

"What's your name?"

"Ray. Raymond Cobb."

"You have another name?"

"Another name?" he said, before realizing he'd asked a question, "Uh, no. Well, not as far as I know. But we call Tom Feder Tommy Cat Piss. Pretty sure he doesn't know that."

"Your name don't sound familiar, Cobb."

"I try to keep a fairly low profile."

"That is, 'til now."

"I'm sorry?"

"I'd say beatin' the shit outta someone in broad daylight ain't exactly what I'd call keepin' a low profile."

"Well, sister, that's why I'm here. A friend of mine's dead and I'm just trying to get some answers. My path led me here. I'm usually not one for this secret society stuff you all have going on, but my buddy is missing his hands, his shiny pink peepers, and his life. I figure if he went through something as painful as that, I can deal with wherever this particular voyage happens to take me."

"You seem a'ight."

"When the wind's blowing in the right direction."

"You ever fucked somebody who didn't want you to?"

Ray stopped walking. "Pardon?"

"Answer the question, Cobb."

Sudden impatience turned Ray's interrogator into a different person.

"Can't say that I have."

The hood was torn from his head and his eyes blurred as they adjusted to the new light. He blinked the darkness away to see he was in a parking lot, empty of cars, the bright overhead lights shining down around him. He wasn't one-on-one with his captor. He was surrounded on all sides, a circle of bodies with him in the center. In her anger, she had given away her tactical advantage, but also let Ray know should he choose to be bold, he was in for quite a fight.

"Have you? Not even once thought 'bout what it'd be like to fuck some stupid chick while she screamed 'No'?"

The question pummeled him, every word soaked in bile. She was a good foot shorter than him and her head was covered with a black ski mask. The rope he held in his hand was attached to her waist. She had deep brown eyes that looked right through him. The pain and resolve there frightened him.

"No," he whispered with soft sincerity, afraid of incurring an unknown wrath. Her eyes didn't leave his, checking for a twitch of untruth. She didn't find the lie she wanted in his dark pupils and the hood was replaced as quickly as it had been removed.

"Let's go," she said, jerking him forward. Now that he was listening for it, he could hear the soft footfalls of those around him. There were ten or twelve of them, perhaps more behind him.

They walked in silence for twenty minutes. The questions had stopped and after her rage-filled confrontation, he didn't dare pose any of his own. Under his feet, the concrete gave away to grass, making Ray wonder if they had just been leading him around in circles, only to abandon him back in Lindberg Park. A hand went up to his shoulder, stopping him. The grip was softer than it was before, but still firm.

"Gimme your weapon," she said to him.

"I don't have weapon."

"You've come this far, Cobb, don't fuckin' lie to me now."

He started to panic before remembering the sword hilt.

"Oh, um, here," he said, reaching into his jacket pocket and handing over the white linen package, "but it's not a weapon, or at least isn't intended to be a weapon. It's an offering."

"An offering?"

"I was told... in order to see *Her*... a gift should be brought."

There was a pause.

"You heard right."

He heard the creak of a heavy metal gate before him and was led through it.

"Watch your step and follow close."

Her gloved hand touched his and choked it up to the next knot on the rope. He could feel her body heat in front of him he was so close to her. Every once in a while, he would widen his stride and his foot would catch a hard surface in the grass. The slope of the terrain changed and his breathing increased as they went uphill. Her hand stopped him once more.

"Kneel."

Ray did as instructed. The rope left his hands. He could feel the dew in the grass seeping through his pants.

"Take the hood off," a different, softer female voice instructed him.

Ray reached up and pulled the canvas off of his head, slowly and with no sudden movements.

Two torches blazed at the foot of a large marble statue. Ray was in the middle of a large cemetery. The smooth surfaces he'd stumbled on were headstones, recessed in the vast lawn. In the distance, beyond a large wall of volcanic rock, the city lights speckled the horizon. Dark figures were perched all around him. At the foot of the statue sat The Queen.

She wore a sleeveless blouse that revealed her tan and well-muscled arms. He could see she was petite, but strong. Her bright green eyes shone in the light of the torches and her red hair flowed onto her shoulders like a cascading waterfall.

"Raymond Cobb?"

"Yeah," he said, his voice cracking.

"I've been waiting for you."

"Then you know why I'm here."

"On the contrary. I don't know why you've come now and not a year ago or a month from now. We've watched you."

"Watched me?"

"You're different, Ray. You don't belong in this world."

"My bank account says otherwise," Ray said without thinking. She laughed before he had a chance to apologize for speaking out of turn.

"Don't look so frightened, I don't bite."

"I'd heard−−"

"That insolence is met with fury? That I'm a mythical beast, segregated to my forbidden city? What do you outsiders call it? The Dark Territory? Myths and stories can be used both to explain the world and to confuse it. Thanks for the sword hilt, by the way, I'll be sure to put it in the pile with the others."

Ray looked at her, confused. The stories of The Queen always had variations, like a bad game of telephone, but every one created a jigsaw puzzle image of a titan, equal parts Catherine the Great and the Queen of Hearts from Alice in Wonderland. He'd pictured a large beast of a woman, sweet when pleased, but a fiery ball of rage when upset. She took glee in the receipt of gifts reinforcing her status as self-imposed royalty and punished those who undercut her authority with gifts not befitting her stature. Madness dictated her decisions. Pain, torture, and hatred filled all the stories, causing fair warning to the listeners. Ray didn't see this at all.

"I was told you have the final manuscript of Ernie Politics' manifesto."

"I do," she answered.

"May I have it?"

The Queen rose from her position at the base of the monument and walked toward Ray, who still knelt in the wet grass.

"Why should I give it to you? I heard you were sent here on an errand by Benny 7-11."

"You've been misinformed," Ray said boldly, waiting for the sweet facade to disappear and the raging bull to emerge, but it never came. She merely kept her smile fixed on him.

"Have I?"

"I gave Benny 7-11 quite a rattling before he spilled the beans leading me down here. I had a feeling he was feeding me a load, but despite the disdain for him you and I seem to share, his info was good. So, yeah, Benny sent me, but this errand is mine."

"You've got a lot of confidence, but are careful not to let it translate into arrogance. I like that about you, Ray."

She took a step away from him and looked out into the vista of the cemetery, calm and peaceful. Her operations took place in the wide-open spaces of lawn, the civilized world standing just beyond the iron fence. Her lack of fear in the open exposure made him uneasy. If these theatrics could be performed in plain sight with no security or police alerted, The Queen had more than this small band of hooligans on her side. Ray could feel his chances of survival slipping away into the ether.

"I caught Benny bothering one of my people at a convenience store in Palms. The filthy bastard almost started a territorial war. When he found out it was me he'd offended, he pissed himself for fear that he had nothing to offer me––nothing but the latest copy of Ernie Politics' manifesto. When I let him go, he'd assumed he made a good offering, not too different from that glittering sword hilt you brought me. Unfortunately, my strategy backfired. Rather than scaring him away, I created a doting fool. Every time he got a new copy, I found it inside the train in Lindberg Park. I never saw Benny and he never saw me, but I can assure you that when he pointed you in my direction, he was more than confident I was going to kill you or at least keep you from being his problem ever again."

"Are you?"

"Going to kill you?" She turned to him, one thin auburn eyebrow rising mischievously, "What do you think?"

"Hard to say. I had my arm broken once for half a beer found in the street."

"Do I look like I'd break your arm for a beer?"

"Depends on how badly you want the beer."

The Queen, laughing full and low, looked down at him for a moment. The laughter died naturally and she yelled to her minions, who still hovered in the background.

"Bathe and dress him. Bring him to me in the grotto when you're finished."

He was suddenly surrounded by dark figures and lost sight of her as she walked deeper into the cemetery. He certainly could use a bath and a change of clothes, but his confusion still lingered. Like a sacrificial lamb being prepped for the slaughter, he was led away into the darkness behind the large rock wall.

11

Quarters Halpern had passed by the house on the corner of Montclair and 6th too many times to count. The white stucco was stained yellow by water damage and rust. The front windows, each boarded up with heavy plywood, had a crown of soot where the flames had burst through the glass and licked the sides of the building. Even the "reduced" sticker on the real estate company's FOR SALE sign had faded to a sun-bleached cream, speckled with dirt the ocean breezes swirled in from the Hollywood Hills.

Quarters had started to move his things in slowly. The back door, where the fire never touched the structure of the house, was left exposed, devoid of plywood barriers. It wasn't difficult to work the lock open, even with his poor breaking and entering skills. The ease of his entry made him think he'd waited too long to pounce on the property, forfeiting his squatter's rights, but it was empty.

Though the fire had been extinguished long ago, the house still smelled of ash and must. Mold grew in the crevasses between the wet walls; life springing forth where the fire hose had put out the flames. Lucky for Quarters, though the air was wet, the floor was dry. There were no puddles breeding swarms of mosquitoes and flies to plague him. The only bugs in the house he would bring with him. Even the cockroaches had abandoned the property, looking for more viable food sources among the neighboring homes. The previous owner had probably tried to sell the property for the land and foundation, but had abandoned all hope once the insurance settlement came through.

There was a serene feeling about the place. The enclosure should have turned the joint into a hot box during the stifling summer heat, but the humidity never turned, keeping the large living room damp and cool. Shortly after rolling his bundle of dirty blankets and torn sleeping bags out on the dusty hardwood floors, he'd found a box spring on the street, torn, but unsoiled. Then he had discovered a mattress in similar condition; stained, but relatively free of offensive odors.

Every day he'd come home, having solicited enough change to fill his belly and purchase a fifth of cheap booze to take him off to sleep, expecting his things gone, or another person sleeping in his bed. But he always found his bed in the same state, the lock on the back door just as he'd left it. The ash smell was becoming familiar, and for the first time in as long as he could remember, Quarters had a home.

But he was different. The prospect of finally having a roof, not having to pack up his life every morning and move to the next location, made him suspicious and paranoid. Instead of trying to come up with a different lie every day as to where he went when daylight disappeared, he stopped talking to people altogether. His only human interaction became his dull, low mantra to passersby of, "Gotta quarter?"

He made his money and then went back to his home sweet home, alienating anyone who tried to befriend him, constantly looking over his shoulder to make sure no one discovered his perfect sanctuary. He was friendless and penniless, but no longer homeless. A sacrifice he was more than willing to make after years on cold concrete, unsure if he would wake up the next morning.

The glow of a single flashlight couldn't be seen from the street and Quarters began to amass quite a collection of books left on public transportation or abandoned after an unsuccessful rummage sale. The living room of the house looked like a mad man's library. The mold mixed with the must of old books. Stacks of magazines discarded at the end of the month from bookstores and supermarkets lined the walls. Manuscripts found in dumpsters behind the offices of literary agents and random writings tossed in the trash were scattered across the floor. It was there, reading in his bed, in his house, that Quarters' fear and hopelessness started to disappear.

Potter Park's trash bins were usually a waste of time. They were full of discarded fountain drinks rather than bottles and cans. The bags of chips and snack cake wrappers were picked clean by the high schoolers playing basketball, every crumb of sustenance fueling their overactive metabolisms. But one day, on his way home, Quarters found something there to add to his collection. The document did a thorough job of keeping him entertained as well as informed. Whoever the anonymous author was, he had an interesting perspective on the world.

... *The Buddha may have been enlightened, but Jesus Christ was an alien. Why should our bodies be burned or imbued into the ground when Christ was taken up into the Heavens. Mary was impregnated by alien souls walking the earth. Aliens first created man by manipulating the DNA of apes and hoped to achieve once again the creation of Supermen. Unification of religion will never happen because of the absent harmony of Karma trapped within each of us. We have all been hypnotized, trapped within our heathen selves, unsure of the places that we occupy. We cannot transcend ourselves without trying to realize what we are. The true self is all around us, but invisible to our modern purpose. Is it blasphemy if I curse the God I do not follow? Is it heresy if I reject the system by which I have never abided? Why do you think God created clouds and animals and minerals as inferior to us? Why should any soul within any body be superior to another? Were we truly meant to dominate the earth and its other dwelling beings? Why would a soul be born to suffer without the justification of reincarnation? The world needs its balance. Reincarnation is an explanation, not a justification. What's the difference between the two? The fat, the blind, the pale-skinned have the choice to wallow in their state of darkness, of obesity, of pigmentation, or use the power of their free will to either change or accept their lot in life. What you see is what you have, as Jesus said. Raise your children to give positive energy out and to treat the world with harmony. The idea of Adam and Eve is absurd. Respect for the evolutionary process causes us to reject it. We will do insane things to respect our evolutionary rights to*

exist. The original genetic alterations drive us to protect that truth.
Our heritage...

Quarters lifted his eyes from the paper. Any other time he wouldn't have noticed, but the silence of the house, the only noise his fingers on the dry pages, magnified the scratching sound. Someone was at the lock, jimmying the mechanism just as he'd remembered doing a short while ago.

The flashlight clicked off and sweat popped on Quarters' skin. His hands grasped in the darkness for the 2x4 gathering dust at the end of the bed, lying in wait for the day the comfort of his home was violated. Quarters rose, leaning in the right spot to prevent the mattress springs from squeaking, trying not to give away his advantage. The sound of his breath and movement muted the lock pick's familiar sound. Quarters had to stop moving and hold his breath to make sure the threat was still present, but the noise had stopped. Either the assailant was too drunk to try harder or Quarters hadn't moved as soundlessly as he'd hoped.

He crept around the hallway corner to get a better view of the kitchen, to see if the back door had been breached. The door wasn't open and the house was silent once more, save the sound of his heart beating swiftly in his chest. It was ten minutes before he moved from his post, his muscles sore from paranoid tension.

Certain the intruder had left, he went back to his mattress, feeling around the heavy blankets for his flashlight to return to his papers. Depressing the thumb-hold to illuminate the room, Quarters Halpern caught a brief flash of powder blue before a wide blade pierced his skull through the forehead; the metal so sharp the penetration was akin to stabbing watermelon rather than bone. The flashlight dropped from his hand, creating a silhouette of his murderer on the far wall, a dancing shadow pulling the weapon from his victim's head and wiping the blade clean with a rag.

The intruder sifted through a pile of papers stacked on the bed, found what he was looking for, flipped through it quickly, and with a grunt of frustration, discarded it amongst the rest of the junk. He left as silently as he'd entered, but not before clicking off the flashlight, the sound echoing through the empty house, leaving the body in the darkness. Quarters Halpern was finally alone with his only friend in the world—his house.

12

Ray was clean for the first time in months. Wrapped in a towel, surrounded by flowers and the interred dead, he looked back at the pond they had cleaned him in. When he'd first approached the water, it was murky and full of algae, looking like a neglected hazard on a country golf course. With the turn of a spigot, the water drained and the fountain spewed fresh water, warm and clear. By the time they were done with him, the water was back beyond brown.

They gave him the choice of a shave, which he denied, thinking it may have been a veiled attempt to get him to willingly expose his neck to a stranger's razor blade. He was handed a set of clothing that seemed no nicer than the rags he'd given up, but he could smell the fabric softener on them and knew they had been recently cleaned. It made him think his own clothing may soon be laundered and given to the next victim who happened upon The Queen and her court. The oddest offering was a cup of mouthwash and an individually wrapped toothbrush. A clean mouth was a welcome change, but if they were prepping him for some strange primeval sacrifice, being minty fresh didn't seem like a ritual prerequisite.

The night seemed colder than before, his clothes and body no longer coated in dirt and sweat, taking away the extra layer of protection he had long taken for granted. Ray was pointed in the direction of the grotto and left to walk. No bodyguards or rope to lead him, he was free to make his own way. Part of him wondered if there was a chance he could make a break for it, perhaps get lucky enough to bypass any sentries The Queen may have placed hidden throughout the cemetery grounds, but he thought better of it, remembering how invisible his assailants were on the playground, knowing he still didn't have what he came for.

He took his time ascending the short set of stairs and saw the glow of a torch set into the stone wall as he passed by a small statue of the Virgin Mary. The Queen had returned to the statue where she had first greeted him, sitting on a stone bench, smoking a cigarette, a navy blue hooded sweatshirt sheltering her bare arms from the cold. She didn't look intense or mysterious now. She was just a girl in a park. The pomp and circumstance were gone, as was her entourage.

"Feel better?" she asked him, blowing smoke in a long stream out of the side of her mouth.

"Much. Thanks."

"Sit down, Ray."

He did as he was told.

"You want a cigarette?"

"Thank you."

Ray had recently cut down on his cigarette intake, finding better ways to spend his time than scrounging for discarded butts, but didn't want to refuse her offer. She held out a match and covered it with her hand to shield it from the wind. Behind the waft of sulfur and tobacco she smelled of lavender and cloves. It was enticing without being overpowering.

"Cold out," Ray offered, not sure where to begin.

"It's amazing how quickly the atmosphere can change," she pondered, inhaling the wisps of smoke from the wind, "but daylight is L.A.'s mask; the pleasant sunshine hiding what lies beneath. We only see her true face under the cover of night."

She spoke with the lilting rhythm of a poetess. Ray noticed her careful choice of words.

"What is this place, if you don't mind me asking?"

"Holy Cross Cemetery."

"No, I figured that out. I mean, what's it you're doing here, because, with all due respect, I don't see you collecting treasures and screaming 'Off with their heads!' at everyone."

She smiled, but her eyes were sad.

"Do you see the inscription on the statue behind us?"

Ray turned, the unfamiliar drag from a new cigarette filling his lungs and clouding his head. A green, oxidized copper plate stared back at him.

He read the inscription aloud.

"*For all who come to the Garden of St. Joseph, May you find Solace here.*"

"And all who've come to this garden have found solace in its sanctuary."

"Sanctuary? The way people talk about this place? Sanctuary isn't how I'd describe it. Quite the opposite, in fact."

"Did you choose your life, Ray?"

"Choose it?" Ray looked at her, not sure how to answer, "I suppose we all do, in a way. I'd like it if things had gone differently for me, I guess, but I'd be lying if I didn't admit that my decisions, good and bad, led me to this point."

"Early in life, I didn't have many choices. When I was twelve years old, my father died."

The Queen took a drag on her cigarette. She watched the smoke dance, and then dissipate into the cool atmosphere.

"He lost his job at an auto plant in Michigan, loaded whatever we could into his Plymouth and drove the two of us out to the West Coast, looking for a job. He joked that we could stay in Michigan and look for work, but the car's busted heater wasn't going to do us much good with winter coming. He tried to keep my spirits up, regaling me with stories of the gold rush and the Okie migration, romanticizing The Grapes of Wrath, careful to leave out the nasty bouts of reality. Swimming pools and movie stars. The whole nine yards."

"But it wasn't like that when you got here."

"He got sick. Could have been the flu, pneumonia, TB, I still don't know, but he died with a cough caught in his throat. I managed to scrape a job here and there, until my employers found out my real age and told me to take a hike. Tried burglary for a while, got pretty good at it too. Met a guy on a job once who eventually became like a second father to me. I started to think I'd found a family again. But he was a con man with a mean streak and a lot of debts to the wrong people. One day he couldn't pay up, so he put me up as collateral. At fourteen years old, I was raped by seven men."

Ray's heartbeat quickened and a lump jumped into his throat. His eyes offered her sympathy, but he had no words to give her.

"They left me torn and beaten, all but dead. I awoke the next morning in a hospital bed. A Christian relief group took me in and did their best to fix me up. They clothed me and fed me. Gave me the medical care I needed. I was grateful to them for everything. But they wouldn't let me destroy the monstrous thing that one of those seven had put into me."

"What?"

"They put me under twenty-four-hour watch. I stopped being their patient and became their vessel, a shell to give life to the demon spawn from my nightmares. What was my sanctuary had become my prison. I refused to push when the labor came and they had to drug me and cut the baby out. I never saw it. I hope that somewhere it has the life I never got, but I never forgot what happened to me, how I was treated."

Ray listened in rapt silence, letting her continue.

"I may have had a chance at a better life, but I was branded as heathen and turned away. I started gathering women from the streets with similar stories. When they could remember their attackers, we found the savages and gelded them, leaving them for dead. But it didn't heal the pain. The revenge just made it worse. I had been denied my sanctuary, so I decided to create one. Let people choose what kind of life they want to lead."

"Hence the bathing and clothes? I tell ya, I appreciate the hospitality, but I don't need saving."

"The bathing wasn't for you, Ray. It was for us."

"I smelled that bad, huh?"

"I've smelled worse."

"So, what? This is a shelter run for the homeless, by the homeless?"

"No," she said, "we do offer protection and community, but we also offer opportunity. I may've ended up in my position under the worst of conditions, but I learned from my experience. As a homeless pregnant teen, I was given the best medical care, and the opportunity to turn my life around. I didn't take what was offered, but some women deserve that chance."

"I'm not following," Ray squinted his eyes at her, trying to understand.

"My practices may come off as sexist, strange, amoral, or even a bit repulsive, but the ends justify the means. I'm merely using these relief groups' double standards against them. An organization is happy to take care of women raped and battered on the streets, only under the hypocritical condition that they have to have a religious value system imposed upon them. Why not use that hypocrisy to our advantage? Control the variables?"

"Control the variables?"

"Create conditions which warrant aid."

"Wait, wait. Let me get this straight. Women come to you... to get pregnant? On purpose?"

"I'm going to do my best to make sure that all women who want it can benefit from the relief that's out there, regardless of what they believe in. Here, nothing is done against anyone's will. Possibilities are offered and can be taken or left without praise or retribution."

"And what happens to the babies?"

"Pardon?"

"You seem so concerned with the mother's well-being. What about the kids? Aren't you clogging an already full orphanage system? What about their choices?"

"Are you speaking from experience, Ray?"

"Not to subvert the good you *think* you're doing here, but--"

"But nothing, Ray. You think I came to this point, all this protection, this elaborate ruse, by not thinking of every detail? The organization we deal with places every child into a good home. Every child," her anger was welling up, "I wouldn't condemn any child to the fate I suffered. Never."

Ray could see the fire burning in her now, but he hadn't been killed for his insolence yet, so he decided to push his luck.

"So this organization isn't as evil as you implied. They're doing some good."

"I never said they weren't. I just question their moral reasoning."

"Some might say the same thing about you."

She didn't respond. They sat on the bench, the breeze caressing their faces, waiting for the cigarettes to burn into strands of ash. A wordless tension hung thick like a shroud between them.

"I'm sorry if I upset you," Ray offered under his breath as he dropped his cigarette to the ground and put it out with his heel, nothing left but the filter.

"On the contrary," she said, turning to him, "I'd be more upset if you followed into this without challenging it. You don't apologize for who you are and neither do I."

"Now that I know who you are, at least, as much as I'm sure you're willing to reveal, what's the deal? Why all the stories? Why the elaborate deceptions? I may not seem like much, but I can see some holes in your little tale there. I don't doubt something bad happened to you, but you sure as hell don't talk like someone raised in an alley. You sound like a goddamn guest analyst for *Meet the Press*."

"All part of the ruse, Ray." She adjusted her body slightly, slumping one shoulder down, maneuvering the way she held her cigarette, cupping it inside her hand. Curling her lips to the side, she spoke, her manner transformed.

"You want that I should, like, talk like you 'spect me to?" It wasn't a caricature of a different person; she'd transformed herself before his eyes like a method actor absorbing a part.

"So, you're whatever fits your mark?"

She relaxed back to her previous posture.

"We're endeared to reflections of ourselves, Ray. Human nature."

"What you're saying is that you're running a game on me, even now?"

"Priority one is protecting the people who come to me. Which means protecting them from the crazy, the violent, the diseased, and all other manner of person who might be wandering without a home after dark."

"And that means getting inside the heads of whatever specific brand of John you run across."

"I merely do my research."

"This isn't about the manifesto at all, is it? I just went through the screening process of potential mates."

"We caught wind of you a few years ago. I believe you saved a woman from being set afire in the Pacific Palisades and you got moved to the short list."

"If your only criteria is preventing someone from being burned alive, you have some higher standards to work on."

"You'd be surprised how many people would see that and keep walking. You and I both know you're different. You aren't a common hustler. You're not a predator. You're not prey. You, Ray Cobb, are something entirely unique."

"Enough about me. Why the Mad Queen of Hearts nonsense?"

"Smoke screens. Everyone accepted is sent away with a story. Rumors are easily fueled and those we deem good enough to let into our circles have not betrayed our trust. Half of the things I've heard that come back to me were created without my knowing. The myths and legends grow like weeds and I'm happy to sow the seeds. Likely you'll leave here with the impression that I'm noble and educated."

"You don't get a vocab like yours without trying, lady. You may be making an effort to put on a personality you think I'm comfortable with, but honestly, I know as well as anybody that it's a shit ton easier to be smart and play dumb than the other way around."

"I knew we chose correctly with you."

Ray shook his head and smiled into the ground. "I suppose I should be honored to be chosen for this."

"Well, we've determined that you're not crazy, overtly violent or diseased."

"How you know I'm not diseased?"

"Like I said, we've been watching you. It's been a while."

"Darlin', truer words have never been spoken, but I came here for Ernie's papers, that's all."

The Queen reached under the bench and pulled out a dirty hunk of crumpled papers.

"I've tried to keep them as ordered as possible, but sometimes it's like putting together a jigsaw puzzle where all the pieces are blank."

"I just hope this puzzle isn't a dead end. I wouldn't know where to start over if this doesn't offer some answers."

"Why is this so important to you, Ray?"

He searched his brain, looking for a rational answer, something that explained why he needed to find out what happened. But he honestly didn't know. Maybe he wished he could have taken Ernie's place. Maybe he was sick of his life, living as a vagabond day to day. His most honest answer was probably that he didn't care whether he lived or died. Hadn't for a long time. He figured if he was going to go out, it might as well be for a good reason. But he didn't say those things.

"You mentioned me saving a girl from a fire. Not too long ago, I wasn't the kinda guy who would've stopped. I would've made a different choice. But Ernie was the kinda guy that didn't keep on walking when he saw something similar happening to me," Ray looked down at his feet, pushing the extinguished cigarette butt around with the toe of his shoe, "I used to think that we should only look out for Number One, because the world is gonna come crashing down no matter what you do, so you just need to take care of your own shit."

She offered him another cigarette and he accepted it before continuing.

"One day, there I was, mindin' my own, but... you know how it is out here... wrong place, wrong time. Little white fucker appears outta nowhere, arms flailing, spewing some god-awful batshit nonsense; I'm about half an inch from getting a knife in my guts. Some gang initiation bullshit."

"So you owed him your life?"

"Nothing so cliché, but we did look out for each other. I couldn't return the favor. I wasn't there for him. I couldn't save him," his voice was quiet and regretful, pausing with introspection between sentences, "I don't know if this is the right thing to do, or if it's gonna make a difference, but it seems like I gotta do something."

"Now you understand my situation, Ray," she put her hand softly on his shoulder.

"Ahem."

They both looked over to where the sound of a throat clearing jolted them out of their conversation. A young girl stood next to the statue of the Virgin Mary. Ray caught a glimpse of her eyes in the flicker of the torch's fire. They were a familiar brown.

"It appears Sarah is ready for you."

"No offense, ladies, I'm flattered, but this isn't what I came here for. Besides, I'm still struggling with how I feel about these little organized rendezvous."

"Look at it this way; you and this very willing woman are going to share a few hours of mutual companionship. Once the sun comes up, you'll leave. What happens after that is none of your concern. Enjoy your time, Ray. Both of you have earned a night of intimacy. Now I'll leave you to it. There are blankets in the grass, use them, it's getting colder."

The Queen got up and walked past Sarah, kissing her on the forehead with her blessing. She turned to face him one last time.

"One more thing, Ray. Benny sent you here thinking you'd never return. When he sees you back and unharmed, he may do something desperate. Watch your back."

"Good to know. Hey, I never got your real name," Ray stopped her.

"And you won't. Have a good night."

With that, she disappeared into the darkness. Sarah ascended the steps slowly. The two of them stood awkwardly, trying not to make eye contact with one another.

"Um... sorry I was so difficult earlier," he offered.

"It's a'right. Just glad I didn't hafta hurt ya."

He laughed. "I'm glad you didn't have to either."

She looked up at him with her big brown eyes and took him by the hand.

"You gonna be a problem?" she asked him flirtatiously.

"I'm not gonna be a problem," he answered her, smiling, "Lead the way."

She pulled him toward the blankets lying in the grass nearby.

13

Penny waved at Nick from a booth in the far corner of the restaurant when he walked through the door. There was a basket on the table and she was through half a beer already.

"Sorry, I couldn't wait, I was starving. Fries?"

"Sure," he said, sitting down across from her. He was amazed at how different she looked. She wasn't wearing much make-up, but what she did apply managed to make her eyes jump and her lips full. Nick noticed that she was this little ball of energy, almost like she was having trouble sitting still, a quality she didn't exude when huddled in the police station bawling.

"Hope you haven't been waiting long."

"No, I got here early. I'd always rather be somewhere twenty minutes early than five minutes late."

He managed to get the attention of a waiter.

"I'll have one of the same," pointing to Penny's tall, half-full pilsner glass. He turned his attention back to her, "I've gotta catch up."

"You'll have to hurry up then, this is number three for me."

"Really?" he said, genuinely surprised that someone as small as her could drink three beers and still be able to walk and talk.

"I don't want you to think I'm an alcoholic or anything, it's just that I'm sorta celebrating, you know, not going to jail for murder forever and also I'm actually really shy and if I didn't have something to drink beforehand you'd probably have had one heck of a time getting me to open my mouth even to do something as simple as making small talk so I thought I'd take the opportunity to loosen my tongue a little, as they say, and I'm rambling so you can shut me up at any time," she spewed out, finally putting a hand to her mouth and rolling her eyes at herself.

"You know what?" Nick said, a bit blown away by her barrage of words, "I'm glad you decided to loosen your tongue a bit, because I don't really do this much. Well, I mean, go out. I mean, I go out, you know, to places. It's just that I don't go out with... um..."

"Women."

"Clients," he spouted quickly, "witnesses, suspects, and well, yeah, okay, women. Gosh, where's that drink of mine?"

The waiter made his appearance as if on cue and placed the tall pilsner glass down in front of Nick. He did a quick "cheers" to her and took a big gulp.

"Saved by the beer."

She snorted out a laugh in a cute, but I'm-three-big-beers-in-and-may-laugh-at-anything sort of way.

"You ready?" the waiter asked politely, but obviously in a rush to get their order, as Penny had been camping in his booth.

"Oh, yes yes yes," Penny sing-songed, clapping her hands together tight in front of her, "I'll have the Rosemary Turkey Burger and could I get swiss instead of cheddar and light on the avocado and would it be possible to get red onions instead of regular onions, still caramelized, but on the side, not on the burger?"

"Sure, and you sir?"

"Diablo, medium rare, please."

The waiter snatched the menus from them and disappeared into the kitchen.

"Wow, that was quite an order," he said to her, taking in another healthy dose of beer.

"Jeez, you must think I am such a pig, but I'm starving. Like I said I've had trouble eating lately and please tell me to shut up every time I'm rambling like now."

He laughed at her. "Don't worry about it, it's fine. I'm glad you're talking and not crying."

"Very funny."

She made a mock mean face at him.

"What I meant was, all the rules with your meal."

"The waiter must totally hate me right now. I sure hope he doesn't spit in the food. How'd you become a cop?"

"That was quite a jarring transition. You'd be good in an interrogation room, catching people off guard."

"Sorry again, sometimes my mouth moves faster than my brain."

"Well," he said, sipping his beer and chewing on a french fry, "it's kinda embarrassing."

"What'd you do? Trip and fall into the police academy?" she asked, laughing at her own joke.

"I'm sure you'd love to hear something about how I thought it'd be great to help people, do good for the community, but really, it was because of TV. And not the good shows, mind you, the super cheesy ones."

"Did you think you'd have a smart talking sassy female partner or a down and dirty street insider helping you out with cases?"

"So you obviously know the kind of shows I'm talking about."

"I spent many afternoons growing up sucking up reruns. The TV was like a babysitter in my house. But, I'll admit, I liked watching middle-aged white guys trying to do kung fu."

"You won't get such pleasure from me."

"You're hardly middle-aged," she winked at him.

"True, but it gets closer every day. I really liked the idea of becoming a private eye, not having to abide by the rules, working just under the law, but my mother lost her job and the police academy provided the security that a seedy office in Echo Park didn't."

"You take care of your mother? That's so sweet."

"It's sweet on paper, Penny, but in reality, I'm a man in his mid-thirties who lives with his mother, and despite the fact that I don't smoke, I always have the haze of tobacco on me."

"Nick, you wear it well. The combination of aftershave, mint, and the faint hint of tobacco on you, is strange, and comforting. Like coming home."

Her eyes went wide as she realized what she had said, placing way too many cards on the table.

"Okay, I think I'm done with these," she said, pushing the rest of the beer away from her, "I'll be right back."

Before he could answer, she was on her way to the back of the restaurant.

Penny pushed into the bathroom and bee-lined for the nearest open stall. She shut and locked the stall door behind her and sat down, her face in her hands.

"Stop throwing yourself at this guy," she hissed, scolding herself in frustration. She admitted that he wasn't the best-looking guy she had ever met, but he was sweet. He was a nice guy. She wasn't awkward around him, though the booze helped, something she couldn't say about any of her other dates in the past few months.

"Just stop being a spaz and quit talking so much. You've never talked so much in your life, just calm down," she pep-talked herself into getting up and out of the stall.

She checked her makeup and breath, made some adjustments to where her outfit had moved to mask her figure and headed back out into the restaurant.

When she got back to the table, he was sitting there with both of the burgers. He had his hands in his lap and was waiting politely for her to return before he began eating.

"Hi, I'm Penny Searle. Can we start over?"

"Pleased to meet you, Penny. I hope you're hungry," he smiled up at her, gesturing for her to sit down across from him.

She sat down and cut her burger in half. Picking up three onions with her fork, she placed them daintily between the bun and cheese, before grabbing the half-burger, still too big for her hands and took a bite.

"Mmm, God, that's so good," she mumbled between chews, "How's yours?"

Nick picked up his whole burger and took a big bite of it, sauce dripping onto his chin and hands. He put the burger down and wiped his hands and face.

"Good," he said, trying not to talk with his mouth full, "Spicy."

"About before," she said, grabbing a handful of fries, and sticking them between the bun and turkey patty, "Let's just call it *Mia kusenveturilo estas plena je angiloj.*"

The phrase stopped Nick in mid-sip of his beer.

"Excuse me?"

"Okay, there I go again," she sighed, "A few years ago, I was bored, thinking my life was uninteresting, granted not much has changed since that little epiphany, and I weighed a bunch of different things to inject some adventure into my life." She took another bite of her burger. He waited for her to finish chewing and continue her explanation.

"I pondered sky diving, but would never even think of jumping out of a plane, learning to play the banjo, but I don't have the fancy finger skills, or learning a new language. After much time wasted online, most of it on company time, I decided it'd be fun to learn Esperanto... fun and completely useless. So, I found this site with common phrases, like 'My name is Penny' or 'Where's the bathroom,' you know, stuff you'd get in a guidebook if you went to a foreign country. At the very bottom of the page was the completely out of place phrase, 'My hovercraft is full of eels,' *Mia kusenveturilo estas plena je angiloj*. It's sorta become my mantra if I say something ridiculous in a normal situation."

"My hovercraft is full of eels?"

"I know, completely random, right?"

"So say something else in Esperanto."

"*Tiu ĉi sinjoro pagos por ĉio.*"

"What does that mean?"

"This gentleman will pay for everything," she smiled at him and took another bite of burger.

"Sorry I asked."

They sat quietly for a few moments, each of them concentrating on their meals. The silence wasn't uncomfortable; they both knew it was a natural pause.

"How's the wonderful world of real estate these days?"

"The real estate world is about as boring as it gets, but life at work has been nothing but interesting."

"Murder mysteries tend to liven up water cooler discussions."

"After this thing with Margie, at first everyone was in a somber mood, and then happy because, though we hate to speak ill of the dead, she was a nightmare. Once this thing with the M&M's happened, I became shunned, like these people who I thought were my friends actually thought that I'd be capable of murdering her. I'm sorta stuck right now. On the one hand, I wanna to stay there, because I like what I do, I just didn't like working for Margie, but now I know that I really don't have any friends there. I'm almost tempted not to tell anyone I've been exonerated when I go back into the office. It sucks not having anyone to talk to during the day, but there's this power in having people afraid of you. Weird, right? I'm sure you know what that's like, having to question suspects all the time?"

"I have a confession. I actually haven't been doing this very long. A few months ago, I was just a beat cop. Most of the time they have me sorting through paperwork, filing cold cases."

"That has to be exciting. Solving old cases?"

"Hate to burst your bubble, but there's really nothing exciting about it. Just a sea of names, unsolved mysteries to be sorted and placed back in their respective boxes."

"There must be some thrill involved in that?"

"You must know some secret about sorting through twenty-year-old paperwork that I seem to have missed."

"Cold cases are cold because there's, what, a lack of evidence, the trail stopped, or nothing could be found in the details, right?"

"For the most part."

"So, now you have the opportunity to offer a fresh perspective. The people who worked on those cases have probably long forgotten about them. I know when I stare at a listing for too long, it starts to lose the excitement and luster it had when I first got it, but pretty soon somebody comes along and sees all the great things in a property that I had dismissed a long time ago. Maybe this is a chance for you to come across something in those files, provide some long needed relief to somebody's loved ones."

"With these things you gotta be careful, though. After a while people have to come to grips with something staying buried."

"Listen, Nick. When I was about twenty-three, a friend of mine committed suicide. He was building houses for displaced natives in South America. He had a girlfriend he was very much in love with, great friends, and all of the villagers had an amazing love and respect for him. One day, without prompting, warning or indication, he was found by his host family hanging from one of the beams in his house. It was investigated, deemed a suicide, and the family decided to leave it at that. Granted, I never got all of the details, I'm sure that his parents got all of the information needed, but they chose not to put further investigation into it because they wanted it to be over. If they had gone through all of the pain of looking into it and found out he had been murdered or had indeed committed suicide, it would've drawn out their pain for months and they wouldn't have their son back. So they let it stay buried. But I'm sure that if tomorrow someone knocked on their door and said, 'Your son was murdered, I have the proof, and we've caught the people responsible,' they would fall to their knees and cry. Not because that wound had been reopened, because something like that never closes, but because he was still the man they always remembered and not the stranger who, without warning, took his own life. The people responsible for snuffing out that light would be brought to justice. You can't bring anyone back, but maybe you can take the weight off of some of the heavy hearts in this town."

"I guess I never thought of it like that,"

"Great first date, conversation, I know," she let slip, then stopped herself, her eyes going wide again.

"Glad you said it and not me."

Once the tension was broken, they were both relaxed enough to continue their conversation and enjoy themselves.

"I had fun tonight," she said to him when they were through with dinner, standing out on the empty curb.

"You okay to drive?" he asked her, trying not to sound over-protective.

"No, I think even with the water, I'm still a little tipsy, but I'm not parked in a tow zone, so I'll just get a cab."

"Or, I could give you a ride home," he mumbled, trying not to appear too hopeful.

"That's sweet, but it's way out of your way. There's a cab stand at the corner."

"All right."

His response was resigned, but disappointed. She could see the look of dejection in his eyes, got up on her tiptoes and kissed him softly on the corner of his mouth.

"But I do want to see you again," she said, still pressed against him.

"I'd like that," he offered in quiet sincerity, not giving away the gleeful bright colors swimming through his head.

"You aren't breaking any sort of suspect-detective privilege, are you?"

"Nope, you're no longer a suspect, so I'm pretty sure we're safe."

"Unless, of course, new evidence comes to light that I did it."

"Then I'd be close to you, ready to pounce when the time is right."

"So it's a win-win," she gave him another quick peck on the cheek before turning around and heading toward the first available cab sitting at the corner. She looked over her shoulder and gave him a little wave before disappearing into the car.

He watched the cab pull away and merge into the sea of taillights on Hollywood Boulevard before turning around and heading to his own car parked down the block. For the first time in a while, there was a smile on his face and a spring in his step.

14

Ray basked in the afterglow, looking up at the stars. Sarah was asleep with her head on his chest. He had his arm around her, his fingers slowly tracing imaginary lines on her shoulder blade.

They'd made love gently, but with a clumsy excitement; the way it was the first time with someone you really cared for rather than the fiery passion shared one night with a stranger. Though they both knew the final purpose of their union, neither of them rushed to get the job done, or neglected to enjoy the act as it was. She appreciated his tenderness and told him so before snuggling up to him and drifting off to sleep. There wasn't much talk between them; everything was said with their eyes and bodies. For the first time since the tryst was suggested, he hoped his seed found purchase and that both mother and child received a better life because of it.

The lavender light of the sun began to tickle the horizon, staining the darkness of the night sky as Sarah awakened slowly to greet the morning with a groggy smile. The sun bathed her small body as she arose from the blankets, wiping the sleep from her eyes.

"We gotta be out by sunrise," she said, starting to gather her things.

Ray didn't move. Instead he split his attention between the transition of night into morning and watching her dress.

"Thanks for last night," she said.

"I should thank you," he said, rolling over onto his elbow, "that was the calmest I've felt in weeks."

"You sleep?" she asked, playfully tugging at the blanket underneath him.

He took the hint and got up, gathering his new clothes and letting her fold the blankets up and tuck them under her arm.

"No, but I rested."

"I'll tell her you were everythin' we expected. You ever need anythin', come on back to her. We remember folks who help us."

He was only half-dressed when she stood and started to walk away. He grabbed her gently by the elbow and pulled her back to him. She did her best to maintain the professional tone she had obviously been instructed to use upon awakening, but couldn't help but nuzzle into his chest one last time.

"I hope you––" he stopped, not sure what to say, "I hope you get everything you wish for."

He knew he'd chosen his words correctly when she brought her head up to him with tears in her eyes. She kissed him on the mouth, not with passion, but with honor and friendship.

"Finish gettin' dressed. Don't forget your story."

"What do I tell people?"

"You're smart enough. You'll think of somethin'."

She sprinted away from him like a bounding hare, her bare feet kicking up dew as she went, and was gone. In the distance, Ray heard a groundskeeper kicking on a lawnmower and knew it was time for him to disappear too.

He finished putting on his shirt as he walked and made it to the back of the cemetery. The green grass gave away to a field of wild flowers, thoughts of the city melting away until the smoggy haze of skyline appeared over the hill, reminding him of where he was.

Making his way back to Robertson Boulevard, Ray found a bus stop, sat down, and started to flip through the document in his hand. The numbers on Ernie's will were 1152 1323 1352 1372 1568 1800 and 1944. He knew they couldn't be page numbers because this copy of the manifesto only had 1389 pages, unless the first four numbers were page numbers and the last three referred to something else. Or all of the numbers were page numbers and he was still missing half of the document in its final version. Whatever the numbers meant, the nonsense on the back of the note still didn't look familiar.

Ray found that The Queen had placed enough cash for bus fare in his pocket and made it onto the Robertson bus going north. It was still too early for weekly commuters and he was the only person riding. The tired bus driver gave Ray a suspicious look; worried he might cause some trouble. Ray made his way to the back of the bus and huddled up against the window. He flipped through Ernie's manifesto, turning to page 1152. Leaning his hand against the bus window, he began to read:

...and that's how we are stuck in the ruts society poses upon us. What's my social position? What's your social position? Because I don't have the wealth and power of someone who works in a multi-national conglomerate, that doesn't make me any less of a human being than that person. In fact, I am more of a human being than that person. I am closer to my various roots. The Pharos of Alexandria had a height estimated between three hundred eighty and four hundred and ninety feet, thought to be the tallest structure on earth for centuries and called one of the Seven Wonders of the Ancient World. Now that we constantly build upwards and outwards, this Wonder of the World, by our common standards, would be no more than merely a tall lighthouse. The earthquakes knocked this great structure down, and man in his infinite glory as the purveyor of great technology was once again bested by nature. The mean length of four hundred and thirty five feet became the world's longest pile of rubble for centuries. So what am I? Am I a man, less so because I have not been blessed with pigmentation of the skin? I will stand on the rubble of modern society. Greatness now will pale in comparison to the revolution's new future. I have progressed past living in a cave of dirt or a castle without modern amenities, but I also have been left behind as stronger, braver men surpass my social and economic standing. Or am I a new man, a precursor to a time when the harmful effects of the modernity that so many call sacred will turn against us and level us to nothingness. I call upon myself and the people of the streets to be pioneers of this new frontier. We know how to live on and survive in the case of nuclear holocaust, which will happen in our lifetimes, or great plague which we have seen time and again, or even something as far-fetched as a robot uprising, which some will scoff at as the works of science fiction writers trying to concoct stories of fear to sell books and movies and

television series, but my friends, if a robot can take over an assembly line and put hundreds of humans out of work, they can take over the world and put millions of humans out of life. The database lifestyle has...

The run-on sentences and dizzying logic let Ray only get so far before he drifted off to sleep.

When he finally woke up, the sun was much higher in the sky, and the bus was full, heading back south on Robertson rather than north. Ray blinked and looked at the LED ticker at the front of the bus. He'd been asleep for almost four hours, exhaustion blacking out his dreams, but still didn't feel rested. No one tried to rouse him, but considering the look the bus driver had shot him earlier, they were content to leave him until he shit himself or assaulted someone. He was still clutching the manifesto in his hand, but instead of continuing to read it, he rolled it up and stuck it in his pocket. The last thing he wanted to do was fall asleep again, riding the bus for the rest of the day. Looking out the window, Ray could see that they had just crossed Wilshire, close to Crispy's territory. Ray needed some sage advice and maybe a tip on a free breakfast. Pulling the cord to stop, he caught the bus driver's sigh of relief.

The bits and pieces of Ernie's work were always a challenge to sift through, but this version seemed denser. Cryptic. Angry. If he had to slog through all fourteen hundred pages, he'd be at it for a month, and even then, he had no idea if the manifesto was part of a wild goose chase orchestrated by

Benny 7-11. The note could've meant something completely different. It might have meant nothing.

The exhaustion and hunger clouded his mind. Was he creating this complicated puzzle for himself to justify how convoluted he wished his friend's death was? Maybe Ernie was just killed by some nutball. The Los Angeles streets certainly didn't have a lack of those. He passed at least three people who would stab him for a sandwich on La Cienega alone and he was in Beverly Hills. There was definitely a lower caliber of survivalists creeping around downtown.

Each step felt heavier than the last as he approached the corner of Beverly Boulevard. He caught Crispy's gaze and held a hand up to greet him, like a warrior returned home after a long battle. Instead of extending his hand in usual politeness, Crispy wrapped his arms around Ray, embracing the man who had come back from the dead.

"Thought you was dead fo' sho', mu'fucka. Goin' down there... what were you thinkin'?" he asked, gripping Ray's shoulder, making sure he was real.

"I guess I was just lucky."

"Lucky? What's it like down there?" he backed off Ray a little, "You smell weird, man. Like clean almost or some shit."

"Can we sit? I'm dog tired," Ray offered, trying to come up with a good explanation. In the end, he decided to just verify to Crispy what he had feared all along.

"They stripped me down, Crisp. Took my clothes. *She* was happy with her offering, but I made the mistake of saying I'd tell everyone I knew of *Her* kindness. *She* snapped like some kind of feral beast and screamed to *Her* followers, the most awful beings you could imagine," Crispy listened in rapt silence, "They bathed and anointed me, saying they were prepping me for the sacrifice. Somehow I overpowered one of my guards, and stumbled upon the cavern where *She* keeps her treasures. I found Ernie's manifesto, stole the clothes off one of the guards and have been running north ever since. Crispy, don't ever go down there. Don't ever send your friends down there. I thought I'd seen Hell on these streets. I was wrong."

Ray was sure he'd painted enough of a picture to serve The Queen's purposes. He felt awful lying to his friend, but knew Crispy could never pass up an opportunity to tell a good story. His recount would be widespread through the community by the end of the day.

"That shit's fuckin' unreal, Ray. Thank God you made it outta there in one piece. What'd they dip yo' ass in? You stink like sweat and sex."

Ray looked away quickly, "I don't know what it was."

"Some kinda animal fat, prolly. They mighta eaten you if you hadn't broken outta there."

Ray reflected on the circumstances under which he had actually been captured, wondering if Crispy would believe him if he told the truth.

"I got news, Ray," Crispy's attitude changed from one of concern and astonishment to unsure pity.

"News? Good?"

"Bad. Bad news in every way."

"Well, it isn't going to get any worse by you postponing the inevitable. Spill it."

"They found Ernie's eyes."

Ray's mouth went dry.

"They did? Who is they?"

"Caravan Kevin."

"Who did it?"

"I ain't said who did it, Ray, I said they got his eyes. I don't know no more deets."

"Where's Kevin?"

"Kevin ain't got 'em, he just knows where they at."

"Crispy, don't rile me up with information like this and then bat the answer around like a cat with a ball of yarn. Who the fuck has Ernie's eyes?"

Crispy shook his head, hesitated and finally spoke, his eyes avoiding Ray's.

"Pretty Boy D'Arby."

Ray's hands went to his face, clutching his forehead hard, as though he'd suddenly gotten a splitting headache. They both sat for a moment, saying nothing.

"That can't be right. He's too careful for something like this."

"You ain't listenin', Ray. Pretty Boy's got the eyes. He don't got the hands."

"Pretty Boy didn't kill Ernie? He just happened upon them? I didn't realize a dead man's eyes were such a hot commodity."

"I know Pretty Boy's capable of a lotta shit, and I don't doubt he mighta snuffed out Ernie for lookin' at him cockeyed, but like you say, he's too careful to go 'round flauntin' a trophy like that if he was involved."

"I gotta talk to Kevin."

"Kevin's gone."

"What do you mean Kevin's gone?"

"If Caravan got outta Pretty Boy's game, means he managed to get out with some scratch. You don't get that kinda luck twice. Dude split with whatever he got. Only reason I saw him is he owed me a trade, took it outta his stake, gave me the info on the eyes and was gone, man. Caravan's halfway to Omaha by now."

"Where's the next game?"

"Ray—"

"Where's the next fucking game, Crisp?"

"You tired and you hungry. You just escaped death and now you wanna go right back into the lion's den? A mu'fuckin' lion that got two heads and rabies. What you thinkin'?"

"I'm gonna get some breakfast, Crispy," Ray stood, brushing the dirt from his new pants, "See what you can dig up on the next location."

Crispy just looked up at Ray.

"Why don't you just let it go, Ray?"

"If somebody killed you tomorrow and took that hand of yours as a trophy, you wouldn't want retribution?"

"I'd be dead, Ray. Wouldn't want nothin'. I know what he done for you, Ray, but––"

"The game, Crispy."

"Ray..."

"The game."

The steel in his eyes told Crispy he wasn't going to back down.

"You gotta give me some time. There was a game two nights ago, so there's another one tonight. Table fills up fast. I can't get you a seat tonight. It ain't possible."

"Find a way."

"I ain't no miracle worker."

Ray chose not to speak. He just stared through Crispy with resolve.

"You'll get a spot," Crispy relented, his voice low, "Go get some food. Get some sleep. SOVA's open today. Get some fresh food. Don't go pickin' through the leavings at the King's Road Cafe."

"Thanks, Crisp."

"This'll be the second time I send you to your death this week. You survived this morning, but won't be gettin' that kinda luck twice."

"I know," he extended his hand to shake, but Crispy didn't return the gesture. Ray lowered his hand in understanding and walked away.

Crispy Morgan sat there, watching as Ray shuffled down Beverly. When Ray was out of his sight line, Crispy stuck a quarter into the pay phone and dialed, waiting for death to pick up on the other end.

15

"Jesus Christ, it's taking you forever to go through these things. If I ever decide to put you on a case, is it going to take you a month to file your reports, too, Archer?"

Jenkins' beer belly stretched the weight limit on his belt. Nick was pretty sure he'd used a screwdriver to put a couple more notches in the far end of free leather instead of ponying up the ten bucks to get a new one to fit his ever-expanding figure.

"Who's the detective heading up Cold Case Special Section nowadays?" Nick asked, trying to not get riled by Jenkins' comments, knowing it'd frustrate him more if Nick didn't play the game.

"Kuhn has a full roster, Archer, so don't get any ideas. I'm just doing him a solid 'cuz he doesn't have the manpower to sort through this shit. Figured I could spare you 'til you catch a body in the rotation."

"I was just..."

"There are plenty of new cases to solve before we decide to go dancing into forty years of back logs. CCSS is low priority right now. Budget cuts. Tag the unsolved opens that aren't already tagged as cold and stick 'em in the dark file. Forget about 'em and move on with your life."

"So these are just going into a box to be forgotten?"

"Until somebody gets curious."

"What if I got curious?" Nick asked.

"It may not seem like it, but this paperwork assignment ain't gonna last forever and I'm not gonna let you waste your time investigating this bullshit when I might need you for something tomorrow."

"Come on. CCSS has their hands full and you haven't part-nered me up yet. There's nobody to drag down with me. Maybe all these cases need is a fresh set of eyeballs. Half the shit in this pile isn't even officially cold. They should be in Homicide active files. Here, look at this."

Nick pulled a file out of the top drawer of his desk and handed it to Jenkins.

"So what?"

"So what? Ernest Gaffney's body was found weeks ago, not years. His name isn't on the big board. You wanna know why?"

"We've got plenty of bodies up there, Archer."

"Freddy Regent retires, he's got three open cases. Two got reassigned. This one ends up here."

"Homeless assholes die all the time. Half of 'em don't have enough paper in the system to I.D. Why is this my problem?"

"Because when these were sitting in a pile in the corner, no one gave a shit, but when they start getting organized..."

"You trying to load me up with red names to drive down my numbers? You miserable piece of shit."

"No, I'm saying we keep 'em where they are. Just give me some room to look into a few."

"No way."

"Here's the thing, boss. This detail is shit. You and I both know it's shit. I could file them away, just like you want. And, say I look into one of these and I don't solve it? No harm, and it goes right back into the CCSS file for when the budget's bigger. But, say I do solve it, especially one of these that's less than five years old? That body goes on your win list, driving your numbers up."

"You're serious?"

"As your impending heart attack."

Jenkins sat down on the edge of Nick's desk. They both heard the loud creak and Nick could see it buckling in the middle, ready to split down the seam and send papers flying everywhere. He knew he had Jenkins' attention.

"I'll make you a deal, Archer. You can pick a case. *One case.* And you can work it. But it doesn't interfere with you getting the rest of these cases into a cardboard box, and it doesn't interfere with you helping out on the real cases when we catch a body. It also doesn't give you free reign to run around this department wasting other people's time and resources. You understand me? I want all your time accounted for. This ain't a free pass to fuck around."

"Yes, sir."

"And no overtime. You want a passion project? You do it on your own dime. This isn't a double-time holiday excuse."

Nick cringed a little at the thought of working on a case with no pay, but tried to focus on the potential benefit if one of them panned out.

"No fudged hours. Promise."

"Don't make me regret this one, Archer. And just because you got permission for this, doesn't take you off my shit list, you got that?"

Detective Everado Naches interrupted them.

"Cold one, 3614 Montclair, abandoned house. Vagrant got a blade in his brain. Who you want on it?"

Jenkins swore under his breath and took a quick look at Nick.

"Give it to Caldwell," he said over his shoulder, not breaking eye contact with Nick, "Get back to work, Archer."

Nick silently saluted as Jenkins relieved the pressure on his desk and got up to walk away. The easy part was over, now he had to dig through the dirt to find that one diamond-studded case. Instead of trying to decide what to do, he picked up the phone and called Penny to see if she was available for lunch. This was her idea; maybe he could pick her brain a little. It was also a great excuse to see her again.

16

A dull *splat!* on the sidewalk beside his head roused Benny 7-11 from a short sleep. His one good eye opened slowly, the other swollen shut from lack of medical attention. A wet, brown streak stained the pavement inches from his face and the smell woke him fully before another *plop!* hit the ground, this one in danger of splashing into his mouth. Forgetting his injury, Benny propped himself up on his broken finger, pain shooting through the newly set splint.

"Son of a bitch," Benny growled, grinding his teeth. He scrambled out of the layer of blankets, searching for his shoes. Finding them under the pile of jackets acting as his pillow, he hurled one at the Sunset bridge over Silver Lake Boulevard. The sole of the shoe caught Danny Ambush squarely in the nose as he popped over the cement edge, another handful of shit ready to dive bomb onto the sleeping figures below.

"I'm comin' after you, you sick fuck!" Benny screamed, ignoring the cars passing his naked body in the early Los Angeles morning.

Danny Ambush clutched his sore nose with the hand not currently filled with feces and tossed his last load over the bridge before running off.

"Why you let 'im get to ya?" a raspy voice asked from beneath the heap of fabric.

"Get to me? Maybe I don't wanna wake up with a face fulla shit. You don't think I've suffered enough in the last twenty-four that I need some corn and hepatitis in my cuts to round out my day?"

Betsy Over-Under turned to face him, her greasy hair matted flat from her concrete pillow. Her low-hanging, veiny breasts poked out from the blanket. One scarred, brown nipple settled on the pavement in some dried chewing gum.

"Come back to sleep. He's gone."

Benny waddled his hairy ass back in her direction, ignoring her request, and sorted through his pile of clothes, looking for a pack of cigarettes.

"Son of a fuck!" he yelled, finding the largest of the dook missiles had hit the crotch of his new Goodwill jeans. Benny emptied the pockets and threw the pants into the bushes, yanking his stained undershorts on over his acrid balls. He plunked down hard on the curb, smoking a cigarette and looking at his crooked finger.

"Whole fuckin' day with this thing set proper and it's ruined in two minutes by some asshole who thinks he's a fuckin' howler monkey."

After his visit with Nestor, Benny couldn't take the pain anymore and made his way to the L.A. Free Clinic. The hours spent waiting there probably brought more risk of infection than if he had gone into Griffith Park and rubbed some dirt on it. A bath of cheap, stinging peroxide cleaned out his cuts and a disgruntled intern, forty-six hours into her shift, set his finger. He wouldn't let them put a bandage over his mustache for fear the removal would pull out even more hair, so he just let his upper lip crust with dried blood and scab over, giving him what looked like the world's greatest cold sore. His rude awakening destroyed all the work done on his finger and he didn't have enough scratch to afford a drug strong enough to help him forget the pain.

Seeing that Benny wasn't going to come back to bed, Betsy Over-Under threw the blankets off, exposing her skin to the cold. Her gigantic belly was crisscrossed with a roadmap of stretch marks and it acted as an awning for her ever-expanding mane of pubis. Betsy was wider than she was tall and had a knack for wearing undergarments found on the street over her pants, hence her name.

"Is today the day, Benny? Is it?" she asked him with childlike innocence, pulling some dirty underoos over a torn pair of purple sweatpants.

"You ask me that every day, Bets, and what do I tell ya?"

"You say soon."

"So what you think 'bout today?"

"Can't today be soon?"

Benny wasn't really paying attention to anything she said. He hadn't had much time to view Ernie's note before the wind was knocked out of him, but he was trying to remember what he saw on the paper Ray had flashed at him the previous morning. He was kicking himself for taking up a position of violence rather than trying to sit down with Ray to figure the note out, maybe getting the drop on Ray instead of the other way around.

Benny was counting on Ray never making it back from his visit with The Queen, so he would have to go find another copy of the manifesto himself. It likely wouldn't be the latest version, but he had to start somewhere. Despite Nestor's suggestion to err on the side of caution, he guessed that Nestor wasn't waiting around for the documents to land in his lap either.

Benny handed the remainder of the butt to Betsy, who was distracted by the infinite contents of her own belly button. She accepted the gift as though she had never seen a cigarette before and took languishing puffs of the remainder of tobacco until the flame extinguished itself on the filter. Benny placed the contents of his pants into the pockets of his pink windbreaker and started to walk away, pants-less and short one shoe.

"Where you goin', Benny?"

"Gotta get some new pants and see Flak Jacket, you stupid cow."

"Bring back some muffins."

She waved at him, a blank grin of empty thoughts following his movements as he walked down the street. The sad, simple mountain of a woman didn't know how to register Benny's indifference as anything but love and was happy to go back to her various arts and crafts. No matter what Benny said to her, he always made his way back to her bed.

17

Nick ordered a coffee, adding cream and sugar while he sorted through the folders laid out in front of him. The handful he'd grabbed on the way out the door was completely random, a full stack still waiting in the office. Jenkins had yelled after him, wondering where he was going with the paperwork, and he'd yelled back that he was going out to lunch. Looking at him as the elevator closed, Jenkins' face showed the instant regret in his decision to let Nick do what he wanted.

Penny slipped through the diner's glass door, dressed much more conservatively than she had been for their previous date. He could see she carried herself differently. She shrunk into herself, navigating through the crowded restaurant, doing her best not to touch anyone or get in anyone's way. She finally made it to him and sat down in the booth.

"Hey," he said to her, smiling.

"Hello."

He could barely hear her. She swallowed her words, eyes focused on the floor.

"Everything okay?" he asked, wondering why she was having trouble making eye contact with him.

"Fine," she said.

"You sure?"

"Mmm-hmmm," she nodded to him.

"Can I get you something to drink, hon?" the waitress asked Penny loudly, trying to speak over the noise in the diner.

"Just a water, please," Penny said quietly, unconsciously adjusting her clothes.

As the waitress left, Nick stopped shuffling through his paperwork and looked at Penny, trying to get her to raise her eyes from the ground.

"Am I gonna have to get you drunk so you'll talk to me?" he joked.

"That's not funny," she bit back at him.

"Sorry, I just... did I do something?"

"No," she raised her head, realizing that she had snapped at him.

"Bad day at work?"

"No, it's just," Penny took a deep breath in, trying to find her voice, "this is me. I mean, this is the real me. Shy, plain Penny."

"Sure, you may be shy now, but you're hardly plain."

She bit her lip and blushed.

"Listen, I know people, all right. I've seen Penny."

"That was just drunk me. I'm really sorry, but that isn't me, all talking and wit and well... you know."

"You're telling me you have a Jekyll and Hyde personality? Ne'er the twain shall meet?"

"Yep," she grabbed for her water, chewing nervously on the ice cubes.

"I think that's the real you. I think you use the beer as an excuse to let your real self out, and if people don't like it, you can just blame it on being drunk and retreat into your safe shell."

"I should go. This was a mistake."

She moved to leave and he placed his hand on her forearm to stop her. He could feel she was tense at his touch, but didn't pull her arm away.

"No, I," Nick tried to find the right words, "you don't have to hide your outgoing self. I like that. Hell, I'm a loud mouth, sarcastic bastard. It's comforting to have that shot back at me."

"Then I guess I'll have to be drunk whenever I see you."

"Were you drunk when you sent M&M's that said, 'Fuck off and Die' to your boss?"

Penny's face turned a deep crimson.

"No."

"So, there you go. That part of you is always there. I like seeing both sides of you, but I need some bold Penny right about now. You think you can help me out?"

She pulled her hand back from him and clutched her purse, but instead of bolting out, settled back into the plush seat of the booth.

"I guess so."

"If you want, I can have the waitress change your order to vodka. You can pretend you're drinking water."

She laughed, "No, I think I'll be okay."

"Then at least get something spicy for lunch. Baby steps."

"Stop it," she raised her eyes to him smiling, "Okay. I'll try."

"Good, now, first things first. I had a great time at dinner with you."

Her eyes returned to the floor, but the smile didn't disappear, "Me too."

"Though, you do talk too much."

"Shut up."

"Hey, I liked it, obviously. What can I say? I'm a glutton for punishment."

"Are you just going to sit there and make fun of me now?"

"You can take it."

"Can I ask you something?"

"Shoot."

"Why me?"

"What?"

"I mean, this is L.A.––I'm sure you have a bunch of beautiful people in your office all day long. Why'd you choose me?"

"Obviously, you haven't spent much time with the Los Angeles Police Department. Not much beauty floods our halls."

"You know what I mean," she said, honestly looking for some verification from him.

"For one thing, unlike most of the people I see daily, you're innocent."

"The jury's still out on that one," Penny tried to joke.

"You're also multi-layered. Hard to get past the surface with a lot of people in this town."

"I guess that's why I like you, too. Though, I thought you were a bit smoother," she said, "Drink much?"

He looked down at his shirt where she had pointed to him and saw a big coffee stain right above his pocket.

"I thought it would enhance my bumbling detective persona," he said, grabbing a handful of napkins.

"How's your paper sorting going?" she asked, trying her best to avoid the subject of feelings, regretting bringing it up in the first place.

"Actually, that's why I called you."

"Oh God, did I say something last night I didn't remember? I might have just been quoting something I saw on one of those lawyer shows."

"No," he laughed, "No, what you said last night about the potential I have to provide relief to some family living with nothing but unanswered questions."

"Oh, that."

"I managed to convince my boss to let me reopen one of the cases."

"One of *these* cases?" she asked, pointing to the paperwork in front of him.

"Or one of the many scattered on my desk or on the floor by my desk or in any number of boxes surrounding my desk."

"So how're you going to pick which one?"

"I thought that's where you'd come in."

"Me?"

"You ready?" their waitress interrupted.

"Um, yes, I'll have a turkey club but with no tomato, mayo on the side, whole wheat toast and could I also get extra salt on the fries?"

Nick rolled his eyes at her, adding a clowning scowl.

"Quiet," her eyes went thin, amused by his mocking.

"Reuben, please."

The waitress grabbed their menus and left.

"How am I going to help you pick?"

"I've been staring at these things for almost a month now, they're all starting to blend together. And, though I hate to say it, I've become a bit numb to the details."

"I'm not exactly the deductive type."

"You can leave the detecting to me. What I want is the humanity you provide. All I see in these anymore are the facts, names and numbers. I'm better at reading people than paper. I need you to help me see the people in here."

"I have a fairly weak stomach."

"Well, then let's weed out the really gruesome murders."

"Is this legal?"

"Is what legal?"

"You discussing these cases with me?"

"Actually, some departments across the country have put up cold case websites describing cases without giving away detailed evidence or compromising investigations. Just think of this like getting a summary of cases and something just happens to catch your eye about one. Fair?"

"Fair."

"All right, Courtney Allende, disappeared March 14, 1990 outside of The Derby in Los Feliz. Witnesses saw her getting into a black SUV with an average height, average weight, Hispanic male. No leads. No plate number on the vehicle."

"How old was she?"

"27."

"Married?"

"Yep."

"Kids?"

"At the time," he looked at the file, "a newborn. Baby girl."

"So the little one is now in her twenties and never knew her mother? Pass."

"Pass? Why pass? That sounds like just what you were talking about. A great story. Find this woman, reunite her with her now adult daughter, or if she was murdered, give them a sense of closure."

"Nick, think about it. Do you think the father of that child has been completely honest with his daughter? What if he always told her her mother left when she was young and they had to fend for themselves together? Maybe he remarried shortly after and the stepmom is the only person she has ever known as her mom. If this is going to be your breakthrough case, you need to take on something that'll cause the least amount of upheaval in the least amount of lives. Get through this first one and they'll let you have more, right?"

"Yeah, but--"

"But say you dig up all those bad memories without any hard evidence. They won't let you near another case for a long time."

"Good point. See, I knew I called you for a reason."

She beamed at him. He made her comfortable and she was startled at herself, at how easy the words came when they talked. He seemed to know exactly how to get her to open up, even if he didn't realize he was doing it.

"Next."

"Garrett Barnes. Shot at close range in his apartment. No sign of a struggle or burglary. September 9, 1985."

"He lived alone?"

"Yes."

"Did they find the gun?"

"The gun was left in the apartment. No prints. Ballistics was only able to identify a partial bullet fragment. A girlfriend was brought to trial, but was acquitted, looks here like it was due to evidence tampering."

"So, reopening that one could possibly bring scrutiny to the LAPD?"

"Save that one for when I'm not worried about job security?"

"It sucks you have to think that way."

Nick shuffled the file to the bottom of the pile. This was going to be harder than he thought. Likely there was a reason not to investigate every single one of the cases piled up at his desk.

"Franklin 'Chipper' Willis. Transient found stabbed to death at the corner of 4th and Main, downtown. Traces of heroin found in his system. Case assumed to be gang related. Initiation ritual commonly seen among certain cliques."

"No witnesses?"

"It says here, no talkers."

"Talkers?"

"One of our biggest problems with unsolved murders, especially this type, murders on the street, is that nobody wants to be a snitch. Somebody could've seen a dude murder his own brother, but he'd rather the guy walk free and have somebody else take care of the problem than snitch on the guy to the police and be branded for life."

"So, there was evidence, a full report, just no eyewitness testimony?"

"You sound like you've done this before."

"Too much TV."

"You must watch more TV than I thought."

"You said transient, right? No family to upset? No protocol to break?"

"But how're people going to remember a vagrant who was killed five years ago?"

"Just because people live on the streets doesn't mean there isn't a community. I've seen a lot of properties reclaimed from squatters. There are a lot of people on their own, and a bunch of people too mentally ill to consort with others, but there are definitely those who stick together. All you need is one snitch."

"A snitch who knew Chipper Willis half a decade ago? Talk about a needle in a haystack."

"I thought you said these sort of murders happen all the time. You have all the files on your desk. Maybe a pattern will emerge if you look at all of these crimes together, just from the last five to ten years. Maybe you won't get a witness in this case, but maybe you'll get a witness from another similar case to break this one. It's worth a try. And you wouldn't waste any police resources other than your own time."

He smiled at her wide, seeing how animated she got while talking to him. Like all she needed was an interesting subject to talk about and the shy shell just melted away.

"Will you marry me?" he said, joking, but still starry eyed.

"Let's just get through lunch first," she stopped him, her lips pulled to a tight pucker, hiding her delight, "then we'll see."

"Not the answer I was looking for, but it'll have to do."

Nick moved the files onto the seat next to them when their sandwiches came. The ice broken, they had a nice conversation, each of them managing to steal food from the other's plate. Nick was able to finagle a kiss goodbye out of her as the end of their lunch hour grew near and told her he would call her soon.

"Thanks for lunch," she said, "Next time, I'm paying though."

"Only if you agree to let outgoing Penny appear more often."

"Deal."

He could see her trying to adjust her posture walking down the street, catching herself when she began to hunch over and lower her gaze to the sidewalk. He headed back to the station, hoping that nothing had come down the pipe while he'd been gone, leaving him free to dig through the pile around his desk.

18

...The great debate amongst our leaders, both in government and community, is the everlasting battle between Science and Religion. These enemies who should be allies create a rift between the faithful and the intelligentsia. The clash being that Science and Religion both have their place, but often they don't, nor should, occupy the same argument. But there are those of us who will not bow down to this heretical chess match. Just as the 199th Pope, Innocent VI passed between the fires to purify his air of the plague -- I have walked through the fires to the other side of knowledge. Science has been destroyed by corporate greed and the mass extinction of the perpetration of ideas in favor of profit. Religious government officials balk at progress in the name of heresy as pharmaceutical companies hold back the cure for the common cold in favor of mass profit gained by the marketing of analgesics and vaccines. There is a community where Jonas Salk is not a savior, but a great Satan, taking away the moneymaking machine of modern plague. Penicillin is the atom bomb of cash flow possibilities, doctors now giving out incorrect prescriptions, shorting the dose of antibiotics to cause incomplete cycles, breeding the new super virus. Will there be a cure for AIDS or cancer? Only once there is something worse to fear, but until then there is no money to be

made when the four horsemen aren't around to breathe fire into the
constant flames of humanity...

It was late afternoon before a young boy with long, unkempt hair kicked Ray on the sole of his foot. Managing to get a loaf of bread and a large can of SPAM out of SOVA, Ray found a spot in the shade under a tree in Pan Pacific Park. Glutting himself on sandwiches, he chose to start at the beginning of the pile of pages in his possession. The enriched wheat flour and salty meat product raised his blood sugar and quelled some of the exhaustion threatening to overtake him. When the skinny kid interrupted his reading, he was on page 132, the scattered text and sunlight giving him a headache. The kid threw a folded piece of paper into his lap, nodded to Ray without speaking and walked away toward CBS Television City.

Ray set the manifesto down and opened the paper, damp from the sweat of the messenger's hands. An abandoned warehouse off of Abbot Kinney would house the next game, one of the few buildings that remained untouched by the gentrification of Venice's seedier areas.

Sending a message through a strung-out errand boy was Crispy's final act of disapproval. There were no wishes of good luck, no pleas trying to talk him out of it, just an address, seat number, time and password. Ray couldn't even send thanks back Crispy's way. The messenger had disappeared into the crowds waiting in line to be an audience participant on *The Price is Right*. The cold gesture was a plain sign that he would be on his own the rest of the way. Crispy knew he couldn't get involved with Pretty Boy's business, lest he go out of business himself.

Ray's sudden compulsion to get into the game worried him a little. Consequences of getting involved with Pretty Boy never had a positive outcome.

Pretty Boy D'Arby didn't live on the street; he only did business there. Heavily involved in the Los Angeles slave trade, Pretty Boy's base of operations was in a well-guarded loft on Spring Street in the heart of downtown. Most of his "cargo" involved illegal immigrants looking for work. His favorite trolling place was outside Home Depot, preying on the unsuspecting workers looking to do eight cheap hours of plumbing repair.

Those he managed to con into trusting him were housed in prison camp warehouses, later purchased by unknown vendors. Some were used in local enterprise, illegal and off the grid, but most were used by legitimate businesses to increase productivity while driving down costs.

Corporations ran their public factories by the book, the bosses carefully adhering to the statutes and codes of the California Department of Labor. The conditions were satisfactory and the wages were usually union-regulated. Then there were the alternate factories, staffed by Pretty Boy's cargo; where up to 40% of production took place. Third World working conditions, living quarters not unlike the workhouses of Charles Dickens' industrial Britain, and no chance of escape. Illegal immigrants bore the brunt of the work, there were also a number of kidnap victims––both children and adults––hookers "rescued" from their pimps, and, of course, the homeless. Vagrants aren't as easily enticed into a strange car as a whore or someone offering plumbing service, so Pretty Boy had a different way of acquiring them.

The brilliance of his conniving was its simplicity. Homeless people are naturally suspicious of everyone and everything, so Pretty Boy removed their apprehensions. He laid everything out in the open.

Participants had the option to join a biweekly game of chance. Omaha, sometimes Pai Gow, most often Texas Hold 'Em, as its popularity and simple rules tended to entice the most players. A spot at the table meant a starting stake of five hundred dollars, provided gratis by Pretty Boy D'Arby. Winners took home enough money to change everything. Losers forfeit their lives. Pretty Boy could ship you to Indonesia, kill you on the spot, or torture you for fun if he felt like it. The game was fixed, everyone knew it, but hope is a powerful drug.

Everyone played the game, including Pretty Boy. If he stayed in the game until the end, he played the best player heads up for the pot. If he was knocked out early, the remaining players continued to play until there was a champion, and then he got to exercise what he called Buyer's Rights. The champion then had to play Pretty Boy in a game of heads up, potentially doubling his stake or being cast into the pit with the rest of the fallen. No one questioned this particular rule because D'Arby was putting up all of the money at the top of the game. It was his right to win his money back.

Pretty Boy rarely lost, and when he did, it behooved the winner to get the hell out of Dodge before they met with an unfortunate accident; the reason Caravan Kevin headed for

---

the hills at first chance. No matter what happened, Pretty Boy always claimed a minimum six new souls a game, so even if the winner happened to walk away with eight grand, Pretty Boy made plenty of profit. He always played to win. He never got angry. And he had the greatest poker face known to man, because half of it was gone.

He had eyes and a mouth, but where his nose should have been, was a large gaping hole. No one knew how it happened, or if he'd just been born that way, but it looked like someone shoved two sticks of dynamite into his nostrils when he was a kid and blew his face apart, bones and all. His cheekbones were the only things holding his upper jaw on.

Rumors of his favorite intimidation tactic were wide spread. There was always a bowl of trail mix handy and whenever someone got too bold or decided to be a tough guy and hold eye contact, Pretty Boy would gather up a handful of trail mix and start chewing. Inadvertently, some of the chewed substance would make its way up into his gaping sinus cavity and he would shove a thumb and forefinger into his face to scoop the slop out. He was playing with a caliber of opponents who had seen some horrible shit in their time on the concrete. This gesture made them all turn away.

Ray managed to panhandle enough bus fare on his way down Fairfax to catch the bus west. The kitschy amusements and eccentrics plying their cheap wares on the Venice boardwalk dissolved into reality once night spread over the canals. The aging hippies all retreated to their homes, once bought on the cheap in the 1960s, now worth millions of dollars.

Ray weaved through the streets, thin and clogged with the overpopulation of cars, finally finding Pretty Boy's warehouse. A security guard wearing a light linen suit and a dark shirt stood outside an unmarked door.

"Ray Cobb, I'm here for--"

"Password."

Ray pulled the note out of his pocket.

"Amistad."

"You carrying any weapons on you?"

"Don't think so."

Ray wasn't in the mood for the bouncer's bullshit. He looked down at the rubber gloves the guard was wearing.

"I'm not hiding a grenade in my asshole, if you're interested."

"I don't wanna catch some weird shit from you filthy bastards," the guard grunted at him.

"This coming from the guy who works for a dude missing his face. I think I'm the least of your worries, pal."

The security detail patted him down. He took a quick glance at the manifesto and threw it back at Ray. Once finished, he stripped off the gloves and threw them to the ground before drawing a new pair out of his jacket pocket and opening the door.

"You shouldn't litter like that," Ray said, joking flatly.

The guard ignored him and shut the door once he was inside.

The warehouse was empty and dark, except for a single poker table illuminated by an overhead light. To Ray's benefit, there were no faces at the table he recognized, save one. Sammy Traffic was positioned at the seventh seat, just to the right of where Pretty Boy would be sitting. His concept of a good time was running down the middle of Cesar Chavez Avenue during rush hour and seeing if anyone would hit him, with the idea of suing them. Obviously, he wasn't bright enough to realize running out into traffic wasn't exactly a litigable defense.

Fortunately for Sammy, he'd be betting into Pretty Boy on every hand. But for Ray to continue to have an audience with Pretty Boy, he'd have to do his best to get Sammy knocked out of the game. He knew all of the poor souls surrounding him chose to be there, but it was difficult knowing he was going to have to forfeit their lives in order to win.

Pretty Boy entered with an overabundance of hullabaloo, a king entering his court. Instead of a crown and scepter, he held his bowl of trail mix in one hand and, in the other, a small mason jar containing the formaldehyde-preserved eyes of Ernie Politics. Ray clutched his chair to keep from leaping across the table to grab the jar.

Pretty Boy set his treasures down on the table on either side of him and made it a point to greet everyone at the table with full eye contact, making sure each of them got one good solid look at his face. Everyone met their obligation in kind, but averted their eyes as soon as contact was broken. That is, everyone except Ray. Ray was the fourth seat, so he'd be positioned right across from Pretty Boy all night. He wanted Pretty Boy to know that he wasn't about to be bullied just because the man had a crater in his skull. Pretty Boy dealt the first hand and the two players to his left put out their blinds.

"Stare much, Cobb?" Pretty Boy smirked across the table at him as he snuck a peek at his cards.

The bet came around to Ray and he mucked his cards without looking at them. Pretty Boy took the time to learn the names of all of the people he was playing with, a detail Ray ignored. It would make beating them easier.

"Noticed your little parcel over there," Ray nodded in the direction of the jar.

"You like that?"

The lanky man to Ray's left raised almost half of his stack.

"Prize from a man you managed to knock out of the last game?"

The table stopped, waiting for Pretty Boy's answer, hoping and praying that he denied it, whether it was true or not.

"What good to me would labor be without any eyes?"

"Good point," Ray said, without smiling, "Seems to me you'd be looking for a different body part to replace anyway."

"They told me you were a smooth talker, Cobb," Pretty Boy smiled wide at him, "You can talk all you want. Your cards don't go right, it won't matter."

"Well, maybe if you weren't such a shitty dealer, it wouldn't be a problem."

Pretty Boy laughed at his comment, but chose to focus on the betting instead of retorting. He called Lanky and let the cards flop. The bet was to the twitchy fellow who stayed in on the big blind. He folded and Lanky went all in. Pretty Boy paused before calling the bet.

"This could be a first. I've never been knocked out on the first hand, Ross. But, hell, I can't help but keep you honest."

All of Pretty Boy's money went into the pot, to match what Lanky Ross had put in. The air went out of him. He was obviously bluffing, hoping no one would be stupid enough to call an all-in on the first hand, ready to scrape up the loose chips the table had left behind. The players flipped up their cards and Pretty Boy laid out the turn and the river. Pretty Boy ended up with a pair of queens to Lanky Ross' pair of sixes. Lanky wept uncontrollably as he was escorted from the table by Pretty Boy's security detail. As they bent to grab Lanky's arms, Ray saw they were packing tasers in their shoulder holsters instead of firearms. Pretty Boy wanted to keep them from permanently damaging the goods if something got out of hand.

Pretty Boy picked up the jar, shook it a bit and gave the glass an eerie smooch. In one hand of cards, Ray had learned several things: he wasn't likely to get shot, Pretty Boy was using Ernie's eyes as some sort of sick good luck charm, and their host played loose and stupid. It made him dangerous and difficult to read.

Lanky Ross' boldness also had an effect on the rest of the players at the table. Fast and aggressive might have been their early strategy, but now most of them would be slow and patient, a tactic Ray had hoped to exploit to get a few people out of the way before he had a chance to really step up and capitalize on a hand. The deal moved on and Pretty Boy prompted the blinds, basking in the stack in front of him, now double the size. Ray knew the smug bastard was likely to play even looser now that he had the obvious advantage. Ray would play the blinds and fold for the next few rounds, knowing Pretty Boy was going to play any cards put in front of him. He had enough money to burn to take some chances on playing shit and possibly turning it into gold.

A few hours into the game, considerable money had changed hands. Another player was out, a woman Pretty Boy called Bea. Sammy took her out with an inside straight draw on the river. It was down to Pretty Boy, Sammy, Ray, a plump guy Pretty Boy called Yeltsin, Twitchy, and a Mexican kid who couldn't have been more than sixteen years old.

"Bet's to you, Beans," Pretty Boy grinned. He was still chip leader, but his flippancy on a few hands had reduced his stack considerably. Ray was even able to take a few hands he'd felt confident enough about to throw some money at.

"Two hundred. That's all I got," the kid pushed in. He was sweating considerably and Ray knew there was no confidence in his bet. Pretty Boy was circling him like a shark on chum.

"Call," Pretty Boy splashed the pot.

The cards went up and the kid's face went white. Pretty Boy didn't apologize or acknowledge his annexation of another poor soul as he bent over the table and raked in the large share of chips. The security detail moved from their affixed positions and went over to grab the kid. He sat staring at his cards as their hands hit his shoulders. Then he snapped.

A makeshift knife came out of nowhere and stabbed one security guard several times in the belly. Blood sprayed out onto the table, hitting the chips and cards like raindrops. The kid was clobbered across the back of the head and was immediately unconscious.

"I thought you assholes frisked these pricks before letting 'em in here!" Pretty Boy screamed, backing away from the table, his hired help losing blood fast.

"We do! We did!" yelled the other guard, trying his best to stop the blood gushing from his comrade's series of new holes.

"Obviously not good enough. Get both of them the fuck out of here. Beaner goes into containment, unharmed. Tell Max to take this pincushion to the hospital."

The guard did as he was told, a short trail of scarlet following them out the door. Pretty Boy grabbed the dripping shiv up off the floor and brought it back to the table with him.

"Any more of you slippery fucks want to get your machos out now, here I am!" His arm was strained clutching the knife.

The table remained silent.

"Good. You all knew what you were getting into when you walked through that door. Any more of this shit, the game is over, and you all come with me. You got it?"

A single bodyguard returned. His shirt was stained through. Ray had missed an opportunity to take on Pretty Boy, but there were now two less people to deal with, the injured man and the guy who took him to the hospital, which meant there was only one guard standing between Ray and some solid answers.

"Looks like those eyeballs didn't bring you too much luck after all," Ray quipped, having been the only person to remain seated during the altercation.

"On the contrary, Ray," Pretty Boy said, wiping his blood-stained hands on Sammy's jacket as Sammy docilely let it happen, "I'm still alive *and* I'm going to enjoy tearing the toenails off of that little wetback after our game tonight. I'm down one security detail that wasn't very fucking good at his job. Looks like everything's coming up D'Arby. The Chinaman was right about these things."

Kissing the side of the jar, his sneer contorted the features of his missing face.

"The Chinaman?" Ray asked, trying not to show his surprise.

"Got these pretty pearls off some gook down in Chinatown. Was gonna take his daughter, but he gave me these instead. Good thing, too. That whore was so goddamn diseased I wouldn't let my dog fuck her."

"When did you get 'em?"

"Why the fuck do you care when I got 'em?"

Ray leaned back in his chair, trying to appear conversational to keep Pretty Boy talking.

"I heard you lost a game earlier this week, if you had them before then, they must not be that lucky."

"Au contraire, Mister Curious," Pretty Boy leaned forward in his seat and tossed a handful of trail mix into his gob. He smacked through the peanuts and raisins as he talked.

"I got wind that Kevin couldn't keep his mouth shut about his future destination. Little fucker cheated me and now a friend of mine in Jakarta is slowly skinning him. So, I hope you weren't thinking about cheating here tonight, gentlemen," he grinned, scooping a hunk of half-chewed trail mix out of his face.

"Needless to say, I managed to get all my money back."

Ray did his best to hide his fear, but couldn't help but notice he was right properly fucked. Pretty Boy had done plenty of killing in his day, but Ray knew he had nothing to do with the murder of Ernie Politics. Someone in Chinatown did. Ray had the information he came for, but he was still stuck in the game. If he lost, he'd be a slave, or more likely, a dead man. With every hand, he could see Pretty Boy liked him less and less. If he won, Pretty Boy would hunt him down and figure out a way to get his money back. He was running out of options and time.

Yeltsin was bagged by Twitchy on the next hand, his face pocked with dried droplets of blood from the security guard's gut as he watched the cards fall. Sammy was gleefully playing with his chips, his simple mind grasping only the concept of how much money was in front of him. When the bodyguard led Yeltsin out of the room, Ray managed to catch a small look from Twitchy across the table. He didn't know how deep the look went, but could tell Twitchy had also taken to heart his odds of coming out of the game on top. Ray hoped Twitchy didn't plan on doing anything stupid before he had a chance to capitalize and get the hell out of there.

The four of them played the next few hands in relative silence. No one seemed to go up or down a significant amount of cash until the blinds reached the point where every player had to either play or have their stack quickly chipped away. The deal was to Ray, which made Pretty Boy big blind. Ray looked down at his 9-10 suited hearts and decided to bet the blind, see where the power sat. Sammy raised. Then Pretty Boy raised. Twitchy stayed in to see the flop, but Ray could tell Sammy was itching to re-raise Pretty Boy. Ray mucked his cards and Sammy's chips were pushed forward before the cards landed in the center of the table. Pretty Boy called, and so did Twitchy, leaving him in a short stack situation that would force him all in after the flop. Ray burnt a card and flipped 8-J-K of hearts. He would've had a flush and tried not to curse himself under his breath for not staying in on the action.

Sammy checked to Pretty Boy, waiting to see his move. Pretty Boy checked through to Twitchy. They'd all been watching how the table played. If Twitchy followed his usual pattern, he'd have gone all-in on a winning hand. He checked through, giving away his weak position. Ray burned a card and turned the queen of spades. Sammy checked to Pretty Boy again, careful not to seem too eager about the potential straight on the table. Pretty Boy threw out the minimum bet, which was ample, considering how high the blinds were. Twitchy mucked his junk, left with barely enough in his stack to cover the next hand. Sammy looked at Pretty Boy's bet and went all-in. Pretty Boy had enough to cover and matched the bet. Sammy flipped over his A-10 off suit, hoping that Pretty Boy wasn't sitting on a flush. Pretty Boy tossed another handful of trail mix into his gaping maw with one hand and turned his cards over with a snap on the table. Pocket eights. Sammy guffawed across the table, thinking he had a damn good chance of winning the hand, giving him enough of a stack to wait patiently until Twitchy and Ray were hen-pecked off the table.

Pretty Boy chewed his snack deliberately, staring down Sammy Traffic, his hand absentmindedly fingering the glass jar enveloping the eyes of Ernie Politics, knowing any face card would give him the full house. Ray swallowed hard as he burned the final card, knowing the pot was good. All noise disappeared in the room when the eight of diamonds took the final position on the table. Ray didn't know how Pretty Boy had managed to will that card to the top of the deck, but there it was.

"No," Sammy whispered to himself, all the air sucked from his lungs before the words burst forth like a backdraft, "NOOO!"

The remaining security guard grabbed him and pulled him away from the table. He kicked it hard on the way up, sending Pretty Boy's chips flying everywhere. The security guard held him under his arms, dragging him kicking and screaming toward the exit. He was afraid to let Sammy go long enough to knock him out, for fear he would charge at Pretty Boy like the room's previous tenant. He was having trouble keeping him under control with the other two gone to clean up the mess the Mexican kid had left them with. The players could still hear Sammy's muffled screams behind the heavy door.

"There isn't anything I hate more than a sore loser," Pretty Boy chuckled as he began to gather up his chips from the floor around the table. Twitchy saw his chance, lunging for the knife Pretty Boy had forgotten he'd left sitting on the table. Twitchy was at his throat, a trail of red already draining from his vein, before Ray knew what was happening.

"Wait," Ray's voice stopped his hand, "Don't kill him yet."

With Twitchy's hand poised for the kill, Ray moved to the door where the security guard would soon be reemerging.

"Why not?" Twitchy's eyes had gone wild, his fear and rage turning him into a feral beast.

"Because we aren't done with him. Just keep him quiet," Ray hissed at him, hearing footsteps coming back toward the open room. In the dim light of the single lamp, Ray knew the wrong move would send that knife right through Pretty Boy's trachea, giving him more than one gaping hole in his head.

The guard came back through the door, the sleeve on his suit coat torn open at the shoulder. He was focused on the exposed cotton and it took him a moment to see Twitchy with a knife at Pretty Boy's throat. In his reaction, he didn't notice Ray's absence at the table and went down hard when Ray tripped him, his teeth biting through his tongue as his head hit the concrete.

Ray drove a fist into one of his kidneys and then grabbed the back of his head, driving it into the floor several times until the moans stopped. Ray checked his pulse to make sure he hadn't killed him. He was alive, but beyond unconscious. Ray turned him over and grabbed the taser out of his holster, emptying it of its batteries and tossing them to opposite sides of the warehouse. Finished, he stood slowly and made his way back to the table. For all the twitching his new partner had done during the game, his hand remained steady, like he was about to give Pretty Boy a shave.

"Who'd you get the eyes from?"

"You better hope this little dickshit kills me, Cobb, or I'll hunt you down and make you feel pain that'll make your nightmares look like teddy bears humping," Pretty Boy growled at him, trying not to move.

"That wasn't an answer," Ray said, picking up the bowl of trail mix and dumping in into Pretty Boy's face, making him look like a living candy dish.

"Old Chink is dead anyway," Pretty Boy spit out, his voice muffled by a septum full of raisins and peanuts.

"His daughter then. Where's his shop?" Ray asked, sitting down in the chair previously occupied by Twitchy. He punctuated his question by plucking a nugget out of Pretty Boy's face and eating it. Twitchy found the gesture amusing and tightened his grip, the knife digging deep into Pretty Boy's neck, causing a slow stream of dark red to flow down to his shirt collar.

"Cunt's name is De Zheng. Curio shop. Alpine and Broadway."

"And he didn't say how he got 'em?"

"Just told me they were the red eyes of a dragon and they'd bring me luck. Can't wait to see how they get me outta this one."

"They won't, since they aren't yours anymore," Ray said, picking up the jar and putting it in his pocket. He stood up and looked around the room.

"I don't care what you do with him, just don't do it until after I'm gone. Keep the money. Cover your tracks. And don't forget to release the others."

Twitchy just nodded to him. Ray left and stepped into the dark morning, the air passing over him like the black river Styx. As the door closed, he didn't look back to see Twitchy's hand buried wrist deep in trail mix, a rusty blade embedded in Pretty Boy's brain stem.

Ray could feel the heft of the jar in his coat pocket. He had the manifesto, the will, and the eyes. All he needed were Ernie's hands, and the solutions to a whole mess of unanswered questions.

Before he could decide on the best way to get back to Hollywood, he saw a flash of light blue out of the corner of his eye, followed by a sharp pain at the crown of his head. Ray's world blurred before he saw the dark shadow that had relieved him of consciousness.

Nestor Tyre stood over the limp body of Ray Cobb, a blackjack in his hand. Slipping the weapon back into his pocket, he threw Ray's body into an old Ralphs shopping cart and covered it with a blanket. He whistled as he wheeled it up Abbot Kinney toward Venice Boulevard.

19

A vacuum whirred in one of the nearby offices as Nick rubbed the sleep out of his eyes, the nighttime cleaning crew the only other sign of life. The night shifters were out in the parking lot, getting a buzz on while the radios squawked from their cars. Nick tried to make friends by saying he'd man the phones while they went, but was already arousing suspicion with his unpaid late night diligence. He wouldn't be surprised if there were rumors flying by morning that he was an Internal Affairs spook, keeping an eye on the departmental goings-on after hours.

Images of manila file folders were blending together and he was having trouble concentrating. In a period of ten years there were over one hundred different cases of unsolved transient murders. The numbers weren't shocking, considering how many bodies the department caught yearly, but it didn't make his inquest any easier. There seemed to be no viable pattern to any of them, with several different methods of death: stabbings, shootings, stranglings, beatings, dismemberment. If by some odd chance all of the murders were perpetrated by the same culprit, the murderer had a flair for variety. He'd decided it'd be easier to take each of the cases for their common ground, focusing on the method of death first, hoping by some random chance that several possible suspects would emerge from the cases in front of him.

The shootings he put aside immediately. Some victims were shot at long range, some at short. There were precision shots and scatter shots, different caliber bullets, dissimilar entrance and exit wounds; nothing at all to indicate that any of the killings were done in any sort of calculated manner. Any moron on the street could get a gun without a registration or serial number and shoot someone for any reason ranging from dishonor to a stolen dinner. It was the most impersonal of murder weapons, sowing the deadly seeds of impulse and accessibility. Each case was likely perpetrated by a separate individual, who, given their social situation and itchy trigger fingers, probably later became victims of crimes themselves.

Gang killings also had to be ruled out. Violent gangs like MS-13 still had a strong presence on the streets and one of the easiest ways for a member to prove his mettle or move up in the ranks was to commit a random act of violence, most times a brutal beating followed by a shooting. If an established citizen was the victim, the file usually ended up in the Vice or Narcotics division, depending on the gang's particular specialty. The rest of the victims ended up in Nick's pile.

The style and pattern of the gangland murders were as plain as day, but there was no leverage to them, so the unknown remained unsolved. Sometimes the district attorney would pull a random file to push a life sentence past the possibility of parole. Reasonable doubt could be jarred both ways and if the prosecution needed a case to put the cherry on top of a meaty conviction, the cold case pile was a good place to start. Nick figured if he did this job long enough, he'd become quick friends with the assistant D.A. He devoted his lower desk drawer to these candidates, sure to remember where they were when the State of California came snooping around.

Dismemberments and stabbings received most of his attention. Having the courage to get close enough to put a knife into someone, or to remove body parts, gave a murder a certain intimacy. The victims got a chance to look their killers in the face, seeing the evil in their eyes as the death dealers watched the life drain out of them. He'd removed everything from his desk but his untouched cold dinner and eight files. Nick spread them out, looking at the different degrees of wear on the name tabs of the manila folders: Franklin "Chipper" Willis, Ernest "Politics" Gaffney, John Doe 8/7/08, Abigail Drummond, Jane Doe 11/14/10, David "Freewheelin" Adder, John Doe 4/23/09, and Yolanda "Zippers" Bateman.

Gaffney and Bateman were both found missing appendages, all removed after death. None of the female victims were found sexually assaulted. All were found with multiple stab wounds from various sizes of blade. The weapons were new or clean because there were no signs of rusting or dirt in the entrance wounds. The clean blades brought Nick back to these eight. With most murders on the street, the stabbing took place with a makeshift instrument; a shard of glass, a rusty knife found in a dumpster. Various sizes of the knife wounds indicated the use of different murder weapons, but whoever the murderer or murderers were, they kept their weapons clean. No blades had been found at any of the crime scenes.

A common history of mental illness also tied the victims together, not too odd given half of the homeless and transient population of Los Angeles had some sort of mental disorder. They all also had scars from what looked like previous attacks, again, not an uncommon sight. Yolanda Bateman was HIV positive, David Adder had the early onset of syphilis, and one of the John Does tested positive for tuberculosis, but none of those pre-existing ailments seemed to have had any effect on their untimely demises. All of the identified victims had mild criminal records, mostly misdemeanors like disturbing the peace. Ernest Gaffney had recently been arrested for aggravated assault and spent a week in holding due to a paperwork glitch. Abigail Drummond had a history of being picked up for public nudity, but those incidents were prompted by her schizophrenia. She commonly used the defense that the government was bugging her clothing.

Nick pored over the final eight for hours, nothing jumping out to give him cause to reopen the case. The clock in the upper right hand corner of his computer screen told him it was time to break for the night. Nick shut down his laptop and shoved it into his messenger bag with the eight file folders. Perhaps a good night's sleep and a real dinner might jostle his brain into seeing something new. The cleaning crew gave him a wave goodbye as he stepped into the elevator and headed home.

20

Benny 7-11 didn't manage to get a bead on Kenny Flak Jacket until the afternoon sunshine was a distant memory. The Belmont Tunnel encampment was devoid of the small campfires and barrels that usually speckled the overgrown grasses and dirt of the abandoned railway. High risk fire warning in the hills put the LAPD and fire marshals on alert, causing the nightly residents to choose being cold over inviting the unwanted attention. A plastic flashlight Benny had picked up at the 99-cent store lit the faces hiding in the shadows. It was cheap and would hardly provide enough light for his purposes, but would be a treasured trinket for Betsy Over/Under if she resisted his advances the next time he wanted access to the fetid flower between her legs.

"You seen Flak Jacket tonight?" Benny asked a woman who was lying in the dirt. She was trying to rewrite the sign she held up to cars at a highway off-ramp, the glow of buildings in the distance her only source of light.

"In there," she grumbled, not looking up, her finger pointed steadily at the darkness of the tunnel.

There were no secret spots in the Belmont Tunnel anymore. Once a central point of the long-abandoned Los Angeles Subway and Street Car, it was a reflection of the crumbled hope of a public transportation system destroyed by a city that couldn't accept it. The tracks were all but buried, every inch of the tunnel covered in graffiti art; an urban canvas where artists and vandals met to create a collage of expression. The works were so diverse and detailed, it was strange the Los Angeles County Museum of Art hadn't claimed the space officially and turned it into a park. There wasn't a blank space that hadn't been tagged or explored. The side rooms and access panels, which once held engineering hardware, were now penthouse suites for vagabond campers.

The cargo pants Benny had stolen that afternoon hung over his mismatched shoes and dragged in the sludge formed by mud, contaminated water, and urine. Pain exploded in his head from the swollen goose egg, increased by the effort it took to focus on the pinpoint of soft light from the worthless flashlight. The tags and murals adorning the walls hid the access panels well and he had to turn his flashlight off occasionally to register any light that might emerge from any cracks in the sealed doorways.

The first door was easy to find. A street artist chose to accentuate the entranceway with the image of a carnival barker standing at a rundown podium, his tuxedo and top hat in tatters, pointing at the door painted to look like the dark opening of a large red circus tent. The grin on the barker's face was inviting, but haunting; the eyes wild, the smile littered with broken, brown teeth.

Benny pounded hard on the door before yanking it open without waiting for an answer. The beam of his flashlight illuminated a man cooking a squirrel over a small fire. He was naked from the waist down and was ineffectually playing with himself, a lazy entertainment while his dinner cooked. He looked up at Benny without fury or apology and told him simply, "Get out," before returning to the task at hand.

Benny did as he was told, glad the masturbating chef didn't charge at him, squirrel in one hand, cock in the other.

Behind him there was a shuffle that kicked up dirt. Benny swung the light around, hoping to catch the other figure in the darkness. The beam shone on nothing but the tags on the wall across from him. His heartbeat increased and he could feel it pumping hard in his cranial contusion and crooked finger. Another noise almost jerked the flashlight out of his hand as he turned to catch a large rat gnawing on the remnants of an old can of soup, its pointy, yellow incisors piercing the tin to soak up every scrap of food still left in the metal.

He knew the next door was only a few yards away and shut off his light to make his way toward it, phantoms of the light beam bobbing in his vision until his eyes adjusted to follow the next beacon in the darkness. Pacing turned into a brisk walk, then a run. Images of what was lurking in the dark were worse than what could be there, but Benny didn't dare turn his light back on until he reached the door. He feared seeing what manner of creature might be lurking in the black, waiting for him to make the wrong move.

Benny's foot caught something solid and he went down hard, catching his head on an exposed bit of track, his gash splitting under the bandage, wetting the gauze with a fresh spread of sanguine inkblot. Crying out in pain, Benny's voice was cut short by a low moan in the darkness. He stopped moving, the warm thick liquid running down his forehead, puddling in the hair of his eyebrow. The moan came again, not far from him, like some flesh eating undead, shuffling its way toward the smell of fresh blood. Benny's hand went slowly to the flashlight, the plastic cracked from his tumble. His thumb found the little white switch on the bright blue plastic and the beam of light, now refracted oddly by the broken lens, lit the source of the moans.

A pile of dirty clothes lay at his feet. The ruddy face of a drunken fool moaned without awareness or purpose. The sauced bastard barely noticed Benny had tripped over him, dead to the world, his face covered in snot and vomit. Frustrated, his adrenaline draining, Benny gave the drunk another kick for good measure. The pile of clothes let loose a dull grunt, but the blow didn't rouse him. Dabbing the blood on his forehead with his sleeve, Benny returned to his feet, his flashlight blinking on and off, the wires jostled out of place by the fall.

When he arrived at the second access door he didn't bother to knock before entering. Bleeding and covered in muddy sewage, his apprehension and fear were gone, replaced by anger and frustration. The floor beneath him crunched when he took his first step into the room. Crumpled and smudged bits of paper were strewn about the floor. In the short interval of working light, Benny recognized the handwriting.

He shook the light and smacked it with his palm, but the bulb's life was gone and he tossed it to the ground. When it landed, the echo of the clatter stirred something behind a stack of equipment and Benny bent down to retrieve the discarded plastic wand, raising it as a weapon against the shadow moving in the dim, hidden light source. The litter of papers underfoot crackled like dry leaves in autumn.

The head of a small dog emerged from around the corner. A ball of matted fur, missing its tail and left ear, the dog's head was cocked in curiosity. The mutt neither posed a threat nor suspected Benny of being one. Satisfied with its findings, the dog returned to its berth, limping. Benny shuffled through the sea of papers to see what the dog found more intriguing than him.

Beside a fading kerosene lamp, the slumped body of Kenny Flak Jacket stared back at him. Flak Jacket's cloudy eyes were half shut and one hand was clutched in rigor mortis to the sheet metal that hung over his torso with bits of twine. It was dull and scratched, like an antique sandwich board. Blood spattered the muzzle of the dog. It alternated between nuzzling Kenny's cold flesh and lapping at the deep slice across his neck, hoping Kenny would wake back up.

Benny sat down in the pile of papers, picking up random pages of Ernie's manifesto.

...Consequences are the only things keeping us from devolving into absolute savagery. The hidden truths will be revealed as the nation's news outlets run by the secret societies of the Ivy League elite will be toppled as the people grapple with their own sense of reality. Their

own personal truths will overwhelm their places in life. Greed will overcome as our society shrivels into itself. Greed breeds Greed. When you have none, you want it all and when you have it all, all you want is more. The inevitability of vice. To deny your basest urges is the most inhuman thing you can do. Sickness of creativity masked by the forebears of Greed...

Scribbles and margin notes crisscrossed the text and indicated a much older version. Scattered and left behind, Benny knew the pages were worthless, just as Flak Jacket's killer had known.

The dog laid its head in Kenny's lap and looked at Benny, raising one eyebrow at him, then the other in swift succession. Nestor was one step ahead of him, refusing to play the waiting game, obviously willing to dispose of anyone who got in his way. Benny stood up and grabbed the dog by the scruff of the neck. It growled at him, but didn't bite as he dragged it through the paper carpeting and shoved it out the door, closing it behind him. Disappearing into the darkness, Benny did his best to keep up with the mutt, listening for footfalls as the dog made its way out into the open air.

Benny 7-11 emerged from the stale gloom of the Belmont Tunnel, now bathed in the lights of the buildings downtown. His only hope for retrieving a copy of Ernie's manifesto was getting to Ray Cobb before Nestor did. He knew he was running out of time.

21

Driving through the city had become a reflex rather than a conscious act. Nick didn't care where he was going, his mind focused on other things while his body performed the in-grained process of getting him from Point A to Point B. Every few blocks he'd come out of his stupor, minutes gone from his consciousness, knowing his mind was focused elsewhere, but unable to recollect his train of thought. He realized he was almost home, sitting at a red light, trying to will himself to make the left turn back to the old, smoky house. Watching the time tick off the walk signal on the corner, he couldn't help but feel it was also a countdown for him. When the light finally changed to bright green, Nick flipped off his ticking turn signal and continued forward.

The car rolled past the fluorescent white light of The Rusty Kilt several times before Nick swallowed his pride and pulled into the parking lot behind the bar. Sitting in the used sedan, the radio off, Nick caught his eyes in the rearview mirror, illuminated by the bar's smoking patio. Weary sadness stared back at him, a man stranded between worlds. He didn't know what he was doing there, but he didn't belong at home, and every moment at the station felt wasted.

Part of him wished he hadn't seen the familiar rust of Hank Drees' Toyota pickup, the truck that helped him move out of the nice one bedroom in Silverlake into his current living situation. Hank loved to complain about being the guy who helped you move or drove you home after one too many, but he never said no, and Nick knew Hank secretly found comfort in being the guy everyone could count on. It was why Nick was in the parking lot, debating whether to go into the bar, instead of at home; he needed to disappear for a little bit with someone who wouldn't judge him.

No one could explain how The Rusty Kilt became the premier off-duty cop bar. Likely it was the offer of free deep-fried cream cheese balls and half-price tappers for anyone who flashed a badge, rather than the atmosphere. Dark tartan tapestries covered the walls, the plaid crimson broken by hunter green paint. A suit of armor sat at the far corner of the bar, holding an empty mug, wearing traditional Scottish garb, complete with a tam o'shanter sitting atop its metal dome. The locals had dubbed the mascot "Seamus" and for a few of the patrons, Seamus was the only guy at the bar who'd tolerate their inane conversation. It was late enough in the evening that the bar had cleared, except for a gaggle of sheriff's deputies playing a game of 501 at the dartboard and a few singles scattered at the stools.

Hank Drees' forearms held the rail at the end of the bar, fingers lightly clutched to a half-empty pint glass. Hank didn't look away from the day's sports statistics on the mounted television as Nick sat down next to him. A frothy pint was set down in front of Nick before he could ask for it.

"I miss the days when L.A. had a pro-football team," Hank said, as though Nick had been sitting beside him all night.

"Haven't you heard? We do. It's called USC," Nick replied, sipping at the dark beer before him, a nod thanking the bartender for remembering his usual even after a long hiatus.

"I suppose they pay 'em enough to be considered pro," Hank said.

Nick could tell Hank had been there since going off shift, but wasn't drunk, just lubricated enough to lose the tough guy cool and slump into the bar stool.

"So, is it exciting?" Hank asked.

"What?"

"Dating a murder suspect?" Hank looked over at Nick for the first time, his eyes eating the shit his grin wouldn't reveal.

Busted, Nick hung his head, clenching his teeth.

"That didn't take long."

"We work in a police station, genius. There ain't much that gets by us."

"Yeah, well, by that logic, the city would be devoid of crime."

"We gotta take time off, my friend, or we'll go crazy."

"You're the first to know, I haven't even told Mom yet."

"Told her about a few dates? You need to slow down, Champ. I know it's been a while, but you're gonna scare that fine weepy thing away if you think she's the end all be all."

"I know, man, but there's something about this girl. Like she makes me want to be better, have purpose."

"You sound like a fucking Hallmark card. You been watching Lifetime?"

"No, I'm serious, man. This detective job is killing me and all the sudden this girl comes along and says two words to give me focus."

"Focus? You getting better at paperwork?"

"Cold cases, buddy."

"That? That's your focus? She got you to look into a bunch of old dried up files that have no chance of moving your career forward?"

"I don't know what it is. Maybe she helps me see why I started doing this in the first place. Most times I feel like this worthless hack."

"You don't need a girl for inspiration, Archer. You were born for this shit."

"Yeah, yeah."

Hank turned on his stool, finally making eye contact with Nick.

"Listen, the boys give you shit because you were once like us and got a chance to move up. That isn't jealousy, fool. They envy you. Most of those fuckers are too scared to even sign up for the test. You've got the skills they don't and it pisses 'em off."

"Bullshit."

"No, bullshit on you. You think I'm fucking with you? Stroking your ego?"

"Any one of those guys could do what I do."

"Don't try to be modest, Archer. It makes you sound like an asshole."

"I'm not, I..."

"You can't turn that shit off and you know it."

"I just wanted a beer, man. Not a fight."

"I'm not fighting with you," Hank said, "Okay, here. Here's an example. I wanna know why you haven't stopped glancing over at that dart game in the corner since you walked in here. You don't think you have the skills? Bullshit. All I see is a bunch of brown shirts playing darts."

Nick avoided Hank's eyes, knowing Hank had bested him in the argument, like always.

"C'mon, man--"

"Spill it."

He exhaled, expelling the carbon dioxide like it held in his apprehension, wishing to avoid what the detectives in RHD called being a Cocky Sherlock.

"Those two," Nick pointed to a mustachioed sheriff in his late thirties passing a handful of darts to a younger female deputy.

"So?"

"Every time they pass the turn, their hands linger a split second longer."

"Why's that intriguing? They're drunk and flirting. Happens every day."

Nick took in a deep breath, knowing what Hank was driving at.

"She keeps playing with her hair, trying to straighten out the kinks from the tight knot it's been in all day. When she came back from the bathroom, she had a fresh layer of makeup, not extreme, but enough to make her eyes pop and her lips glisten.

He keeps unconsciously rubbing the point where his ring finger meets his palm, knowing there's something missing, pretending to check his phone when he's really making sure the wedding band is still deep in his pocket. And I caught one of his bad jokes. There's no way she could find him that funny. They're just waiting for that game to be over. Neither of them are paying attention to the time, but they're both impatient, trying to speed the game along."

Nick went back to his beer, staring up at the television.

"And you think that's something anyone would notice?"

"If they're paying attention."

"Nobody's paying attention, Nick. Not even you. Who gives a fuck if that guy cheats on his wife? But you saw it. You see it. You saw it when they caught The Strangler. You see it in the department every day. You don't need some new chippy to inspire you for that."

"Some days I just don't know what I'm doing, man."

"Fuck that," Hank said to him, getting agitated, "I wish I had your problem. I know exactly what I'm doing. I do my job, drink my beer, and try not to die before my shitty pension kicks in. That's it. That's what I got."

"You're a good cop, Hank. Don't give me that 'another day another dollar' crap."

"You wanna talk, Archer? You couldn't come in here without your brain working overtime, but you still need a pep talk from your old buddy Hank. Where the hell did you leave your balls?"

"Why are you so pissed right now? I just wanted to talk," Nick said, defensive.

Hank stood up, reached into his wallet and threw a few bills on the bar.

"I want you to stop feeling sorry for yourself. You need to start trusting the details. Quit looking at the things you don't have, start loving the things you got. You're paying attention to everything around you except yourself. Do me a favor, Nick? You wanna work on cold cases, ride the desk at CCSS? Fine. But don't just be another asshole spinning his wheels. Start looking at the shit only you can see."

"Hank––"

"Naw, man. Give me a reason to envy you. Not just to be jealous of your paycheck. See you around, Detective."

Hank pushed through the back door of The Rusty Kilt and disappeared into the parking lot. Nick wondered if he was going to manage to lose any more friends for this job, if it was really worth it. Finishing his beer, he watched with bittersweet fascination as the woman playing darts accepted the seemingly innocent offer from her male counterpart for a ride home.

22

...Time is nothing but a restriction we have put on ourselves. It will take time, but time is on our side. The Dutch cared not for time as they toiled eighty years against the dreaded Spanish. Eighty years? I would fight a hundred eighty years if it meant an end to corruption, tyranny, and lies...

Ray's eyes opened slowly, Ernie's words resonating through his skull, his shoulders and knees in severe pain. He was in a wooden chair, his hands bound behind him, the rope pulled taut and tied to his ankles. He tried to push back on the chair to relieve the pressure on his joints, but it didn't budge. Tight knots caused the rough hemp to cut into his wrists.

"Ernie always did have a knack for the hyperbolic," Nestor said, flipping through the pages of the manifesto.

The back of Ray's head was swollen and tender where the blackjack had hit him. The smug, smooth sound of Nestor's voice sent a pounding ripple through his brain, enough to transfer the concentration of pain from his hands to his head.

"You seem to have a death wish, Ray. You pay a visit to *Her*, then Pretty Boy? I'm amazed there's anything left of you.

How'd you manage to get out of that game alive? There was certainly no cash on you. Only this lovely document and a pair of freshly cut albino eyeballs."

"Fuck you," Ray growled out of his dry throat, while his fingers did their best to wriggle out of their bindings.

"Always the elegant one, aren't we?" Nestor's eyes narrowed to a crease as he leered underneath his mask. Pacing in front of Ray, he was sure to maintain a certain distance. Flicking the wilted and dirty Post-it note between his fingers, Nestor mused at his captive.

"Clever use of Achilles numbers by Ernie, don't you think?"

"Achilles numbers?"

"1152 1323 1352 1372 1568 1800 and 1944. They're Achilles numbers. Numbers that are powerful, but not a perfect power."

"What the hell are you talkin' about?"

"Ray, it seems to me that the folks on the pavement have talked up your intelligence so far beyond its true capacity that you have actually started to buy your own hype. You see, Ernie wasn't only intrigued by the conspiratorial nature of humanity; he also had an obsessive desire to spark his psyche into mathematical autism. As Galileo said, 'Mathematics is the language with which God has written the universe.' He loved numbers, their simplicity, but was never a genius with them. He would latch onto some obscure mathematical theory and ponder it for years. Just discovering that Fermat's Last Theorem existed almost made him catatonic. You didn't know that about him? What kind of friend were you?" Nestor laughed at him.

"The name of his killer is buried in mathematical calcula-tions?" Ray asked, trying to get Nestor to revel in his hubris.

"The name of his killer? Mathematical calculations? My friend, you give Ernie too much credit. As I told you, he wanted to spark genius mathematically, but couldn't. Likely he chose those numbers because of their mathematical signif-icance, but didn't think beyond that. I assume, like me, you've taken a look at each of those page numbers?"

"Yeah, but––"

"The pages only go to 1389."

Ray nodded in agreement, sweat mixing with tears as he tried to adjust to the strain put on his tendons.

"I've also checked 19, 44, 180, 15, 68, 156, 818 and other various permutations," Nestor said.

"You killed Ernie?"

"Blunt. Very blunt. I like that you get to the point, Ray. I hate to disappoint you, but Ernie and I agreed on far too many political points for me to dispose of such a gracious ally. I'd have to say I was nearly as disappointed by his passing as perhaps you were. In fact, this lovely room we're in was one of his many safe houses. At the time of his mutilation he was about to have me start surveillance on one of the enemies of the movement somewhere nearby. Never did find out who it was. Maybe that's part of the mystery."

"Then why––"

"You had the map," he said, holding up the Post-it note, "and the key. I couldn't, in good conscience, let you find the pack-age, as you obviously didn't know Ernie as well as you claimed.

It isn't befitting that someone of your particular stature should have access to such riches."

"Maps? Keys? What the fuck are you talking about?" Ray was genuinely confused and interested, and he needed Nestor to keep talking. Pain streaked down his arms in an electrical surge, but his fingers never stopped working on the knots.

"You certainly are good at playing dumb. If, in fact, you're playing."

Nestor stepped close to him, their eyes meeting.

"A last will and testament usually implies transfer of wealth, doesn't it?"

"Wealth? You're a fuckin' nutball. Ernie was just as goddamn dead poor as the rest of us," Ray huffed through his tears.

"You're telling me you beat half the life out of Benny just to find out who killed Ernie? Not to find the package he left behind? That seems a bit far-fetched, Ray. Altruistic, certainly, but completely unbelievable."

"Is that who put you up to this? Benny?"

"Oh, no. I take full credit for this interrogation. You and I both know that Benny isn't worthy to take up the mantle and follow the revolution to the end. My guess is he's currently submerged under the bloated body of Betsy Over/Under, awaiting instructions from me. Which will never materialize, of course. The fortune Ernie left will serve as an excellent nest egg for the beginning of a glorious new era. Benny wouldn't understand that."

"You're completely Looney Tunes, you know that?"

"Sanity is relative," Nestor shrugged.

He stepped away from Ray and went to a small table on the other side of the room. When he turned back around, he was holding a sickle, not unlike the one adorning the old Soviet flag.

"I was hoping you'd share your information with me, relieving both of us of this unfortunate situation, but since you don't seem to know anything about how to read the map buried in these pages, I'm afraid I'm going to have to proceed with my original purpose."

"Which is?"

"Gutting you and taking the items to figure out on my own," Nestor responded, smiling as though he had just asked if Ray wanted a cup of tea.

"If you kill me, you'll never know what the phrase on the back means," Ray bluffed, watching light reflect off the clean, sharp blade.

"*Komenci kie la soldato evolui al granda forxi*," Nestor said, having memorized the text on the back of the note, "What is it, Ray? Pig Latin?"

"No," Ray answered as Nestor progressed ever closer.

"It's a wonderful world we live in. When I'm done with you here, I'm going to pop over to the nearest public library. You might be shocked to find out that our libraries can be used for more than naptime. Filthy places, I'd never set foot in one, but I'll send someone in for me and have them enter that phrase into Google. One of those words is likely to tip me off to the language. And, if it isn't a language, and happens to be another complex code, I'm sure I'll also figure that out eventually. Ernie wasn't exactly the Enigma machine."

Ray couldn't believe he hadn't taken the time to just go online and look up the phrase. Then again, he was keeping busy getting involved in poker games of slavery, a charity pregnancy farm, and being tied up and gutted like a hunk of beef.

One of his hands was sore and scraped, but Nestor's pontificating gave Ray enough time to work it free.

"Sorry to have to do this, Ray, but I can't have you going after the package."

Nestor rose the sickle to strike and Ray brought his fist up to catch Nestor on the chin. It stunned him briefly and the trajectory of his swipe sent the sickle from his hand. Ray pulled hard to free his other hand from his feet and his shoulder tore from the joint, causing him to howl in pain, but it gave enough slack to slip his wrist out of the bindings. Nestor dove for his weapon as Ray managed to wriggle his disabled hand out of the rope.

"Slippery fellow," Nestor cackled, the sickle back in his hand, "I suppose I shouldn't have been so complacent in my capture. You escaped The Queen and Pretty Boy, it only holds true that you'd escape me."

"Bring it, you crazy bastard," Ray taunted, struggling to maintain leverage with his feet still bound together.

Nestor charged at him, but Ray ducked, sinking his fist deep into Nestor's gut. The wind left him as his diaphragm crumpled, but the force of his fall brought the sickle down hard into Ray's already torn apart shoulder. Blood was flowing steadily down Ray's arm from the gash in his back, but he flung himself at Nestor's midsection, both of them slamming into the floor. The sheer force of the blow against the concrete lodged Ray's shoulder back into the joint with a resounding pop. Adrenaline was the only thing keeping him conscious.

Nestor swung the curved blade again, barely connecting with Ray's cheek, taking out a chunk. Had he been closer, Ray would have been as faceless as Pretty Boy.

Ray's hand grabbed Nestor's wrist and slammed it repeatedly into the ground until the bones crunched from the impact and the reaping tool clanged to the floor. Ray knelt down hard on Nestor's gonads and threw the weight of his barely functioning elbow into his attacker's Adam's apple, constricting his breathing. Nestor's eyes bulged out as shorter and shorter breaths puffed beneath the stained light blue of his surgical mask.

"You wanna know why I was able to escape The Queen?" Ray asked him, blood flowing down his cheek and dripping onto Nestor's fatigues, their faces almost touching, "She wanted me to give you this."

Ray ripped the surgical mask from Nestor's face, exposing a patch of beard and skin, untouched by a razor or sunlight for years. Nestor shrieked at the removal of his mask, exposing a cave of neglected teeth. Ray gathered his saliva and spit a thick wad of mucus into Nestor's mouth, before pushing off of him.

Nestor let out a nightmarish scream, Ray's spittle like sulfuric acid in his throat. He tried to spit all liquid out of his mouth in between screams and scrambled to grab the sickle, sticking the blade into his mouth to scrape the germs from his tongue. He only succeeded in splitting it in two, his saliva mixing with thick blood, his screams becoming more violent.

He ran for the door, his bellows echoing through the room, the sound disappearing into the heavens, consumed by the stars. His fingers grasped at his mouth and throat as he ran hacking and screaming into the night.

"Goddamn germaphobe," Ray said to himself and staggered to the small table in the corner. Grabbing the manifesto, note, and jar, he shoved them into his pockets. The table also had an assortment of different blades, laid out in preparation for surgery. Ray decided it was time he stopped wandering into these situations without a weapon. He grabbed the closest knife, sliced through the ropes still around his ankles, and stuck it into his jacket pocket.

Stumbling out into the slowly cresting sunrise, blood dripped behind Ray's path, seeping from his dead shoulder. He struggled to stay conscious, trying to get a bearing on where he was. From the proximity of the buildings in the distance, he was somewhere downtown. To get there all the way from Venice, Nestor had to have stolen a car. If he could find it parked close, he could make a quick getaway, but his vision began to blur, the adrenaline wearing off, his body going into shock. In front of him, he could make out another figure in the alley.

Dropping to his knees, Ray hoped it wasn't Nestor standing before him. A low whine escaped from Ray's lips, a plea to the stranger for charity, before he passed out against a dumpster, his face pressed into the rust and dirty water.

23

Nick remembered a time when he possessed the constitution of a younger man, capable of drinking several beers before consuming an unhealthy amount of fast food. Performing such a task now rendered him sore, bloated, and exhausted.

Sucked in by the comfort of the couch cushions, he was unable to execute the simple act of switching off the television his mother had left on. He held his distended belly as he smashed his head into the plush arm of the couch.

The glow of the small picture tube stared back at him. His mother was still obsessed with watching The Discovery Channel. Last month it was The Food Network, the month before, TLC.

"This too shall pass," Nick said to himself, not particularly interested in the overblown drama of paranormal investigations, but too lazy to bother changing the channel.

Nick didn't believe in ghosts. There was just no logic to the concept. If someone dies, in the unlikely scenario their soul continues to exist after the body doesn't, why would they spend their afterlife wandering down the hallways of their own home, reliving scenes from their former life, scaring the pants off some old lady brushing her teeth? Ghosts have unfinished business, the so-called experts say. Nick tried to think if there was anything so important in his life that if left unfinished, he would abandon paradise for. Nothing came to mind. Supernatural chicanery coupled with people's inherent fear of death. If the people who feared ghosts saw what Nick saw on a daily basis, they would find out they have much more to fear from the living.

"The rural homestead, built in 1846, appears, on the outside, to be a picturesque image of country living. Well-maintained by the real estate company which purchased the home off of the previous owners, the three-bedroom two-bath estate has been available for sale for the past eight years, with no serious buyer."

The voiceover showed the home, bathed in beams of light spread by early morning, something out of a Rockwell painting, before a picture-negative effect was placed over the exterior shot of the house. An overweight woman with tightly curled blonde hair, wearing a gaudy flower pattern blouse spoke to an interviewer off camera in a thick southern accent.

"The agent mentioned somethin' in passin'. Somethin' 'bout a crime of passion decades ago. Neither me or my husband really took anythin' like that seriously, knowin' there was always stories connected with old houses. After a hundred and fifty years, there probably was gonna to be some history."

After scouring files all day and his fallout with Hank, the last thing Nick needed was to hear this bumpkin prattling on about goblins messing around with her cabinets or moving her morning paper from one room to the next. Managing to rouse himself from his food coma, Nick half-rolled to grasp for the remote control sitting on the coffee table. After several failed attempts, his hand found the black plastic and he pointed the remote at the set.

"The price was amazin'. We was sure there was a catch. Little did we know that murder tends to drive the price down..."

The television went dark and Nick swung his legs off the couch. He switched off the lights in the living room and made his way into the hallway, yawning wide. As his feet hit the staircase, his mind suddenly awakened. The woman's final words echoed through his head and his eyes went wide.

Murder tends to drive the price down...

Turning around, he flipped a small table lamp back on and extracted his laptop from the bag he'd discarded onto his mother's red chair. Nick turned it on as he sorted through the files looking for police reports detailing the addresses of the incidents.

Once the computer was booted up, he opened the web browser and typed in the address where the body of Abigail Drummond was found. The first search result stared back at him.

Commercial High Rise Complex brokered for a steal at 613 South Olive

Nick clicked on the story.

After almost eight months of vacancy, the property at 613 South Olive Ave, not too far from bustling Pershing Square, has found a buyer. Once an abandoned building, rife with vandalism and squatters from L.A.'s constantly growing homeless population, Keller & Hoff Real Estate, in conjunction with the Greater Los Angeles Department of Community Redevelopment, have brokered a deal mutually beneficial for the residents of the area and private enterprise....

Nick furrowed his brow and opened up the next folder in his pile, entering the next address into the search engine.

New Recreational Facility in East L.A. to Build Community Along Whittier Corridor

He opened the link.

During the opening ceremonies of this year's Cinco De Mayo Parade along Whittier Boulevard, the Greater Los Angeles Department of Community Redevelopment will open a new recreational facility, complete with a full staff to mentor children in programs reaching from basketball fundamentals to safe sex practices. Keller & Hoff Real Estate...

Two was a coincidence. Three was a pattern.

Koreatown Warehouse Gone to Greener Pastures

The remnants of an old toy factory, once the center of industry for the small community along Virgil Avenue, and lately a den of drug addicts and transients, will be demolished to make way for a park, an unfamiliar development in the real estate world. Representatives from the Greater Los Angeles Department of Community Redevelopment worked closely with brokers from Keller & Hoff Real Estate to settle on an agreement to increase the greenery amongst the broken concrete of the neighborhood...

Keller & Hoff and the DCR? Keller & Hoff was the company Penny worked for.

"Could she have known about it?" he whispered to himself.

He pulled out his phone and dialed Penny's number. It rang three times before she picked up.

"Mmpfh... hello?"

"Penny, it's Nick."

"Um, oh, hi. What time is it?"

Nick looked up at the time in the corner of his computer screen. It was well past two o'clock in the morning.

"Hey, I'm sorry, I didn't realize how late it was."

"What's going on? You okay?"

"How involved are you in the brokering of properties at your firm?"

"Huh?"

"Do you broker deals? Are you an agent?"

"Can we talk about this in the morning? Are you drunk?"

"Please, Penny. Just answer the question."

"No, uh," she was starting to wake up, realizing how urgent his tone was, "I'm an executive assistant. Paperwork. Occasionally I'll be brought to a site to help with cleaning, but that's only cosmetic, otherwise they bring in an outside cleaning crew."

"But you said you've seen properties reclaimed from squatters, right?"

"I help take before and after pictures. With reclaimed properties, sometimes it helps to give people a vision of what can be done with a building that seems too run down to be worth it. Wait... what's this about?"

"You don't do negotiations?"

"No." She was awake now.

"What do you know about the Department of Community Redevelopment?"

"I dunno. They build parks and stuff. Why are you calling to ask me about this in the middle of the night?"

Nick could tell Penny wouldn't have been directly involved in any of the transactions. At the very least she'd see the contracts, but would never have access to direct negotiations.

"Do you have keys to your office?"

"Nick, you're freaking me out. What's this all about?"

"I think I found that pattern we were talking about. Can you meet me at your office in half an hour?"

"It's two o'clock in the morning."

"I know, I'm sorry, I just... I've gotta get into the files at Keller & Hoff."

"Don't you need a warrant for that?"

"A warrant or a disgruntled employee who gives up the files willingly."

"I wouldn't exactly call myself disgruntled. You wanna tell me what this is about?"

"Will you please trust me and meet me there?"

"All right, but beware, I'm not gonna be presentable."

"Unfortunately, this isn't a social call."

"You really know how to flatter a girl."

"Thanks, Penny. I really appreciate it."

"See you soon. And you better bring coffee."

Nick hung up the phone, grabbed his keys and the files. Locking the door behind him, he realized he was no longer tired.

24

She was already outside waiting for him when he pulled into the empty parking lot. Her hair was up in a bedraggled ponytail and she had obviously thrown on a pair of sneakers and a jacket over her pajamas. In the overhead glow of the outside light, she hopped from one foot to the other trying to keep warm.

"Took you long enough," Penny said to him as she turned around and stuck her key in the front door, setting off the alarm. She ran inside the glass doors and punched in the alarm code quickly so that the security company didn't have to make a check-in phone call.

"Sorry, I wasn't right around the corner like you," he joked to her.

"I was beginning to wonder if this was going to be like some stupid camera show. An elaborate set up where Margie steps out of the bushes, scares me half to death and tells me it was all a prank."

"I wish we were so lucky."

They made their way upstairs and Penny flipped on one of the lights. The white tubes flickered a bit before illuminating a small section of cubicles.

"You wanna tell me what this is about, now that you've gotten me out of bed and involved me in some light breaking and entering?"

"It isn't exactly B and E if you have the keys."

"Still, what we're doing isn't exactly legal, is it?"

"It also isn't exactly illegal. Chalk it up to following a hunch."

She led him to her cubicle, unadorned with the decorations other employees used to make their workspace less sterile and bland. She turned on the computer and sat down.

"All right," Nick said, pulling a chair from one of the other cubicles and sitting down next to her, "you know how we looked at all the files and picked out the one that seemed the least publicly disturbing?"

"That Chipper Willis guy, right?"

"Yeah, well, I decided to pull all the files with similar details. By pure accident, I stumbled across a strange connection. All the murders took place in properties that were later brokered into much larger deals by Keller & Hoff."

"Wait," she stopped typing in her username and password, "you think Keller & Hoff has something to do with a bunch of murdered bums?"

"I don't know. That's why we're here. Could be some crazy coincidence, but I thought–"

"You thought since you've got a girl on the inside, why not take advantage?"

"If I got a warrant on a hunch and was wrong, I'd be a traffic cop by tomorrow. And I wouldn't say taking advantage," he searched for the right words, "I'm utilizing your skills."

"Right," she said, still unsure if they were doing anything wrong.

"What kind of information does your database provide?"

"Buyer information, price adjustments, appraisals, incident disclosure records––"

"Incident disclosure records?"

"Yeah, when someone dies, is killed, if a previous resident was HIV positive, stuff like that, the company is legally obligated to let the new tenant know. There's a lot of superstition involved in this business. That's why it took so long for them to sell that Amityville house."

"People afraid of ghosts?"

"I sure as heck wouldn't want to live there."

"So, what usually happens once an incident is disclosed to potential buyers? Are those properties more difficult to sell?"

"It depends. If an old lady died in the house, people don't usually care, but if a family of four has been brutally murdered and there have been spooky twin sightings, it doesn't tend to move. Wait, are you saying––"

"I think these 'disposable' dregs of society were purposely murdered in these properties."

"Because if a property isn't moving, an incident would drive the price down."

"And then a potential buyer on the line can pick it up for a steal."

"That's messed up."

"Of course, it may be some crackpot theory and I got you out of bed for nothing."

"Well, only one way to find out. Gimme the first address."

Nick set the folder down in front of Penny. They both scanned the screen once the results came up.

"That's funny," Penny said, scrunching up her nose, "Under the incidents tab, it says 'None'."

"Did you type in the address right?"

"It's right there."

"Huh. Try the next one."

The incident report was the same.

"Who has access to change the incident report status? Is there a statute of limitations?"

"I think so, but not within ten years. And everyone has access to this, we all have to update our own properties."

"Try this one," Nick said, frustrated.

Penny pulled the third folder from his hand and double-checked the address entered before she hit the return key.

"Okay, this doesn't make any sense."

"What're these numbers here?" he asked, pointing at the screen.

"Those are the prices. Original asking price, potential offers, counter offers, price drops and the dates."

"August 1, the price for this property is listed almost $50,000 more than it was on October 15. John Doe was found killed on that property on August 7. How long does it usually take for a price to drop?"

"A property is usually shopped for a while before the asking price is lowered, but the price didn't drop. That number under October 15th is the offered price accepted by the broker."

"Who was the broker?"

"Hold on... oh my God," Penny said softly, covering her mouth, "Marjorie Wells."

"Go back to those other records."

For each file, the price had dropped considerably after the incident, sometimes taking a few weeks, sometimes many months, but it always dropped. The buyer was always DCR and the broker was always Marjorie Wells.

"Are you telling me that Margie and someone at the DCR conspired to have homeless people killed at properties that had no potential of moving? Even brokering the deal at a discounted price, Margie would have walked with a considerable commission," Penny said.

"She probably also got a hefty kickback from her contact at the DCR. Good detective work there, Miss Searle."

"This is creeping me out."

"Do you have access to Margie's files? The buyer is the DCR, but it never mentions a specific negotiator."

"All her leads were given to Gabriel. Those files aren't shared. Personal contacts are kept private."

"Was everything on her computer? I can't see myself getting a seizure warrant any time soon."

"No, she kept a‑‑"

Penny got up without finishing her sentence and raced over to Gabriel's cubicle. Nick followed her, but by the time he got there, she had already torn through half of his drawers.

"So much for making it look like we were never here."

Penny opened each drawer, shoving things around.

"Got it."

Setting a large Rolodex on the desk, she went through it carefully, hunting for something specific, but not knowing what it looked like. She pulled a card out of the stack and laid it down on the desk. She didn't stop her search, however, going through every entry until she reached the end, making sure there wasn't anything she'd overlooked.

"Here."

She handed the card to Nick.

The card read: *Harry Watson, Greater Los Angeles Department of Community Redevelopment.*

"Looks like we got our man," Penny smiled brightly, the thrill of the hunt sending rubies to her cheeks, making her skin glow.

Nick put the card into his pocket and rearranged Gabriel's desk as best as he could remember it before Penny attacked it.

"Not necessarily, just a great lead," Nick smiled at her.

"This is so exciting. I mean, not like, the murder or conspiracy part, but finding clues that lead to other clues that lead to--," she grabbed Nick and kissed him.

"Hello," he said softly, pulling slightly out of the embrace.

"You know, I do live right around the corner," she took his hand and led him out of the office, shutting the lights off as they went.

Nick thought of what Hank had said to him about getting out of his own way. If this lead panned out, he'd be sleeping with a witness.

"Penny, I--"

"You can't interview that guy 'til tomorrow, right?"

"Right, but--"

"Then let's go."

She kissed him again, all traces of the shy girl he met a short while ago gone. Despite the potential consequences, he couldn't deny he was equally as turned on by the hot lead.

25

Ray awoke with a start, knocking over a tray of food sitting next to him. Someone had laid him on a green military cot and stripped him naked to the waist. There was a bandage over his sliced cheek and a dressing over the makeshift stitches in his back. A sling held his damaged arm to his chest. He was in a small room lit by a single, bare bulb hanging from the ceiling. The shelves around him were full of glass jars and the room smelled of mold and old cardboard. He appeared to be the only thing in the storage room not covered in dust.

The knob of the room's only door started to turn. He jumped back, shooting pain through the wound on his shoulder as he knocked it against some shelves.

"You okay?" a small voice snuck into the room before a delicate hand appeared on the doorjamb. Without waiting for an answer, a young Chinese girl, no more than seventeen, stepped into the room with him. Her nose was crooked and scarred, the result of an improper set after a break. She was missing several lower teeth, but had beautiful dark eyes.

"Who're you? Where am I?" Ray asked, still on the defensive.

"You passed out in the alley. Scared the dumb trick I was with half to death. Yanked his thing out of my mouth and went running down the street, dick flopping in wind. Would have thought it was hilarious, if you weren't dying in front of me."

"The trick you were with? Where are we?"

"Father's shop. Or my shop. But it brings in no money, so I keep working."

Ray's head was still cloudy, but he remembered something Pretty Boy had said. There was no way it could be her. Someone had to be setting him up.

"Are you De Zheng?"

She cowered against the wall, dropping the glass of water she had brought him. Neither of them moved as it shattered.

"How you know that? Who're you?"

Ray reached over to where his jacket was crumpled in the corner and pulled the jar out of the pocket, shaking the eyes at her. She shriveled more until she was almost on the floor.

"No... No... Not my fault! Tell Pretty Boy we paid!" she went into a fetal position and began weeping.

Ray thought he was being played, there was no way he was there by pure providence, but the way she shook expressed true fear. It could have been an act, but he could tell this little whore was no Meryl Streep.

"Honey, no, stop, you got it all wrong," Ray said, setting the jar down on the cot, his movement slow, like he was approaching an injured animal, "I don't work for Pretty Boy. I took these from him. You don't have to worry about him anymore."

"Luck of the Dragon Eyes brought you here."

The tears stopped immediately as she lunged at him, throwing her arms around his neck. He cringed as her embrace irritated the gouge on his back, but managed to pat her with his good hand.

"Don't know about that, sweetheart, but I was awful goddamn lucky to stumble upon you. Just happens to be a coincidence I was headed here anyway before I met with this unfortunate accident."

"You don't believe in the Luck of the Dragon Eyes?"

"No, I don't."

Nestor had said Ernie was watching someone nearby. It had to be Zheng. And maybe Ernie got too close.

"Where did Pretty Boy get those eyes?"

"My father gave them to him as payment. Why?"

"Was your daddy the kind of guy to cut out a man's eyes for keeping tabs on him? Maybe to send a message that he should be left alone?"

"No, someone brought them here. My father, he bought them."

He stood above her, trying to read her eyes. There was a deep fear there, but she was telling the truth. In his quick movements, he had opened his wound and his shoulder was bleeding again, staining the white dressing on his back.

"He *bought* them?"

"I'll tell you everything. First, come," she motioned to him, disappearing out the door.

Dark and musty, the shop was something out of a different world. Streams of light poked through the covered windows, catching flecks of dust in the air. A thin layer of dirt settled on various paper lanterns, dragon statues and smiling red Buddhas. Ray wondered if the Zhengs would have more customers if they pulled out a dust rag every so often.

She sat him down on an ornately upholstered fainting couch and went behind the counter. Moving a few items around, she pulled down a small jar of white powder and a large jar of black powder from a wall of spices and teas, all labeled with Chinese characters.

"Lay on your stomach."

He hesitated, thinking she was trying to get him to let his guard down, but he was already at half-strength and wouldn't do much good defending himself anyway.

She guided him down onto the fainting couch, the worn silk upholstery soft on his skin. He couldn't help but notice how tender she was with him as she wiped the blood from his injury with a wet cloth. His mind began to drift back to the night he'd spent with Sarah, her lithe body and soft caress. Searing pain jolted him from the memory, every muscle strained in reaction. A small tablespoon of white powder was sprinkled into the open sore, bubbling and fizzing. She put a soft hand on the small of his back.

"Please, relax. Let the medicine work."

He sputtered as tears flowed down his cheeks. A phantom smell of burning flesh seeped into his nostrils. His hands dug deep into the upholstery of the fainting couch as the chemicals did their work to kill the infected tissue. De watched him struggle, calm as a nurse set in routine, waiting for the medicine to take hold. Ray thought he might snap his own spine from the strain, before she sprinkled a scoopful of black powder over the white fizzing on his back. The pain was immediately gone and his body relaxed. She placed a fresh dressing on the wound before putting the powders back on the shelf.

"What the hell is that stuff?" Ray asked, wiping the cold sweat from his brow.

"Special medicine."

"Hurts like fuck."

"It's how you know it's working," she reassured him.

"Thanks, I guess," he said, sitting up, his hands still shaking.

"You stopped Pretty Boy from coming here. Least I could do."

"Who did your father buy the eyes from?" Ray asked.

"A man brought them. Put them on the counter, blood still on them."

"What man?"

"Said they were full eyes of rare red. Father knew what they were. He'd never seen them fresh before."

"Albino eyes."

"Eyes of the white ones, yes. Thought to harness the souls of long perished dragons."

"A bunch of mumbo jumbo," Ray said.

"Mumbo jumbo that cured your cut," she shot back at him.

"That's it? Your father just took a pair of human eyes off a stranger, no questions asked?"

"Wasn't a stranger. I didn't know him, but my father seemed to. Gave him all the money in register for them. Those and––," she went silent, knowing she had already said too much.

"And the hands?" Ray asked her.

Her eyes went to the floor. "Hands?"

"Where are they, De?"

"Father gave all he had the for eyes. When Pretty Boy came to collect me, there was nothing left to give, he gave up the eyes and with them went all our luck. Without money or Dragon Eyes, his heart broke and stopped within the week."

"The hands, De."

"They're all I have to not lose this place. I'll be on the streets."

"Streets aren't so bad."

"Please, no."

Ray looked at her. Those dark eyes, beautiful and broken, had seen too much in her young life. Without this dusty haven, they'd likely see much more horror. He thought of The Queen and what happened to her when her father was gone.

"I won't take them from you. I swear. I just wanna see 'em."

She shook her head, but her eyes darted to the jar of white powder, giving her away.

"There? That's them? Ground up to make some medieval Neosporin?" he pointed to the jar, standing.

De darted to the jar behind the counter, standing in front of it with her arms out, as though protecting it with her life.

"You said you wouldn't take them!"

"What's so special about them?"

"Flesh of the white ones brings special healing when combined with herbs and minerals. I already used too much on you."

"What do you mean? How much was the amount you used on me worth?"

"Fifty, sixty dollars. Only thing people come in to buy any-more."

"I won't take it from you. How much for the whole jar?"

She looked at him with suspicion, trying not to move from her position.

"Ten thousand dollars."

"Ten thousand?"

"Worth twice that much."

"I'm sorry to upset you, De," Ray lowered his hands, "I don't have that kind of money, I can't pay for it, but I promise, I won't take them from you."

She didn't move.

"The white one, as you call him, was my friend," he said, trying to be tender, "and he didn't give up his eyes or hands willingly."

De didn't stray from her defensive position.

"Thank you for taking care of me. I'll leave now, you don't have to worry about me."

De stepped forward a little, but didn't leave the vicinity of the jars, thinking he could make a play for them at any second.

"Please tell me who brought them to you."

"A man I didn't know. I told you."

"What did he look like? Was he wearing a mask? A blue mask?"

"No. No mask. He had strange, crazy eyes. Danger hidden under a demon's grin. Wore a jacket and gloves even though it was the hottest day of the summer."

Gloves would explain why there were no leads from the police.

"Anything else?"

"Mustache."

Ray stopped breathing.

"Big mustache?"

She just nodded at him slow.

Ray ran past her, into the storage room, causing her to flatten her body against the jars. He grabbed his coat, shirt, and other items and flew back into the shop, putting his clothes back on and patting his pockets to make sure he had everything.

Pulling open the front door to the shop, causing the little bell above the jamb to ring, he turned back around to her.

"Keep my friend's hands safe, De. And, here," he placed Ernie's eyes on the counter in front of her, "keep these safe, too. Don't sell them. Maybe they'll bring you some luck. I'll be back for them. Both of them."

He closed the door behind him and ran down Broadway, heading toward Echo Park. Ray Cobb was on a mission to find Benny 7-11, the bastard who'd murdered Ernie Politics.

26

Nick woke up early and silently extricated himself from Penny's bed. She moaned a little when he removed his arm from under her pillow, but didn't wake up. After he'd dressed, he went into the kitchen and left her a note, stealing a banana on the way out.

Nick glanced at the clock in his car's dash. It was early enough that Jenkins wouldn't be anywhere near his desk. Nick dialed the office, waiting for the voicemail to click over.

"It's Archer. I'll be little late this morning. Interviewing a witness, more details when I get in."

Nick knew it may have been infringing on what Jenkins referred to as his regular duties, but if Watson panned out, his absence wouldn't matter.

When he pulled into the driveway, his mother was on the porch waiting for him.

"Surprising, seeing you outside." He slammed his car door, checking his mouth for lipstick in the side view mirror.

"Thought I'd get some fresh air," she said, bringing a cigarette to her lips and inhaling.

"Late night at the office?" she asked him, her eyebrow going up.

"Amongst other things," he winked, kissing her on the forehead as he passed.

"You gonna tell me about her?"

"If you're good."

He disappeared into the house to take a shower.

Janice Archer sat in her rocker, smoking a cigarette, enjoying the morning sunshine tickling the edge of the afghan in her lap.

When he made his way back downstairs, she was puttering in the kitchen, taking out pots and pans, making a lot of noise, but not actually cooking anything. She took one look at him and burst into laughter, which transitioned shortly into a fit of coughs.

"What?"

"Did somebody die?"

Nick looked down at himself. Wearing his best Sunday suit, freshly shaved, he looked as comfortable as a six-year-old forced to take a family photo.

"I've gotta interview a suspect, Ma. I'm forced to look respectable."

"How old is that suit? Why don't you go find one of your father's?"

"You mean one of the suits tailored in 1983 that smell like moth balls and cheap aftershave? I think I'll be all right."

"You have time for breakfast?"

"Nope, gotta go. Coffee?"

"In the pot."

"Thanks, Ma," Nick grabbed the decanter and poured coffee into his to-go mug.

"You gonna give me a name at least? Throw an old lady a bone, I have very few things to live for."

"Penny," he said, avoiding her eyes.

"Penny? Like the coin? Sounds sweet," she added to get under his skin, "Is she?"

"Can we talk about this later, Ma?"

"Fine, excuse me for caring."

"I'll be late again tonight."

"Just be sure and let me know in advance before you get married," she said over her shoulder.

"Very funny. Have a good day."

As he rushed out of the house, Nick forgot to kiss his mother goodbye.

27

"Now these ain't the usual dose, but they take the pain away same enough. What you got for me?"

Lo-man greedily grabbed the handful of Vicodin from Crispy and handed over a worn copy of the Encyclopedia Britannica, Volume B.

"Really?" Crispy looked at him.

"I 'specially like the chapter on The Beach Boys. Informative."

Lo-man smiled as he walked away.

Crispy sat down on the curb and opened up the book to the entry on The Beach Boys. A wad of crumpled green poked out at him.

"That's right, mu'fucka," he smiled, shoving the cash into his pants.

The phone above his head rang.

"Crispy here. What you want?"

"It was Benny," Ray growled from the other side of town.

"Ray? Where the fuck you at?"

"Downtown. You have a bead on Benny's whereabouts?"

"I ain't his keeper."

"Shit. I'm gonna have to hit up Betsy."

"Hold up, Ray," Crispy said into the phone, standing, "You need to calm yourself."

"Calm myself? Crisp, did you hear me? I've got him."

"No, you listen here. Pretty Boy's dead."

"Figured as much."

"Was it you?"

Ray breathed heavy into the phone, "No. Might as well have been, though."

"Bodies pilin' up. I found out someone ended Flak Jacket."

"No shit?"

"Someone found him in Belmont this mornin'."

"Could've been Nestor, I just barely got away from him myself."

"Folks said they saw Benny at the tunnel last night."

"Those two are into some fucked up quest for glory. They've lost it."

"Maybe, Ray, but if that's the case, you sure you wanna go after him?"

"Took on his ass once already."

"But he weren't prepped for it then. He's ready now."

"I don't give a fuck. This has to stop."

Crispy rubbed his face with his burnt hand, the smooth scars scratching against his rough beard.

"Flak weren't the only one."

"What?"

"Some dude named Quarters, got it in Jefferson."

"Crispy, I don't have time for this."

"Well, you need to make time, mu'fucka. Both them boys had copies of that piece o' shit manifesto on 'em. Now you the only asshole left with a copy. Don't bode too well."

"Betsy still camp under Silverlake Boulevard?"

"Ray--"

"Yes or no?"

Crispy paused, looking at the Latina in a business suit at the bus stop across the street. She was playing with her smart phone, but if she looked up, she would catch him staring at the dark shadow between her thighs where the fabric stopped. He turned his back to her, trying not to make a scene.

"Yeah, you find her there. You want help?"

"I don't wanna get you killed."

"Just yourself?"

"So long, Crisp."

The phone went dead at the other end.

Crispy hung up the receiver and sat down on the curb. Pulling a small notebook out of his pocket, he opened it to the page marked "Clients."

He'd already crossed off a few names; Kenny Flak Jacket, Caravan Kevin, Ernie Politics, and held a small pencil next to Ray Cobb's name. A lump rose in his throat, ready to strike a line through his friend's existence, but he stopped and put the book back in his pocket.

Crispy took a deep breath and looked back across the street to see if he could get one last glimpse at those fine brown legs, but the woman was gone.

28

Sitting in the waiting room at Harry Watson's office, Nick couldn't get comfortable. The unfamiliar tie chafed against his freshly shaved skin, making his neck red and irritated. Losing the clean look of a collared black shirt and heavy vest was one of the great joys of getting off the beat and he reveled in it by avoiding the razor daily. He could feel sweat seeping through the armpits of the shirt he hadn't worn since his cousin's wedding five years ago and was pretty sure the wetness was starting to sink into the suit coat as well. It wasn't exactly the presentation he'd hoped for.

"Mr. Watson will see you now," the receptionist said, poking her head over the glass-topped desk. For a community organization funded by the mayor's office, the interior design of the place certainly was corporate. Nick could feel he was surrounded by money, something conspicuously absent in most non-profits.

Making his way through the sea of cubicles, Nick passed several young employees in business casual attire making cold calls and updating spreadsheets. A dark-haired, middle-aged man met him in the doorway of the office in the far corner of the room.

"Detective Archer," Watson extended his hand, "Harry Watson."

"Mr. Watson."

"Harry. Please. Have a seat," Watson said, taking his position behind his desk. His smile set lines in the tan around his eyes. He was accustomed to flashing the gleam of his white teeth and had perfected the grin.

"What can I do for you today, Detective?"

"Thanks for meeting with me on such short notice, I know you're a busy man."

"Happy to help," he said, the broad smirk never leaving his lips.

"I won't take too much of your time. I just have a few questions for you about a couple of your recent community acquisitions."

"Acquisitions? Detective, you're talking to the wrong man. If this is an audit, our accounting department would be more than happy――"

"I mean your new community center."

"State of the art. There's never been anything like it," Watson glowed at him, oozing with pride, "I've already fielded calls from five major metropolitan centers about the design and funding strategy. Would you be interested in getting involved with our community action programs? It's always easier to get residents to participate when we have a relationship with local law enforcement."

Watson was good. Nick saw him trying to work the conversation off track, changing the subject, supplying useless information. He hadn't gotten into the details yet, but could already tell Watson was trying to hide something. He twirled his pen, occasionally tapping it on the arm of his chair. Nervous energy fueled the ballpoint acrobatics. Nick could tell his presence made Watson wary.

"Actually, I had some questions about Keller & Hoff."

"Brilliant folks over there. They find some of the best hidden gems in the city. We wouldn't have half the properties we do without them."

Every time he spoke, he punctuated his sentence with a twinkle of laser-whitened enamel. Nick thought it made him look like a sadistic game show host.

"Were you acquainted with Marjorie Wells?"

"Oh, is this what this is about?" His manner tried to turn dour, but there was still a smile dancing a jig in his eyes, "Terrible shame. She was so young."

"So, you did know her?"

"Very well. As I said, she was my contact at Keller & Hoff. Really helped this little community reclamation project turn into a powerhouse. Even connected us with the anonymous donor who helped us with our own little remodel. We owe her almost everything. I wish I'd had the opportunity to tell her that before she passed."

"All your deals were done through her?"

"She was almost as good at her job as I am at mine," he joked, the ivory display returning, "I thought she died of natural causes? Is there something you're not telling me? Did the secretary do it after all?"

Nick tried to bury his reaction to the mention of Penny, but could feel his face go flush.

"This isn't about her death. It's about her business."

"Really?" Watson said, his feigned intrigue almost sincere.

"Were you aware, Mr. Watson, that the properties sold to you by Keller & Hoff had a history of incidents?"

"Incidents?"

"Deaths in the property."

"Certainly most of the properties did have a history of that. Most of them were very old, or had been occupied by transient populations. I wouldn't be surprised if more than one of them was the scene of an unfortunate," he relished the word, "incident."

"What if all of them were?"

"All of them?"

"You were never informed that certain incidents took place at your properties before purchasing them?"

"Perhaps they were mentioned in passing, but we try to keep a vision of what a building *could be* rather than what the building may have been. Opportunity and new beginnings are what we're all about here at the DCR."

"So you wouldn't say that you took advantage of price cuts once an incident happened at any location?"

"We'd purchase properties at the price presented to us, Detective. I had faith that Margie would find us the best properties in certain areas at the best price possible."

"But you *were* informed of the incidents?"

"There were times I was shown so many properties I began to forget my own name, let alone every minute detail."

Nick could see Watson's jaw clenching, straining to hold onto his feigned jocularity.

"So you and her would scout neighborhoods looking for viable properties?"

"They don't just fall into your lap," Watson said.

"Would you say the properties you've acquired in the past would be in the best location to benefit the entire community?"

"Where do you live, Detective?"

"How's that relevant?"

"Humor me."

Nick paused before answering, trying to assess whether he'd be giving anything away.

"Mid-City."

"No doubt just off Washington, in a condo?"

"Don't presume to know me, Mr. Watson."

"I'm just using you as an example to illustrate my point, Detective. Say a community center went up across the street from your condominium--"

"I don't live in a condo. I'm on the wrong side of La Brea," Nick said before he knew what he was doing, letting himself be played.

"Then you'll appreciate my point even more. Say in your residential area of Mid-City, likely on the edge of what we euphemistically refer to as a 'transitional community,' there was no place for teens to congregate, or the less fortunate populations to get the aid they need. Likely your crime rate would increase, yes?"

"It doesn't necessarily correlate."

"But it does correlate that if we put state of the art low income housing across the street from condos in an upscale neighborhood that it wouldn't be where it was needed. Correct?"

"True."

"So you wonder if I scout optimal property? Absolutely. I look for it where we can maximize benefit."

"I don't understand why you're getting so defensive, Mr. Watson, it was a simple question."

"I'm not getting defensive, Detective. I'm merely dissuading you from believing that in order to get a bargain basement price on a property I'd seek out places where a grisly murder took place."

"I never said murder," Nick said plainly.

"No, you keep harping on the 'incident' euphemism. My guess is that 'incident' doesn't necessarily imply a man freezing to death in an abandoned convenience store, especially in this climate."

"Do you have a record of your offers made on properties brokered by Keller & Hoff within the last ten years?"

"Like I said, that's an accounting question."

"I'm just trying to get some information, Mr. Watson."

"What I believe you're doing is implying that I'm some sort of ambulance chaser bent on snatching up prime real estate listed in the obituary page. I'm sorry I couldn't be more helpful, but I have another appointment."

"I didn't mean to be rude," Nick said, standing, "I'm just trying to conduct an investigation and would like access to those records."

"And I don't *mean* to be uncooperative, but those are private records of the City of Los Angeles. Given your line of questioning, it seems to me that you wish to bring slander upon this office. An office, may I remind you, that's in the business of making this city a better place to live. You want my records? You get a court-ordered warrant to look at them. I happen to know for a fact that a judge will require more than coincidences and circumstantial evidence to allow such an injunction. And even if you get it, I have nothing to hide. You'll be wasting a whole lot of time and tax payer money."

"I didn't realize you were a lawyer."

"Well, unlike the LAPD, the mayor's office doesn't just pluck its recruits out of correspondence courses. Good day."

Watson's glass door closed in his face. Nick stood outside the closed door for a moment, doing his best to restrain himself. He was going to have one hell of a time getting those records as it was, it'd be almost impossible if he threw a punch at the guy. Unbuttoning the top of his shirt and whipping off his tie, Nick stormed through the office on his way back to the elevator. He could feel the wide eyes of the receptionist on his back as he repeatedly hit the down button.

Watson opened his door a crack to watch Archer leave. Once the elevator doors had closed, he sat down at his desk and rolled his head to each side, stretching his neck and calming his nerves. Pulling up a database, he entered the name Nick Archer, Mid-City residence, and the cell phone number on the LAPD business card his administrative assistant had given him before he took the meeting. Once the results came up, he picked up his phone.

"Yeah," said the voice on the other end of the line.

"I've got another job for you."

"Where?"

"1676 S. Longwood. Mid-City. Eliminate all residents."

"Usual pay?"

"More if it's done tonight," Watson said, loosening his tie.

"On it."

29

Nick punched the paneling on the inside of the elevator as he traveled back toward ground level. He'd spent almost a month poring over cases where evidence was thrown out because it had been collected under inappropriate methods and now he was going in and doing exactly that. Watson was lying, but Nick had no solid evidence, and now Watson would be taking precautions to make sure he didn't dig any further. Nick felt like he was deer hunting with a bell around his neck.

He needed to talk to Penny. The direct approach had failed. Maybe she could get more information on the transactions from her end. Even if Marjorie Wells changed all the computer records, there had to be another paper trail. When he got out onto the street he turned on his phone to call her. The display read: *20 missed calls, 14 messages.*

"What the hell?" he said to himself before listening to his messages.

"Archer! Where in the fuck are you? Get in here now!" Jenkins yelled at him over voicemail. He didn't bother listening to the rest of them, knowing they'd be fairly similar, each with a different pattern of expletives, all of them driving Jenkins closer to heart failure. He dialed Jenkins' cell number.

"Where in the name of Shit Baked Susan have you been?" Jenkins yelled into the phone without bothering with a hello.

"Following a cold case lead, chief, what's up?"

"God fucking––I told you not if it got in the way of cases!"

"What cases?"

"What cases? What––listen you––son of a," he stammered, "I've got two slaughterhouse-looking crime scenes, a ranting and raving crazy bastard suspect, and a possibly dead missing witness in both cases! This is an all-hands-on-deck situation. Don't ever turn off your phone again! If you're in a fucking coma, with tubes to help you shit and piss, I'll rouse you with the power of my voice, do you understand me?"

Nick held back a snide retort, he was in enough trouble, "Where do you want me?"

"Where are you?"

"Downtown."

"Crime scene two, 870 New High Street, Chinatown. Check out prelims with forensics and then hightail it to the station, interview the witness we picked up down the block before he's committed or loses too much blood."

"You got it."

"Just my luck you decide to go cherry picking in the middle of a shit storm. I needed you there an hour ago."

30

"Based on the amount of blood on the ropes, here, I don't think he was holding the victim too long."

"Victim got free, though, right? They weren't set free?"

Gary Mankowitz tried not to show too much excitement as he explained what he found. Most detectives just asked a few key questions of the forensic techs, and then got the rest of the info from the report later. Archer was following everything he did, joining him on the floor as he bent down and pointed out the streaks on the concrete.

"From the look of the spatter pattern on the floor, there was a struggle, and either one, or both of them, was wounded. Suspect fled out the door first, spraying blood from his mouth. We found a mixture of blood and saliva in a sporadic pattern, like he was trying to frantically spit something out. Victim left after him, turning the opposite direction, the blood trail indicating a wound in the arm or torso, exiting this way," Gary waved a rubber glove in Nick's direction, asking him to follow the trail outside. The droplets continued down the alley, gory breadcrumbs which finally pooled under a Waste Management dumpster.

"Does it go cold here?"

"We haven't done a thorough perimeter sweep yet, but we assume he passed out from a blow to the head. There was a significant loss of blood, but not enough to render him unconscious. The wound may have clotted enough for him to have awakened and wandered away. No emergency service was alerted until after the other suspect was found raving in the streets. Wouldn't hurt to see if our victim made his way to an ER."

"All right, have the lead officer alert all ERs in the area, looking for a stab wound victim, likely deep and in the upper torso. He's either in shock, trying to get as far away as possible from his assailant, or doesn't want to be found. Both are reasons for us to try to get a bead on him soon. You said you lifted some pretty good prints?"

"There are prints everywhere, most of them old, but we managed to lift a few full prints from the knives, floor and ropes. If they're in the IAFIS, we should have a positive I.D. on both of them by early afternoon. It'll take a while to identify matches on the blood samples."

"You said knives?" Nick asked, heading back into the building.

Nick stood over the table where the knife set was laid out. They were in a rollout leather case and were of different shapes and purposes.

"They were well-maintained, cleaned regularly. We're going to do our best analysis for other traces of possible victims, but they're pretty clean. We might luck out if some trace DNA drained into one of the hilts, but that work is meticulous, it could take a while."

"One's missing."

"Probably taken by the victim. Cut ropes were found by the table. One weapon was found on the subject, but it wasn't the tool missing from this kit. Crazy S.O.B. almost cut his own tongue off."

"I need you to email me the photos of this kit. I'm heading back to the station to question our witness."

"You've seen these before?"

"I need to have Charlie compare these with photos of entrance wounds and old autopsy reports."

"I can do that," Gary offered, glad there was still somebody on the force who appreciated his work.

"You don't have your hands full?" Nick asked, trying to keep his promise to Jenkins.

"No, we're almost wrapped up here. Leave them on my desk."

"Can you look at them now?"

"Now?"

Nick ran out to his car and grabbed the extended file. Gary gave Nick a strange look as he took the files from him.

"You keep all your cases in your car?"

"Let's just say you caught me on a good day. And don't lose those, they're my only copies."

"I'll be back at the station in about half an hour. Let you know as soon as I can. You have a trail on this guy for a while?"

"Nope. Just today," Nick called over his shoulder, heading back to the station.

31

"Betsy, I know you know where he is."

"I ain't tellin' you nothin'. You ruined his pretty face!"

"You and I both know his face wasn't that pretty."

"Ray, youse a dirty fighter and a turd. I love him!"

"I have it on pretty good authority that Benny couldn't give one flying fuck about you, Bets."

"Gave me this flashlight. It's blue!" She waved the broken, muddy thing at Ray before shoving it back into her shirt.

"Where is he?"

"Check my butthole," she cackled with a wide grin.

While trying to spend time with Ernie, Ray had been regaled with hours of horribly detailed stories about the kinds of things that Benny did with Betsy after the sun went down. The thought of it, coupled with her grotesque mass and pungent smell, regurgitated bile from his empty stomach into his throat.

"God's here. In this tree," Betsy said, pointing at a small maple tree she had just scribbled nonsense on with a magic marker.

Ray knew Betsy Over/Under wasn't right in the head. Any interrogation would be tainted by the simplicity of Betsy's logic. She loved Benny, regardless of his behavior toward her, and Ray had hurt Benny, so Ray was the bad guy. He'd have to play on her misplaced affections and stupidity. Otherwise, he might as well be talking to the same tree she was.

"I figured out the map," Ray offered, hoping Benny was just as forthcoming to her in bed as he was to anyone who'd listen to the details of their encounters.

Betsy stopped licking the tree's bark and held onto it tight, like a little girl with her favorite doll.

"Dunno what you talkin' 'bout," she said, her eyes betraying her.

"Betsy, don't tell me that Benny never mentioned Ernie's treasure?"

"Ernie was nutso. Thems was just stories," she lied, now wrapping her legs around the tree and closing her eyes tight, trying to make Ray disappear with her mind.

"Maybe they were. But I'm gonna go looking for it and Benny'll be out his cut if I find something. Which means you won't get any more of the pretty things I'm sure he promised in exchange for the sick shit you let him do to you."

"Where's it at?" she asked, eyes open and innocent, giving herself away.

"This is between me and Benny. I don't know what kinda side deal he promised you, but if I don't find him tonight, I'm going after it myself and he's shit outta luck."

"You really figured it out?"

"Of course," Ray lied.

"No, Benny done told me he hates ya, no way he'd let you in on the deal."

"Just business, Betsy. When there's cash involved, nobody has to like anybody. Our deal is mutually beneficial. It's got nothing to do with how much we like each other."

"Why'd you beat him up?" Betsy asked.

"Benny broke our fifty/fifty agreement, claiming because he knew where the will was, he should get more, so we had a little scuffle. In the end, we agreed we'd hold the bargain if I went down and got the manifesto from *Her*."

"Benny was gonna get it hisself. Said you tricked him," she said, getting nervous and defensive.

"Betsy, I saved Benny from going down there. You think *She* would've let Benny out of there alive?"

"You got out alive?" she asked, reality starting to wander away again.

"I'm here, aren't I?"

"Swear you ain't gonna hurt him?"

"I'm about to make both of us very rich men. You're lucky I'm coming to you at all. I could've just gone and found the treasure myself, but I'm a man of honor. I'm keeping my word to Benny, no matter how much I dislike him."

"He had business." The words came out without more prompting.

"He say anything else?"

"That to say if anybody asked, he was with me all night."

"What's he doing, Betsy?"

"Thought it had somethin' to do with the map. Him and Nestor is always havin' secret meetins."

"Nestor?"

"Aw, shit, I done talked too much."

"No, I know about Nestor, Betsy," Ray thought fast, "Benny's afraid of him, so we're working to cut him out of the deal."

"I'm 'fraid of him too."

"He didn't say anything more specific?"

"Somethin' about Mid-City, gonna take him half the day to get down there."

"Where, Betsy? C'mon!"

"Don't know nothin' else. 'Cept..."

Ray was doing his best to not beat the answer out of her, but he figured she'd suffered enough keeping Benny 7-11 as a companion. There was probably just as much of her as there was of him on those coffee cup lids.

"Kept repeatin' Longwood. Somethin' like that so he wouldn't forget. One Six Seven Six. One Six Seven Six. One Six Seven Six. Over and over."

"Thanks, Betsy."

"Ray," she stopped him as he turned around, "we gonna be really rich, like with a house and everythin'?"

Ray looked down at the disgusting creature. He pitied her. She'd been promised all the gold in El Dorado and would end up with nothing more than a couple of broken dreams and a lover who'd murdered his friend for an imaginary pot of gold.

"Sure, Betsy."

"Hope you find him," she said with a broken-toothed smile, tears welling in her eyes.

"I hope I do too."

32

"Why didn't you wake me up?"

"Sorry, had to get to work and wanted to let you sleep," Nick said into his phone as he got out of his car in the station parking lot.

"Well, you're not forgiven, you'll have to make it up to me." He could hear her smiling over the phone.

"Gladly."

"Listen, I decided to do some more detective work of my own," Penny said.

"You didn't riffle through your other co-workers' desks, did you?"

"Maybe."

"What'd you find?"

"All of those database entries had been updated *after* the final transaction had taken place."

"Isn't that normal, having to update buyer info, final price, escrow, stuff like that?"

"I mean after that stuff."

"Margie went in and changed the incident status after the transaction took place?"

"Because if the current resident wishes to sell the property again--"

"They can do it at an inflated rate without worrying about the incident record driving the price down again," Nick said.

"Sounds like quite a scam those two had running."

"Did you talk to Watson?" Penny asked.

"I did, but he's pretty slick. I'm going to need some harder evidence to get a search warrant."

"What happens next?"

Nick was about to get on the elevator.

"What's next is you go about business as usual. I don't want to sound ungrateful, I'd never have gotten this far without you, but I've already discussed this case with you way more than I should've."

"But, I thought they were cold cases? Any information from the public and all that?"

"Believe it or not, something happened this morning that might jump these cases from cold to active real quick?"

"Really?" her voice quickened, "What?"

"Told you, I can't say."

"Fine."

"I'll keep you apprised of how things go. I just can't go into too much detail right now without jeopardizing the investigation."

"Who am I going to tell?"

"Nobody, I hope, but I may've already blown my chance at getting a statement from Watson under oath. I don't want to do anything else that'll send these things back into a file folder for another ten years, okay?"

"All right," she said. She sounded disappointed, but he could tell she understood.

"I'll call you later. Promise," Nick said, trying to sound tender.

"You better. Bye."

When Nick arrived at his floor, everyone was going through paperwork or on the phone. The office was teeming with activity.

"Naches, where's the suspect they picked up this morning?"

"Interview 4. I think they had to sedate him. Good luck with that one."

"Anyone talked to him yet?"

"They just now calmed his ranting long enough to stitch up his tongue. If you do get him to talk, it's going to sound like he has marbles in his mouth. Not to mention the mask."

"The mask?"

"He wouldn't calm down 'til we told him he was in a sterile environment and gave him a surgical mask to keep out continued contamination. That's what we could make out from his gibberish. If you can coax some kind of confession out of his nonsense, you should quit this shit and go work for Homeland Security."

"Sterile environment? How'd you do that?"

"We left the room and told him we were turning on the air purifiers. Turned off the air conditioning, turned on the heat for a minute, then turned the AC back on. Seemed to work."

"Clever."

"Hey, we try."

"Do me a favor? Mankowitz should have some work-ups for me when he gets in. Bring 'em to me right away. Cool?"

"You got it."

Nick made his way toward Interview Room 4. Hank was posted outside the door and didn't look at him as he approached.

"Detective," Hank said, gazing at the opposite wall.

"Hank, I—"

"Suspect's waiting, Detective."

"All right, you wanna keep playing this shit? I just wanted to say, thank you. I needed a swift kick in the ass."

"No shit."

"I may be close to something here."

Hank looked at him without saying anything before breaking his tough guy exterior.

"Listen, man. I was a little drunk, a little lonely, and a lot pissed off. Anything you need from me, you got."

"Thanks, man. I need all the friends I can get."

"Heard you went M.I.A. this morning."

"Following a lead. I didn't know all hell was gonna break loose. Heard you had to dose this one."

"Dose him? They pumped enough tranqs into him to kill a horse."

"You serious?"

"Dude wouldn't stop screaming. Before they cuffed him he was trying to tear his entire digestive system out with his bare hands. Fucked himself up real good."

"Shit."

"Whaddaya mean, shit? No drugs and fucker'd be dead. You wouldn't have been able to talk to him."

"Yeah, but if he gets a sneaky lawyer, he could say his testimony was acquired under duress."

"This guy ain't gonna get much more than an old court-appointed."

"Those are the worst. Even the ones we know are on our side have something to prove. Anything to boost their names to the top of the private firms' recruitment lists."

"Wow. You know what? I take it all back. You can have your detective bullshit political maneuvering, man. I'll stick to the simple police work."

"Days like this, I envy you, my friend."

"And I don't envy you," Hank said to him, opening up the door.

"CLOTHE ITH! DON'T LETH INS THE CONTHAMINENTH!" the suspect yelled, chained to the metal chair.

"Have fun," Hank smiled.

Nick closed the door behind him.

"I've been through the sterilization checkpoint Mr.--" Nick looked at the file in his hand, "Tyre."

"DON'TH COME ANY CLOTHER!" Nestor yelled in a muffle from beneath his mask.

Nick pulled the chair from the table and sat down at what he thought might be a fair distance.

"I'm not going to come any closer, Mr. Tyre, but I need you to stop yelling. I'm right here."

"I didnth do noththin'."

"On the contrary, Mr. Tyre. We tracked your little trail of destruction back to an abandoned grocery store. Seems to me your self-mutilation wasn't the only hack job you had planned for this morning."

"I don'th known whath you're talthing abou'."

"Why were you running down the street clawing at yourself, Mr. Tyre?"

"Conthaminenths! He thpit the poison in me!"

"Who did?"

Nestor was quiet.

"We know there was another person in that room with you, Mr. Tyre. And based on the lack of bruising on your wrists, I'm gonna guess that you weren't the one tied to that chair."

Nestor said nothing.

"Was that your set of knives we found, Mr. Tyre?"

Again, he was met with silence and glazed eyes. There was a knock at the door. Nick took one hard look at Nestor and got up. Nestor screamed again about the sterile environment when he closed the door behind him, meeting Gary in the hallway.

"What you got for me?"

"This shit's fucked up, Archer. I don't know how you happened on those particular files, but there was a knife in that satchel for almost every one of those victims. All except these three," Gary handed him the files.

"The diseased three?"

"Yeah. The HIV, the TB, and the syphilis."

"In all these other cases, this could be our guy?"

"Well, we can't necessarily prove those were his knives, though the evidence is pretty clear. Also, that's a pretty standard set; you could pick one up in any Army Navy store in the city. They're mainly used for field dressing game."

"So, we're gonna need some eye witness testimony on this case to link these knives."

"It'd help. Also, I haven't taken these apart yet. Like I said before, there might be some residual blood traces in the hilts. If we find some and if we match it to the blood type slides in one of these cases, we can get something. But that could take weeks."

"What about the other guy?"

"Here's where it gets interesting," Gary said, "Prints match a guy named Raymond Cobb. Guy we picked up for sleeping in an ice machine. He's had a few misdemeanors, the usual stuff."

"What's so interesting about that?"

"The screamer's crime scene wasn't the only thing we're dealing with today."

"Double homicide poker game in Venice?"

"Right. We got the guy that did that one. Twitchy little fucker named Barry Prestler. Confessed to everything. Apparently one of the deceased was running a dirty slave trade ring out of Hermosa Beach. Vice had a file on him a quarter-inch thick. Ran the game to recruit new blood."

"You're right. That *is* fucked up."

"You wanna talk fucked up? Wait until you see a picture of the guy. Missing his face. And that was when he was alive. Far as I'm concerned, this Prestler is a goddamn hero. But get this;

poker table of eight, six accounted for, plus the ugly bastard who got the stick. One set of prints unmatched. Guess who?"

"Dr. Contamination?"

"Nope. Ray Cobb."

"You telling me we find this guy, we solve two of these cases in one fell swoop?"

"Maybe three."

"What?"

"Check out the rap sheet on Cobb."

Nick scanned the paperwork in front of him.

"Nothing out of the ordinary for a vagrant, right?" Gary asked, smiling like the cat that ate the canary.

"Seems pretty standard."

"What about this?" Gary poked the bottom of the paper.

"Known acquaintance of Ernest Gaffney?"

"One of your illustrious eight."

Nick read the report.

"Cobb was questioned in the short-lived investigation, but was released."

"He might have more to say today."

"Tell Jenkins to get an APB out on this Raymond Cobb, he's definitely our missing link. Meanwhile, get to work on those knives, see what you can find. Thanks for doing this so quickly, Gary. I owe you."

"I accept all forms of payment. Mostly alcohol and cash."

"We catch this guy, I'll get you both."

Gary headed back to his lab.

"See, told you you'd be good at this," Hank finally commented, being a man who knows when to keep his mouth shut.

"Thrill of the chase, my friend," Nick chuckled and went back into the interrogation room.

"Nestor," Nick sat, giving up the formalities, "Tell me about Ray Cobb."

"NOOOO! DISEASTHED! NOOO!"

"Why'd you have him tied up in that room?"

Silence. Nick was tired of playing games, but he also knew sometimes you had to counter crazy with crazy.

"You don't start talking, we can't give you the antidote," Nick said plainly.

Nestor's eyes went wide.

"That's right. We know it was Ray Cobb in that room and you said he spit on you. According to the analysis of the blood we took off of the crime scene, he's infected you with a rare strain of influenza."

Nestor began to thrash in his chair.

"Mr. Tyre, struggling isn't going to save you. We have the inoculation, but unless you give us answers, I'm afraid there's nothing we can do for you."

"PLEATHE!"

"I told you, you don't have to yell," Nick said, trying to be as emotionless and clinical as possible.

"THE MAP! RAY HATH THE MAP!"

"The map, what map?"

"TREATHURE! ERNIE POLITTHICS TREATHURE!"

"Ernie Politics? You mean Ernest Gaffney?"

"Yeath."

"Did Raymond Cobb kill Ernest Gaffney for the map?"

"No."

"Did you kill Ernest Gaffney for the map?"

"No. Ernie my fthend."

"Who did?"

"I DON'TH KNOW! PLEATH GIVE ME THE ANTHI-DONE!"

"What about Chipper Willis? Did you kill Chipper Willis?"

"YEATH! ANTHIDONE!"

"What about Abigail Drummond?"

"YEATH! PLEATHE! I CAN FEEL MYTHELTH DYING!"

"Yolanda Bateman?"

"NO! NO! UNCLEAN! NO!"

"David Adder?"

"UNCLEAN! NO! NOT ME! NOT ME!"

"Who?"

"BENNY! BENNY! ANTHIDONE!"

"Benny Who?"

"PLEATHE! I ANTHWERED YOUR QUESTIONS!"

"BENNY WHO?" Nick screamed at him.

Nestor started screaming incoherently, bashing his head on the table. Nick leapt up and swung open the door, beckoning Hank inside. Hank and Nick were unable to get to him in time and Nestor had managed to knock himself unconscious.

"What the fuck did you do to him, Archer?" Jenkins asked, having run down the hall with the rest of the officers to see the commotion.

"He just freaked out on me."

"Get a medic in here for the douchebag. You get anything out of him?"

"Got him to confess to these," Nick said, throwing several files into Jenkins' hands.

"Sounds like you could've gotten him to confess to killing Mary Queen of Scots, fucker is so hopped up."

"Gary's cross-referencing them with the weapons found at the scene. Even if the confession is deemed inadmissible, any trace DNA evidence will confirm it."

"We got that APB out on Cobb, hopefully he'll put together the missing pieces."

"Good," Nick said, placing the rest of the paperwork on his desk before heading for the elevator.

"Where you going?"

"I've gotta find Ray Cobb," Nick said, "Oh, and if Tyre wakes up any time soon, tell him you gave him the antidote."

"What?"

Nick winked as the elevator doors closed.

33

The sun passed plenty of time in the sky as Ray made his way from Echo Park into Mid-City. It was already a long trek without transportation and the laceration in his arm had begun to ache, adding effort to every step. Whenever he had the chance to find a public restroom, he stopped in and took a look at the dressing, a difficult task with his forearm bound to his chest. The dust made from Ernie's hand had reduced swelling and prevented infection, but did nothing to dull the continuing pain. He had to be careful in his range of motion to make sure he didn't split the scab or pop the meager stitches De had put in for him. It was no wonder her miracle powder went for as much cash as it did. He'd never had such good care at the public hospital.

Even with the address he'd coaxed out of Betsy Over/Under, Ray didn't know what kind of situation he was heading into. Benny having business in Mid-City could've meant anything. He could've been scouting a new murder victim or doing something as simple as checking out an untapped convenience store. If his experience in the past few days had taught him anything, it was to start exercising some caution, starting with disappearing back into the population.

Between his ordeal with Nestor, and the long walk from the eastside, the benefits of the wonderful bath he'd had a few days ago were all but gone. He had to ditch his bloodstained clothes, stealing some out of an unattended shopping cart under the Hwy 10 overpass.

Benny 7-11. Ray'd had all day to stew in his hatred of the mustachioed prick. There were certain people he got a bad feeling about, knowing as soon as he met them they should be avoided. With Benny, he'd always assumed it was his disgusting mustache and habits, compounded with his smug, holier-than-thou attitude. He never saw the greed-fueled murderer.

Ray still had Ernie's manifesto in his pocket, but he wished he didn't. Nestor and Benny apparently believed there was a treasure map buried in the words of the hulking work, leading to a cache of squirreled away riches. Given Ernie's sociopolitical paranoia, it wouldn't be too strange to suggest he'd be keeping a stockpile for when he thought the system would eventually collapse.

It was always Ray's favorite diatribe of Ernie's. He liked to call it his "Meek Shall Inherit the Earth" speech. He could almost imagine Ernie on the corner of Vermont and Franklin, while Benny 7-11 opened doors for people across the street.

...We of the streets, we will have the power, because those that live in their crystal castles and glass houses will not understand what it's like to not have their food laid out for them in a supermarket. They

will not know a world without a warm shower, gas heat, or central air conditioning. The workers of the world will not unite, because they will not have the soap to cleanse their superficial wounds and will perish without the convenience of a sterile bandage. We, however, we will prevail. When the world of men collapses, it will be those on the outside that raise the fallen banner high. Society has progressed past the feudalism of the Middle Ages, but we, WE HAVE NOT. You have your cities, your neighborhoods, your districts. We have our territories. Toss your pennies, your quarters, your dimes. We will find value in that you do not respect. We are the people of We the People. You? You are nothing...

Ray always took Ernie's ranting with a grain of salt, but there was an inspirational power in his words. Certain choices had put Ray where he was, but the thought of everyone going back to zero, having to live by their wits, was a comforting picture of the future. He missed listening to Ernie talk. He missed laughing at his nonsense and nodding along with his truths. Ray missed his friend and he needed to find the man who took him away.

Darkness' spindly hands grasped the edge of the horizon when Ray finally lumbered onto Crenshaw Boulevard. A skinny woman, missing most of her hair and teeth, was bent over a garbage can in front of a Carl's Jr., looking to pick out some dinner from a discarded smorgasbord of large portions.

"Excuse me?" Ray asked with caution. When dealing with an unknown person in an unknown area, he had to be careful. There were all kinds of crazy out there and he never knew when he'd catch one ready to snap.

The woman raised her head out of the garbage and cocked her head at him quickly, like a songbird that can't stand still.

"Looking for a guy, huge mustache, gaudy clothes. You seen him?"

She stared at him, her eyes blank, before bolting away. Ray could see the blue and red bouncing off the brick walls of the Carl's Jr. drive thru before the first siren squawked at him. Two uniforms were almost on top of him by the time he turned around.

"Raymond Cobb, lay down on the ground and put your hands behind your back."

Ray started to do as he was told, then grabbed a handful of garbage from the can in front of him and threw it at the approaching officers. Running behind the restaurant and over the fence, he heard one officer running behind him, the other back in his cruiser, calling in the suspect identification.

34

"We have a positive I.D. on the suspect Raymond Cobb. Resisting arrest. Corner of Crenshaw and Washington. Officer pursuing on foot."

Nick thought it would be best to turn on his police scanner as he headed home for the night. Since leaving the station, he'd stopped every homeless vagrant up and down Hollywood, Sunset, and Santa Monica Boulevards; flashing the mug shot of Raymond Cobb taken only a few days before. Costing him his entire day and the full contents of his wallet, he was still without many real answers.

Most people he'd encountered weren't saying a thing, knowing someday somebody might be flashing their picture around and would like the same courtesy paid to them. Others shook him down for a couple of bucks and then told him they knew Ray, but hadn't seen him in days. One guy said he'd gone to Culver City a few days back and no one had seen him since. The rest were just loons.

He grabbed the talk box on his dash as soon as he heard the call come through.

"Suspect may be armed. Approach with caution. Must be taken alive for questioning in pending investigation."

"Identify, over"

"Detective Nick Archer, Robbery-Homicide."

Nick pulled his car to the curb, parking by a heavyset officer puffing down the street. He got out and flashed his badge to the running cop.

"Where?"

The uniform pointed behind a small bodega and beyond into some neighborhoods. Nick got back into his car and pulled a u-turn, cutting off traffic. In his rear-view mirror, he could see the heavy uniform call it quits and sit down on the curb, trying to catch his breath.

Ray was pretty sure he'd lost the tubby cop following him as he got out of the accusing headlights and meandered into a neighborhood lush with bushes and trees; plenty of cover as long as nobody was having a barbeque. He could feel the hot spring starting to flow down his back. Running had popped the rudimentary stitches and he'd lost his sling climbing over a fence, but he didn't have time to think about that. He had to disappear.

Blood pumping through his chest caused his whole body to vibrate as he paused to catch his breath. He figured they'd gotten his prints out of the warehouse in Venice and he had no way of knowing how discretionary Twitchy had been in his disposal of Pretty Boy. If he was caught, he was probably going to prison. No more fresh air. No more surprise sex sessions at The Queen's grotto. No more of what he called real life.

"Don't move."

Ray heard the safety click off the service weapon before he heard the voice. He went stiff.

"Keep your hands where I can see them."

Ray's hands went above his head, pain shooting through his arm as he raised it above shoulder level.

"I didn't do anything."

A hand grabbed his wrists and bent them behind his back, cuffing him.

"Easy chief. Fucked up my shoulder playing flag football this afternoon," Ray moaned through clenched teeth.

"You have the right to remain silent. Anything you say can, and will, be used against you in a court of law."

Ray was guided to a standing position and led out of the cover of trees and onto the street to an unmarked car.

"You have the right to an attorney present during question-ing. If you do not have an attorney or cannot afford one, one will be provided to you. Do you understand these rights?"

"You gonna read me the chef's specials, too," Ray said.

Ray's comment made Nick shove him against the trunk of the car and kick his legs apart as he patted him down. Nick found the knife he'd stolen from Nestor, as well as the manifesto, tossing them through the open window onto the front seat. Ray was placed in the back seat of the car and locked in.

"You dickheads need to fill your quota today or something?" Ray asked.

"We've got some questions, Ray," Nick said as he pointed the car back to the station.

"Well, you already know my name. I'm a Capricorn. And I like long walks on the beach."

"Nestor Tyre ring a bell, smartass? A map? A torture room? A poker game?"

"And a partridge in a pear tree?"

"You've got a comeback for everything, don't you? No wonder you ended up being tortured in Chinatown. You make the wrong comment about Tyre's mother?"

"Pretty sure that dicknose couldn't give a fuck about his mother."

"We've got him in holding. Sliced himself up pretty good."

"Wouldn't know anything about that," Ray smiled at the eyes in the rear-view mirror.

"We're just curious as to how you ended up at two major crime scenes in one night? You've been a busy bee."

"Didn't you just tell me it was my right to shut up?"

"Just making conversation, but if you prefer, I can throw some Boston on the stereo. You can rock out to *More than a Feelin'* on your way down to the box," Nick said.

Ray kind of liked this cop, he was a just enough of a bastard to not be an asshole, but Ray knew it was time to get out of the car. He couldn't risk losing the lead he had on Benny.

"I always preferred Kansas myself. *Dust in the Wind.*"

"Blasphemy."

"You're going the wrong way," Ray said, staring out the window.

"You hiding a GPS up your ass I missed in the pat down?"

"The real problem's a few blocks away. Dude named Benny 7-11."

Ray was trying to remain calm, but the further the car travelled away from Longwood, the higher his heart rate went.

Nick slammed on the brakes, stopping the car in the middle of street as he swung around to face Ray through the crisscross of metal separating the backseat from the front.

"Benny and the map? That Benny?"

Ray's frustration finally took over, "You want your goddamn map? Right next to you, there, on the seat. All you crazies can try to figure out the cryptic bullshit nonsense and shove it up your dicks."

Nick picked up the manifesto. "What's this have to do with all the shit that went down last night?"

"Listen, pal, I just wanted to find out who killed my friend. And now that I did, you, you son of a bitch, you and the whole fucking LAPD are out chasing *me* while the prick who mutilated him is still out there."

"Ernie Gaffney's killer?"

"You fucking care now? Now that you got yourself a couple of grisly crime scenes you can't sweep under the table? When it was just one freak albino stuck under a dumpster with his hands gone, you couldn't give two flying shits."

"What about Nestor?"

"What about him? Crazy fuck tried to kill me, probably killed a bunch of people, but he didn't kill Ernie Politics."

"But this Benny did?"

"He's supposed to be right up here. You want him? We can go after him right now."

"One at a time," Nick said to Ray, though he had trouble hiding his interest, "Let's get you back for questioning, in a proper environment, and then let's see if we have to go after this Benny guy."

Ray could tell he was losing his footing. If they didn't go after Benny now, he'd go underground once he found out both Ray and Nestor had been picked up. Disappear. Maybe even go so far as to get rid of that ridiculous mustache.

"Wouldn't hurt to check it out. He's supposed to have business up here. 1676 Longwood."

"How do you know that address?" Nick flinched.

"His girlfriend told me," Ray saw how it registered as Nick's ears went red, "Right down the street."

"What kind of business?" Nick asked, hitting the gas.

"You tell me. You picked up Nestor for killing Ernie Politics, but Nestor mentioned Benny, right? So maybe Nestor and Benny are in on the killing together. Who knows? Maybe Benny's down here scoping their next victim."

Ray was grasping at straws, but he could tell the officer's ire was up and they were going in the direction of the south 1600 block rather than toward the highway to the station house.

"If you're bullshitting me, I'm going to make what Nestor did to you look like a cakewalk," Nick threatened into the rear view.

He sped up the car and skidded off of Venice Boulevard onto Longwood, his foot to the floor. The brakes squealed as he pulled up in front of the small house, sending Ray forward, his chest slamming hard against the front seat.

"You stay right here and don't make a sound," Nick said to him, getting out of the car.

Ray couldn't figure out what had changed the cop's mind so quickly and why he panicked to get to the house. Apparently, Ray was better at manipulation than he thought. All the same, he was pretty sure Betsy had fed him a load of bullshit. Watching the cop creep up the front porch, Ray thought the house looked normal. Porch light was on, lights on in the house, rocking chair on the landing. It looked like some old lady lived there.

Ray propped his legs on the back of the front seat, straining to wriggle his arms under his ass, the pain in his shoulder causing him to cry out. Something caught his eye that made him start kicking out the back window without caution. The cop was pulled inside the house, the door slammed behind him, but not before Ray had caught a glimpse of neon pink in the foyer. Adrenaline surged through Ray's body, rage flowing down his legs as the glass cracked, then exploded out onto the sidewalk.

35

"I don't fuckin' care how much you're paying me!" Benny 7-11 screamed into the cell phone, "A fuckin' house! A fuckin' house with not just some old lady livin' in it, AN OLD LADY WITH A COCKSUCKING COP SON!"

The yelling brought Nick back to life, his head hazy. The pain in his chest was severe, a deep gash draining him like a bull hanging in a slaughterhouse. He could see his mother slumped in her chair, as their attacker paced back and forth in the foyer, waving Nick's service weapon to punctuate his point to whoever he was talking to.

"Done? That all you fuckin' care about? Yeah, it's fuckin' done, asshole. But now I'm a cop killer. How do you suggest I get rid of this little problem? The LAPD isn't exactly known for being forgivin' when one of their own gets disappeared."

There was a pause as he let the other party speak. Nick was losing blood fast, but he wasn't as dead as Benny thought.

"I don't fuckin' know. I didn't check the amenities."

Benny went into the kitchen and yelled back into the phone.

"Yeah, it's gas... No... Don't tell me to calm down. You ain't here... No, I'm not *used* to this shit. This is a new fuckin' situation."

Nick had done everything by the book. Pushing the front door open carefully, sweeping the room with his weapon before entering, but when he caught sight of the limp foot of his mother, he lost his cool. He never saw the fist come down on his wrist. As he watched his gun slide across the hardwood floor, a rusty blade was shoved deep into his chest. The knife was still in him, stopping the steady flow of blood from draining him dry. Every breath was excruciating, but Benny had missed his lung by some miracle. He'd seen a sucking chest wound before and had enough presence of mind to know he didn't have one. But he also wasn't getting up any time soon. It took all his energy to open his eyes. He didn't know if his mother was dead or alive, but he wasn't hopeful. This guy wasn't here to play any torture games. He was here to do the job and leave. Like he'd done with all the others. But this house wasn't on the market. Nick had just asked too many questions.

Benny turned on all the burners in the kitchen, covering them with magazines and dishtowels, before moving into the living room and opening up the nozzle on Janice Archer's oxygen tank. He made his way back into the foyer and Nick closed his eyes to play dead once more. He felt the badge Benny had yanked from his wallet hit him in the chest. It took all of his effort to not cringe at the pain.

"You pissed off the wrong people," Benny said to the body of Detective Nick Archer and opened the front door wide. Nick knew exactly who he'd pissed off.

Before he could raise the pistol to the figure charging at him, Benny 7-11 was tackled into the house, the gun flying as Ray's shoulder hit him hard in the solar plexus. Benny's back rammed into the stairwell and he yelled out in pain. Nick opened his eyes wide to the struggle in front of him and mustered all of the energy he could to crawl into the living room. He lifted his good arm to turn off his mother's oxygen tank and brought his fingers to his mother's neck, her old body punctured several times by the dirty blade currently living in his chest cavity. There was still a pulse, but it was staggered and low.

"Ma... Mom... c'mon Ma!" Nick yelled at her limp body as he tried to shake her awake. Every word sent a serrated blade of pain through his chest.

Nick grabbed her hand as he slumped down to a seated position, blood flowing out of his wound and down the hilt of the knife before splashing onto the carpeting. He never noticed how soft her hands were, the skin transparent and nicotine-stained.

"Nicky," she gurgled, a line of dark red bubbling the word from her lips.

He couldn't get up, he couldn't do anything but let the tears go as he rested his head on her shins, her hand still in his.

"Sorry... Ma..." he strained through the tears.

"Love you..." she managed to spit out before the light in her eyes went dark.

His hand dropped from hers as he hit the ground. The last thing he saw before passing out from blood loss was the two figures struggling in the other room.

Ray cupped his cuffed hands together and bashed Benny across the chin like he was swinging a giant mace. Blood and snot sprayed from Benny's nose. Benny brought his knee up and slammed Ray in the groin. He fell back onto the floor, Benny leaping on top of him. He landed hard on Ray's hand, breaking his thumb. Ray grunted in pain as he pulled his busted hand free from one of the cuffs.

"Doesn't feel great, does it? You like pullin' out people's hair?" Benny yelled at him, his mustache almost touching Ray's face, "Wanna know how that feels too?"

Benny grabbed a tuft of Ray's hair, pulled hard and sent his other fist flying into the deep cut Nestor had left on Ray's face. Pain shot through his newly healed jaw, the teeth cracking, razors slicing through his cheek. Ray's head hit the floor hard and Benny was left with a bloody tuft of hair. The sheer force of the blow had torn it out. Benny tossed the hair away and stood up, kicking Ray in the face. Ray's eye was starting to swell shut and he was bleeding heavily from his wounds. One side of his body was limp; his shoulder back out of its socket and thumb bent the wrong way. Benny leapt for the gun in the corner and Ray charged after him.

Managing to get a hand on the gun, Benny brought it around just in time for Ray to keep it from being discharged point blank into his face. The gun went off, scorching Ray with powder and lodging the bullet in the doorjamb above his head. The smoke alarm was going off in the kitchen.

Each of them beaten and bloody, the weary men struggled for the gun. Benny's eyes were wild and all sanity had left him. The tendons in their necks were strained as they struggled to get a grip on the weapon. The gun went off and both of them stopped.

Their grips loosened as Ray staggered backward. Blood gushed from under the limp, broken hand clutching his belly. He tripped over his own feet, landing hard on the floor against the molding of the front door, doing his best to hold his guts in. In a daze, he looked at his free hand to find he'd won the gun in the struggle.

Benny stood in shock, not noticing his other victim had crawled away, or that there were sirens approaching in the distance.

"Shoulda left it alone, Ray," Benny said, standing over him.

Ray turned his head in his semi-conscious state, feeling the life slipping out of him.

"I hate that fuckin' mustache," Ray sputtered, before using the last of his energy to raise the gun and pull the trigger. The remainder of Benny's mustache was blown up through his nose and into his brain. Benny 7-11's body hit the wall behind him, leaving a long streak of blood, skull, and gray matter across the floral pattern wallpaper. Ray managed a weak grin of vengeance before the spider webs spun thick through his skull, turning the room into a foggy blur as he struggled to hold in his torn intestines.

36

"That deal should be done by the end of the day, Mr. Byhn. Margie had all of the paperwork prepared and in order. All you had to do was finalize the offer. I expect to hear the results by end of business," Watson hung up the phone and rubbed his temples.

"Incompetent fruit," he said under his breath. The phone on his desk rang again.

"Watson," he said into the receiver, his glowing smile returning so the caller could hear it through the phone.

"All that planning and at the end of the day you use your work phone? Number was programmed right in. Just had to hit your name in the address book."

"Who is this?"

"I'm sorry, were you expecting a call from Benny? He's indisposed at the moment. Won't be available for any more jobs, I'm afraid."

"I don't know what you're talking about."

"I'm not trying to entrap you, Harry. You've done plenty of that yourself. What the hell were you thinking buying your lackey a cell phone? Even the corner boys are smart enough to use burners. You'd be surprised how easy it is to subpoena phone records when you go after a cop."

"Archer?"

"Surprise."

"There's nothing that can trace that phone back to me."

"Except the paperwork on the dummy corporation you set up. You know, when we met, I could've sworn you were much smarter."

There was a knock at Watson's door.

"Not now," Watson yelled at the secretary who had pushed herself in.

"But, sir, I..."

"That'd probably be the arresting officer. I would've come myself, but as you know, my mother and I had a bit of an accident recently. I'd hate to mess things up by getting emotionally involved. You may want to get off the phone with me and call your lawyer. But my guess is, he probably helped you with some of the paperwork on your shady deals, so likely we'll be investigating him too. Talk to you soon, sweetie."

On the bench outside of the DCR offices, Nick Archer turned off the cell phone and dropped it back into the evidence bag, before peeling off the latex glove and putting it in his pocket.

"You really couldn't have done that from your hospital bed?" Hank asked him.

"Then I wouldn't have been able to see him taken away."

"The doctors were pretty pissed."

"We'll go back soon enough."

Hank's phone buzzed in his pocket.

"Drees... yeah, hold on."

He handed the phone over to Nick, exchanging it for the evidence bag.

"Guess who?"

Nick squinted in pain as he reached for the phone, knowing he was in trouble.

"Yeah."

"So imagine my surprise when I managed to convince the nurse, against her better judgment, to wheel me down the hallway, only to find out my near fatally injured son is nowhere to be found. You wanna explain this to me?"

"I had some unfinished business, Ma."

"Put Hank on the phone."

Nick held out the phone to him.

"She wants to talk to you."

"No fuckin' way."

"C'mon."

Hank took the phone, holding it away from his ear in preparation for the string of obscenities. All Nick could hear from the receiver was a high-pitched squawking until Hank finally hung up.

"You wanna tell me why an old woman with Stage IV cancer, who can barely move, scares the fuck outta me?"

"Because on top of that she walked away from being stabbed nine times."

"I'm glad for you that your mom's still around and all, but she may be a vampire. Watch your back."

"Fucked up, right?"

"Naw, man. What's fucked up is she asked me to pick up a pack of Virginia Slims for her on the way back."

"Don't you dare."

"I ain't crossin' her."

"You wanna help me?"

As Hank helped Nick up, the flashbulbs and camera lights went hot behind them.

"You even gonna see him through all the reporters you called?"

"The son of a bitch almost killed my mother and burned my house down. He's lucky I know better than to jeopardize this investigation, or I'd be up there now. Lemme tell ya, what I've imagined doing to him is a lot worse than what he's gonna go through in lockup."

Nick turned around, the painkillers barely doing their job to numb the fire in his chest. He managed to catch Watson's eye in the barrage of media and flashed him the biggest smile he could muster.

"Pretty sure he just said 'fucking asshole' on the news," Hank laughed.

"That'll help ratings."

"C'mon, play time's over. You do remember almost bleeding to death a few nights ago, right?"

"You heard from Jenkins yet?"

"Would you just let the man do his job and focus on not dying?"

"All right, but if you hear anything you have him call me right away. Stabbing or not, I'm still the lead on this thing. If Jenkins did as I said and let Nestor know that Benny killed his buddy, the sick bastard will probably let loose all the details on his end."

"Just get back in the fuckin' ambulance."

"Good to see I'm still on the PC's good side."

"Waste of resources, you ask me."

"I didn't. But thanks for your help. Seriously. For everything," Nick said.

"Yeah, man. Wish I could do more. I'll come see how you're doing later. If you're good, I'll bring you a file folder with a nice little confession in it."

"Almost as good as a box of chocolates."

"Get back safe."

"Can't wait to eat some Jell-O and watch the evening news."

37

Bright lights shining behind his eyelids broke Ray from a dreamless sleep. White sterility permeated through his blurry vision, giving the figure standing over him a hazy aura. The deep ache in his gut was dulled by the steady stream of morphine, his mind wet with drugs. The bandages in his midsection itched, but he couldn't scratch them, his limbs heavy and covered with IVs.

"You going to stay with us this time, Ray?"

"Yeah," his voice lumbered from his throat, a grizzly bear emerging from a long hibernation, "Can I have some water?"

His pupils finally adjusted to watch the nurse at his bedside fill a glass and bring it to his lips. The water was refreshing, metallic and cold. After the doctor checked his vitals, the medical staff left the room.

"Probably better nourished than you've been in a long time," a different voice said from the corner of the room. Ray turned his head slowly to see the cop who'd picked him up the night of the incident.

"Think they're feeding me cheeseburgers through this thing?" Ray croaked, gesturing to his IV.

"Not likely, and based on that gut shot you took, it might be a while before you're eating them the normal way, too."

"How long've I been out?"

"Long enough that it was touch and go for a while there."

"You all right?" Ray asked, seeing that Nick's arm was in a tight sling.

"Been better, been worse."

"The old lady?"

"My mom," Nick said, "It was rough, but she's already complaining about the hospital food."

"Sorry, uh... I... don't know your name."

"Nick."

"Sorry 'bout your mom, Nick. Wish I'd gotten there quicker."

"If it hadn't been for you, I wouldn't have gotten there at all."

Ray stared up at the white, speckled panels of the ceiling. Tears started to well in the corners of his eyes. Everything just hit him.

"I could've..." Ray couldn't finish.

Nick stood and walked to Ray's bedside.

"Ray, you saved her life. Caught a murderer. Don't beat yourself up. I'm the one who put her in danger. We both gotta forgive ourselves."

Ray could see in Nick's eyes that he was talking about Ernie, too. Ray knew his tears weren't for Nick's mother. He'd been focused on revenge for so long, he'd never let the emotion break free.

Ray tried to bury the lump in his throat. "You tellin' me you aren't just healing me up for death row?"

"Far from it."

"Then you wanna tell me what Benny was doing at your house?"

Nick grabbed the easy chair from the corner of the hospital room and dragged it over to the edge of Ray's bed.

"I got put on the list."

"This was never just about Ernie, was it?"

"Not entirely."

"So, how'd you get mixed up in this nonsense?"

"I was working on old cases and happened to find a pattern in some homeless murders, one of them being Ernie's," Nick said, leaning back in his chair, "I found there was a connection between the murders, a real estate agency, and a lesser known department in the mayor's office."

"Wait... Benny killed people before Ernie?"

"A man named Harry Watson arranged for vagrants to be killed on properties he'd later buy at a reduced price. Benny took the orders from Watson and usually passed them onto Nestor Tyre. But Benny always picked the victim."

"If Nestor was the killing machine, why'd Benny kill Ernie?"

"Usually, when the victim Benny chose didn't fit Nestor's idea of cleanliness, like Yolanda Bateman——"

"——Zippers had the bug."

"Exactly. Nestor wouldn't go near 'em, so Benny did the job. Benny was sloppier, by far, but still knew how to clean a crime scene. Probably why he took your friend's hands."

"What?"

"Likely, Ernie got a hand on Benny in the struggle and got some skin under his fingernails. Easiest thing to do would be to take them with him."

"Ernie got killed because of a real estate scam?"

"That's what we thought. But there was no reason for Nestor to pass Ernie off to Benny. Nestor didn't even know Benny had done it."

Ray laid back and looked at the ceiling, trying to put all of the pieces together in his head. After a short silence shared between them, he looked back up at Nick.

"It all has to do with the map," Ray said.

"In the manifesto?"

"After Ernie was arrested the last time, he started getting paranoid, more paranoid than usual. He wrote out his will in his holding cell, confiding in Benny where it was, in case anything should happen to him," Ray said, trying to find the reasons he had ended up in the hospital bed, "Benny obviously hadn't told me the whole story. Nestor said Ernie told Benny that his will was like a code key to break the map hidden in his manifesto. Ernie assumed Benny had the final copy, could be trusted to retrieve the key, and find the so-called treasure. But I guess Benny got greedy and wasn't patient enough to wait for Ernie to die."

"So next time he got the call from Watson, Ernie was the likeliest of targets?"

"But Nestor wouldn't kill Ernie. Ernie was like his guru on the revolution and Benny knew that, so he had to do it himself."

"Might've been why Benny mutilated the body, to throw Nestor off the scent," Nick mused.

"Benny probably told Nestor that Ernie was killed for the map, but entrusted him with the final location. Nestor would follow the cause blindly."

"But you got in the way."

"Benny left the final manifesto in a dangerous part of the city before he knew its value and couldn't get it himself, so he sent me. I didn't know the story of the map. I still sure as hell don't believe it."

"Why'd you go?"

"I bought Benny's story. Thought there might be a clue as to who might have motive to bump off Ernie."

"What about the poker game?"

"Huh?"

"What does that have to do with anything?"

"Pit boss there thought albino eyes would make a fancy good luck charm. I went to get 'em back."

"You get them back?"

"I buried them, put my friend to rest," Ray lied, "likely you got plenty of evidence in this case, you don't need them too."

"Benny's dead, Nestor's locked up."

"And I take it you found out the dirty details of that late-night poker game."

"Pretty Boy was into some serious shit."

"Another lucky coincidence?" Ray asked.

"So this wasn't just about a real estate scam, it was also about buried treasure?"

"Any way you split it, it was just about money," Ray said.

There was a knock on the door.

"Come in," Ray said.

A small pretty girl holding a bouquet of flowers entered the room. Nick rose and kissed her on the cheek.

"Heard you were awake," she said to Ray, placing the flowers on the windowsill.

"Hi. Who're you?"

"Oh, sorry," Nick said, "Ray, this is Penny, my girlfriend."

"That still sounds weird," she said to Nick, waving at Ray, unsure whether or not she could shake his hand.

"It's a pleasure," Ray said, feeling the morphine drip start anew.

"I just wanted to thank you so much for saving Nick's life. I don't know how we could ever repay you."

"Just doing my job, ma'am," Ray joked.

"Well, Ray, before you're dead to the world again, we wanted to give you something."

Nick got up and with his free hand picked up a messenger bag, placing it on the chair. He pulled out a wad of paper that Ray recognized as Ernie's manifesto.

"Isn't that evidence?" Ray mumbled.

"This is just a copy. Penny has a surprise for you."

Penny took the document from Nick and sat on the edge of Ray's bed.

"*Begin where the soldier evolves to the great forge*," she pointed to the paper, reading it to him.

"Excuse me?"

Penny pointed to each word on Ernie's key, translating.

"*Komenci kie la soldato evolui al granda forxi*. It's Esperanto."

"Okay," Ray shrugged, glad he finally knew what the phrase meant, "so what?"

"While waiting for me to recover, Penny snatched this sucker out of my bag and started reading."

"Before I knew it was evidence," she clarified.

"Good thing you're a snoop, or we never would've figured it out," Nick said, pulling her to him and kissing the top of her head.

"It was 1944 that really did it for me," she said, excited to reveal her findings.

Ray was trying to get a handle on what she was saying, but the morphine drip was doing its worst.

"Look, here's the reference in the text to 1944," she flipped the document open to a point marked with a neon pink Post-it note, "*Across the deep water, taking the hill, as the allies did the impossible, but finally reached their goal, the end of the beginning and the beginning of the end.*"

"Ernie liked to use historical hyperbole."

"It wasn't just that, Ray," Nick said.

"These numbers, 1152, 1323, 1352, 1372, 1568, 1800, and 1944 on the other side were—"

"Achilles numbers."

"What?"

"Achilles numbers. Perfect power something. I don't know, something Nestor said," Ray tried to remember.

"I was going to say dates."

"Hmm?"

"I looked up each of those years and then found a corresponding event referenced in the manifesto, each of them with a distance, landmark, or direction. This thing actually *is* a map," Penny smiled at him.

"You just didn't know the starting point," Ray said.

"Where the soldier evolves to the great forge? How is that a starting point?" Penny asked.

"Achilles. The soldier," Ray smiled, shaking his head.

"Maybe there's a treasure out there after all," Nick said.

There was a knock at the door. Ray had never felt so popular in his life.

"Come in."

The dowdy gray dress of a nun from the hospital's chapel flashed in the doorway. Her eyes studied the floor, hiding her face under her habit.

"I'm awake now, don't need Jesus. Thanks, though," Ray said as loud as his voice would allow, his words caked in sarcasm.

"I'll come back," the small voice said, turning around.

Ray's tone changed immediately, "No, it's fine."

He looked at Nick and Penny, trying not to give anything away.

"Would you mind if we--?"

"Uh... no, we should be going anyway," Nick said, smart enough to know something was going on, but fine to leave it be, "Glad to see you up."

"I'll talk to you soon, yeah?" Ray asked.

"We'll be around," Nick said, lightly pushing Penny out of the room, her smile never disappearing.

"You had to come in that getup? Couldn't just dress normal?"

"Didn't want to rouse suspicion, they still have guards posted at your door," The Queen said, taking off the habit and letting her red hair fall to her shoulders.

"Can't say I'm in the mood for a conjugal visit, but I appreciate the thought."

"Glad to see being shot hasn't killed your sense of humor."

"Would take more than a bullet."

"You think that thing," she said, nodding to the manifesto, "was worth the trouble?"

"Found out what I needed to," Ray said.

She stood and went to his bedside. Adjusting the drip, she turned down his morphine.

"What are you—?"

"I need you lucid. We have to talk."

38

As the car wound through West Hollywood, Ray stuck his head out of the open window, like a dog on a road trip. After weeks of recovery, he still needed a cane to walk, but couldn't take another day in the hospital, even if it was on the LAPD's dime. He didn't realize how much he'd missed the open air. Having access to bath water and three squares a day was nice, but he wouldn't trade the outdoors for anything.

Nick pulled over onto Beverly Boulevard just off of Fairfax.

"You sure you wanna walk from here? That's a long way to go."

"I've gotta pay a visit to an old friend first, let him know I'm not dead."

"You know," Nick looked at him, an eyebrow raised, "you *could* be dead, Ray. Use this as an opportunity to start over."

"Too much unfinished business," Ray said, pointing at the manifesto, now dog-eared and marked with various page holders.

"You sure you don't want me to come with you?"

"No, I think I can maneuver this cane pretty well by now."

"I mean for police protection. That isn't exactly open wilderness up there. You're likely to trip a private security system and the ADT boys are armed. Rich folks on the mountain don't take kindly to trespassers."

"Not if I follow the directions."

"I probably shouldn't go with you anyway," Nick said.

"How come?"

"Whatever you find up there's private. Between you and Ernie. Hell, according to you, it's probably nothing."

"Or it could be the chopped-up bodies of twelve little girls."

"If that's the case, you've got my card."

"You got it. But I think my investigating days are over."

"By the way, almost forgot," Nick said, pulling out his wallet and handing a folded piece of paper to Ray.

"What's this?" Ray asked, opening it.

"Your paycheck. Had to register you as a confidential informant to justify the hospital stay."

"I don't want this," Ray said, handing it back to him.

"Fudged plenty of paperwork to make that happen. Keep it."

"So now you've got me on paper."

"That's up to you. I can keep you on the payroll if you have tips that lead to arrests, or you can disappear. You've done enough, you don't need to do anymore if you don't want to."

Ray folded the check and stuck it into his coat pocket.

"Having any luck on the home front?" he asked, changing the subject.

"Not so much. Penny keeps taking me into these houses, but none of them feel right. Maybe it's time for me to get out of this town."

"Stick around. We need all the honest cops we can get."

Ray opened the car door and stuck his cane out to balance his stand. The scar tissue in his guts still ached when he bent over, but the doctors said he was healing nicely and should be okay. Ray waved over his shoulder and hobbled over the curb before Nick's voice stopped him.

"Hey, Ray."

"Yeah?"

"One thing I wanna know before you go up there."

"Shoot."

"You seem like a pretty smart guy, nothing like most of the people I've seen wandering the streets. How'd you end up out here?"

Ray looked down at his new orthopedic shoes, then up at the bright shining sun before he fixed his gaze back on Nick.

"That's a long story," Ray said, turning around and heading toward La Cienega.

Nick shook his head, laughing as he got back into his car. Ray watched as it disappeared into the flood of traffic. He took the check out of his pocket, staring at his name typed in black print, and then tore it up. The pieces flew into the street, confetti in a tickertape parade welcoming Ray Cobb back home after a harsh and unforgiving war.

39

Staring out over the canyon, the cool breezes of autumn were finally starting to sweep away the oppressive heat of summer. Crispy was eager to continue, but couldn't help but join Ray in admiring the sprawling vista of the valley below. The fauna of the canyon was different from the manicured shrubbery not fifty feet behind them, wild and unfettered by the complex civilization built to either side.

Hobbling up Crescent Heights to the Doric splendor of the Mount Olympus sign, Crispy followed close behind Ray. In another city, such a place might incur a fever of bad jokes, but in Los Angeles, people paid millions for the privilege to live there. The steep climb to the top of the world wore hard on Ray's recent infirmity, and between short breaths, he told Crispy everything he'd learned from Archer. Crispy said nothing for most of the ascent, amazed to find Ray alive after his third brush with death. He was surprised at Ray's endurance as they turned the corner from Hercules Drive onto Achilles Drive.

Ray had spent plenty of time in that hospital bed poring over the well-chosen words of Ernie Politics. It wasn't until they'd reached the top of the world that he'd realized the depth of thought put into everything Ernie had done. Between 7940 and 7939 Vulcan Drive, the axial point of a cul-de-sac, was an empty plot of land. Hidden by a wall of well-manicured brush, a patch of grass—yellowed, but neatly trimmed—stood empty. Between two large mansions, the barren plot waited, once meant for a house to join the surrounding community, its potential never fulfilled. The lot had no address, nor a place in the world of swimming pools and movie stars. As far as property went, it was essentially invisible.

"This the start, huh?" Crispy asked, looking over the haze of the valley.

"Nope. This is the end," Ray said, cradling the cane over his forearm and pulling the manifesto out of his pocket.

"Leave it to Ernie to make shit more complicated than it needs to be. Where we go now?"

Ray turned to the first marker on page 15. The text was highlighted and Ray had written the event Ernie had described in the margins.

1152 - Henry II marries Eleanor of Aquitaine. *Henry the Second of England, first of the Plantagents, wed fair Eleanor, bearing the Lionhearted who went to the Far East, over the mountains of the Balkans to fight the crusades. I now find a holier crusade for the people of...*

"We head east, over the mountain, until..." Ray pulled back several pages until he landed on page 1152, "we reach a rock wall."

"I got no idea how you is followin' that nonsense."

"Directions go in order of events, not pages."

Ray turned the manifesto around and showed it to Crispy.

1323 - The Pharos of Alexandria is destroyed. *The earthquakes knocked this great structure down, and again, man in his infinite glory as the purveyor of great technology was once again bested by nature and that mean length of four hundred and thirty-five feet became the world's longest pile of rubble for centuries.*

Crispy shook his head, looking over the edge of the cliff, "We gotta go down there?"

"Yep."

"Then we gotta follow it 435 feet, huh?"

"You can turn around if you want."

A few hours before, when Ray had pulled the document out of his pocket, wiggling it in his face, asking him if he wanted to go on a treasure hunt, Crispy was still getting over the shock of seeing Ray alive. He never expected to be trekking miles into the Hollywood Hills, only to come back down the other way through the wilderness.

"We this far, what's a few wood ticks and snake bites? You all right with that cane?"

"I'll be better off than you on this steep terrain. Watch your step," Ray warned, sliding down into the dry dust and desert brush.

It had taken them most of the afternoon to get to the top of Mount Olympus and as they made their way down into thicker foliage, the sun was starting to retreat in the west, heat beating down on their backs before they reached a crumbling wall of stones, placed there long ago along a trail now buried by the natural undergrowth.

"You ever think maybe this whole shit was just one big fuckin' joke? Like one last laugh for Ernie?" Crispy asked, leaning against the rocks to catch his breath as he beat the beige dust from his pants.

"I did once," Ray said, placing his feet toe-to-heel in a rough count of 435 feet along the rock wall, "but there better be something up here worth digging for. If there's nothing where X marks the spot, then Ernie died for no reason. He's just another faceless victim of the streets. Don't know if I could handle the futility of it all. For the sake of my sanity, I hope this is the one time Ernie checked his sense of humor at the door."

Crispy was having trouble with the terrain and swore under his breath after nearly twisting his ankle on a loose rock.

"What's this mean?" Ray handed the pages to Crispy once he'd caught up, "We looking for a campfire site or some burned out brush from the last fire season?"

1352 - Pope Innocent VI succeeds Pope Clement VI as pope. *Just as the 199th pope, Innocent VI passed between two fires to purify his air of the plague, I have walked through the fires to the other side of knowledge. Science has been destroyed by corporate greed and the mass extinction of the perpetration of ideas for profit.*

"Anybody startin' a fire up here ain't gonna contain shit. If Ernie was tryin' to make some markers with a box of matches, he woulda lit the whole canyon up."

"Look around," Ray said, keeping his eyes to the ground. The trees and weeds had grown so thick it was hard to tell that a major metropolis was only a small hill away. Ernie probably wasn't the only one burying things out there. One accident and Ray would be there forever, waiting for a mountain lion to take a piss on his bones.

"Yo, Ray," Crispy yelled to him, pointing in his direction, "Look where you standin'."

Ray looked up to see a large bush covered in clusters of bright red flowers.

"So?"

"Come here," Crispy waved him over.

Ray limped to where Crisp was standing and turned around. The leaves had grown over some and a large tree had fallen in the path, but there was definitely a trail splitting down the middle of two large bushes, each adorned with red flowers. The trees looked ablaze.

"Least Ernie got creative," Crispy said, walking through the trees and stepping over the fallen trunk.

"You feel purified, like the mu'fuckin' Pope?" Crispy asked as he helped Ray over the log.

"Nope. You?"

"Shiiit. Well, maybe a little," he stood up straight, "What we got next? This here's startin' to get fun."

1372 - The Battle of La Rochelle. *Our battle will not be easily won my friends. Even when the system has collapsed, it will keep its name. After La Rochelle, the French knew their crossing north was over French seas, though it still bore the name of the English Channel. Their government may keep its namesake, but our Revolution will control the waters.*

"Why couldn't Ernie do somethin' easy, like 1492? Even I know that shit. Columbus sailed the ocean blue. It has water in it. And North America. North. Water. Shit," Crispy said, looking down at the dry riverbed they had to cross, to the right of where the sun was dipping down below the hills, "Battle of La Rochelle? I ain't never hearda that bullshit."

"Part of the mystery, Crisp. 1492 isn't an Achilles number."

"You said that before. Achilles numbers? You smarter than I give you credit for."

"Thank God for the Internet, otherwise I wouldn't know any of this either."

"How many clues we got left?"

"Three."

"Hold up," Crispy stopped, "You hear cars?"

They continued walking until the brush began to clear and they could see the shining metal of vehicles speeding past in the distance. Pushing some branches aside, the two of them wandered onto Mulholland Drive.

"Think we took a wrong turn, Ray."

Ray ran his fingers over the markers made on the pages, coming to the next Post-it note.

1568 - The Eighty Years' War Begins. *Time? Time is nothing but a restriction we've put on ourselves. It'll take time, but time is on our side. The Dutch cared not for time as they toiled eighty years against the dreaded Spanish. Eighty years? I would fight eight hundred years if it meant an end to corruption, tyranny, and lies. We'll let nothing get in our way. The civilized serenity of France lay between the teeming wilderness of war, and both sides crossed to make their purpose known.*

Ray waited for a few cars to pass and then made his way across Mulholland, hoping another car didn't come around the blind curve.

"Where you goin'?" Crispy asked, a horn blaring at him as he stepped out into the street.

"Crossing the civilized serenity of France, back into the teeming wilderness. All there in black and white."

They were losing sunlight and Ray's pace began to quicken. He didn't want to be stuck up in the woods after dark. Ray could tell that Crispy was getting a little impatient and he realized he'd never really seen Crispy with his feathers ruffled.

"How long we gonna wander down Mulholland Drive, Ray?"

"Be patient, Crisp. I want you there when I find what Ernie buried."

Ray pointed at a "No Parking" signpost. A small, faded American flag sticker with an arrow underneath it and the initials "T.J." stared back at him.

"C'mon."

"What the fuck's that?" Crispy asked, following Ray back into the woods.

Ray handed the document over to him, continuing into the brush.

1800 - Thomas Jefferson beats John Adams to become the 3rd President of the United States. *A Declaration of Independence is more than just pages written on parchment. "When, in the course of human events, it becomes necessary for one people to dissolve the political bonds which have connected them with another, and to assume among the powers of the earth, the separate and equal station to which the laws of nature and of nature's God entitle them, a decent respect to the opinions of mankind requires that they should declare the causes which impel them to the separation." These are not mere words. They are a beginning. But just as this document is a beginning, so the declarer waited in patience. First a declaration, then a revolution, and finally leadership. So here, now I declare....*

"So there's only one clue left," Crispy called after Ray, his eyes revealing his excitement. He stopped to read as Ray disappeared down into another valley.

1944 - The Allies invade Normandy. *There will be missteps. There will be distractions. But, some missteps will lead us to greater enlightenment. Some distractions will further our purpose. We will play the game of deception. Saying that we will land our boats on a different beach on a different day and then we will pounce, striking across the deep water, taking the hill, as the allies did the impossible, but finally reached their goal, the end of the beginning and the beginning of the end. But there is a hidden path for all of us. Take the next step that hasn't been revealed.*

When Crispy finally followed Ray's path he found him standing at the base of a tall oak tree, a shining beacon in the desert brush of the Laurel Canyon wilderness. A large "E" was carved into the bark. Ray was sore from all the walking and couldn't tell if the sinking feeling in his belly was from nerves or his recent surgeries. Ernie Politics was killed for whatever lay at the base of that tree. Ray set his cane across the tree's exposed roots and pulled a small spade out of the pack Nick had filled with various supplies.

"Ho-ly shit. It's real," Crispy marveled at the letter engraved into the hard wood.

Ray took his time digging, still unsure if he wanted to see what was down there. He didn't have to go very deep before his spade hit something that wasn't dirt. The dry dust of the canyon stuck to the sweat pouring down his forehead. Tightness in his stomach made every task more difficult and his bed rest had atrophied most of his muscles lean.

Ray got down on his hands and knees, though it hurt him to bend in half, and frantically cleared away the rest of the dirt, revealing an old, tattered suitcase. He stared at it for a moment, not wanting to touch it, still in disbelief that he'd found something. He took a deep breath and heaved the heavy parcel onto solid ground. There was definitely something in it. But he didn't open it.

"What you waitin' for, Ray?"

"Do me a favor, Crisp," Ray said, sitting on the dusty ground next to the suitcase, twilight approaching, "I got one more marker in that thing. Read it for me, would ya?"

Ray pulled a pack of cigarettes out of his pocket. The brush with death had given him a new attitude toward the cancer sticks and he'd managed to convince Penny to grab him a pack of Parliaments when she went shopping for crossword puzzles and snacks. He lit one with a small box of wooden matches from his pocket, crushing the charred wood into the dirt. Sucking the sweet smoke into his lungs, the nicotine sending a low buzz of flies into his mind, he waited for his companion to wade through the sea of pages.

Crispy looked at the final Post-it, knowing they'd been through all of the numbers. Ray had highlighted the final piece of text.

Y2k wasn't the only virus threatening to shut humanity down. There is a greater virus. Greed. Greed and wickedness can be suppressed but never forgotten. A simple act of greed misbegotten does not end the want. Grease to lubricate the gears of treachery. Oil to drench the soul in black ooze. Can you trade away your pain? Can you trade away your want? I will be gone someday. Someday I will be taken away from you by the spectre of Avarice veiled in Amicability. Scars of truth hiding the true scars.

"If I remember correctly Crisp, you burned your hand in 2000, right?"

"Lemme guess. 2000's the next Achilles number?"

"Why'd you do it, Crisp?" Ray asked, not moving, looking deep into Crispy Morgan's eyes, a thin curl of smoke dancing up from between his fingers.

Crispy tossed the manifesto into the open hole, his deep-fried hand going to his face, wiping the sweat from his brow.

"Did what I had to."

"Paying Benny to kill Ernie Politics for some mythical buried treasure? Sounds to me like you weren't obligated to do shit."

Crispy looked at Ray and started laughing, hard and deliberate, the low tones vibrating off the silence of the canyon.

"You think you got it all figured out, don't you? You find one little sentence in the ramblings of a paranoid albino and, apparently, you solved the whole mu'fuckin' mystery. That's why I didn't bring you in from the beginnin', Ray. You ain't never been a big picture guy."

"You're telling me Benny 7-11 was a big picture guy?"

"Ray, you dumb fuck. I wouldn't work with that nasty piece of shit if he served that suitcase up to me on a silver platter."

Ray realized his mistake, but didn't let the shock reflect in his eyes.

"You did it yourself. Benny didn't kill Ernie," Ray said.

"Nope. But he did kill Zippers Bateman and Freewheelin' Adder. So just take comfort in the fact that you still killed a guilty man, you honorable mu'fucka."

Ray took another drag on his cigarette, knowing every tainted breath could be his last.

"You don't have to hide the gun anymore. I saw you grab it before we left."

Crispy pulled an old luger out of his coat pocket.

"You like this piece? Traded a gram of black tar to Chipper Willis for it. Hung onto it for five long years 'fore I got any use outta it. Shame Nestor killed Chipper 'fore I could build up steady business with him."

"All that equal trade talk was bullshit. You're just a flunky pusher."

"Ray, the insults ain't gonna do you no good. I never compromised my principals. I provided a service. Benny and Nestor was killin' off my best customers. Couldn't let that stand. Like to think of Ernie's little stash here as a fringe benefit to all of the good I'm doing."

Ray's eyes were fixed on the luger, slick with new oil, while his brain was calculating the distance to his cane. It was leaning up against the far end of the tree, too far away to grab before Crispy could put two in his skull.

"All the good you're doing? Loading people up with heroin and killing anyone in your way?"

"Ernie's poison wasn't so harsh as Chipper's, but I kept him stocked in antipsychotics. His ass would be bouncing off the walls if it weren't for my little pharmacy. Ernie paid with information. That's how I found out 'bout Nestor and Benny's little side business."

"Ernie knew?"

"How you survived this long by being so goddamn naive? Ernie picked out the victims, man. Those he deemed too weak to pick up the mantle of revolution or some shit. He was just as bad as those two other fucks. I ain't the bad guy here, Ray. Had to put a stop to what Nestor and Benny was doin' and knew killing Ernie would set the whole thing in motion. Guess

Ernie caught wind of my master plan, set him to doing some rewrites."

"And you took his hands and eyes, for what, dramatic flair?"

"Shit. My supplier been askin' for them for years, son. He would see Ernie snooping 'round his place, lookin' for a way to cut me out of the game. Weird old fuck wanted to make himself some magic whitey potion."

"The old Chinaman was getting you the drugs?"

"Yeah. 'Til that little cunt daughter of his came snoopin' back around. Surprised that little whore was fooled by a bushy fake mustache, but tradin' human organs is riskier than narcotics. Figured a shitty disguise was better than none at all," Crispy said, transferring the luger into his burnt hand, "Now, why don't you pick up that there spade and keep diggin'? I don't wanna have to do twice the work when we done here."

Ray didn't move.

The smug look left Crispy's face as he pressed the barrel of the gun into Ray's kneecap, "You wanna push me? Go 'head. I can make it real painful for ya."

Sucking in the last bit of smoke from the butt, Ray flicked it over Crispy's shoulder and reached for the spade, using it as leverage to rise from his seat.

"You've been playing me this whole time," Ray said into the ground, driving the tool into the dirt.

"If your dumbass hadn't got curious and gone lookin' for Ernie's will, Benny and Nestor coulda gotten it their own selves and I'd be up here putting a bullet in whoever won out between the two of them. Fuck if I ever thought that suitcase was real."

"Why not just take the will off of me when I came to you the first time?" Ray asked as he ceased digging.

"Same reason Benny didn't. I needed the manifesto from Lindberg to keep the game goin'. Tried to go around you, but Flak Jacket and Quarters didn't have what I was lookin' for. That copy there was the one I needed," Crispy waved the gun in the direction of the hole, "I don't remember tellin' you to stop."

Ray resumed shoveling dust out of his own grave.

"You could've killed me when I came back."

"Sure 'nuff. But, you'd already gotten the will, gotten the manifesto, and started a rift between Benny and Nestor. You was becoming my best soldier. Figured while you was doin' so good, I'd use you to take out the competition. Ugly mu'fucka was startin' to branch out."

"Pretty Boy was a setup? God dammit."

Ray almost wanted Crispy to shoot him, the quick sting of lead ending the disgust in his own stupidity.

"I happened to offer Caravan Kevin somethin' 'fore he spilt. D'Arby had already given him a free sample. Guess it made Kevin easier to find when Pretty Boy came lookin' to get his money back."

Figuring he had dug enough, Ray threw the spade out of the shallow grave, just wanting it all to be over with.

"Well, that 'bout wraps everythin' up, don't it, Scooby?" Crispy raised the pistol to Ray's head.

"Was it worth it?" Ray asked, ready to take the bullet without fear.

"Don't know," Crispy shrugged, the futility of his response hitting Ray like a kick to the groin, "So long, Ray."

He closed his eyes tight, waiting for the sweet sound of the gun blast to make his world dissolve. The only thing Ray heard was a high whistle in the air, the whine of an RPG before it exploded.

One eye opened tentatively before the second followed suit. Crispy's burnt hand hung low, the weight of the gun dragging the rest of his body to his knees. The sharp, hollow pyramid of an arrowhead stuck out of his Adam's apple, blood gushing down onto his stained shirt before all life disappeared from his shocked eyes. The shaft of the arrow stood up straight out of the back of Crispy's neck as he collapsed into the shallow hole at Ray's feet.

"Took you long enough," Ray groaned, making sure he hadn't soiled his pants.

"I had to be sure," The Queen said, her red hair whipping in the wind. She held a crossbow fixed on the body, making sure it didn't stir.

"You sent me up here on a hunch?" Ray broke his cool, yelling into the canyon, "Am I just a fuckin' pawn to you people?"

"You've eliminated several threats to those we share the streets with. Can't you take comfort in that?"

Ray kicked the limp body of Crispy Morgan in frustration. He caught her stoic gaze and just shook his head before pulling another cigarette out of his pocket.

"You couldn't use a gun, like a normal person?" he asked, trying to regain his composure.

"Guns draw attention," she said, lowering the weapon.

Ray grabbed Crispy's legs and pulled him out of the hole. It would have to be deeper if they didn't want the coyotes getting at him.

"Aren't you curious?" she motioned to the suitcase, now flecked with blood.

"Does it matter what's in there?"

"A lot of people are dead, Ray. Shouldn't we find out why?"

He shoved the spade into the yellow dirt, kneeling down next to the package. Unzipping the suitcase, he flung the top open.

There, stacked in neat little piles, were the various drafts of Ernie Politics' manifesto. It was no wonder Ray couldn't find any copies at Ernie's camp or in his cart. This was his treasure. He had buried them all for safe keeping, knowing the person to take his place would need his riches to take up the revolution. Ray laughed at the sky until he cried and started picking up the drafts one by one to look at them. Each one was dated differently and he flipped through them, smiling with tears streaming down his dirt-streaked face, each page like a eulogy to Ernie's legacy.

"One man's treasure," Ray said, looking up at The Queen, his hands full of reams of crumpled paper.

"Ray," The Queen said softly, nodding his attention back to the luggage.

Ray didn't notice it at first, but a crumpled flash of green stuck out from underneath the stacks of ratty paper. Ray stopped laughing and tossed the bound documents to the side. The bottom half of the suitcase was lined with neatly wadded bills, different denominations, each packet labeled personally with a note of amount by Ernie.

Ray stared at the pile of money for what seemed like an eternity. It had to have been every dollar Ernie had scraped together from his time on the streets. Coins exchanged for bills and placed neatly in the suitcase to be used for future purposes unknown. All of Ernie's hard work and hard earnings buried together. The man Ray *thought* he'd known.

Ray dumped the suitcase over on the ground. He whipped off his backpack and started filling it with the wads of cash now mingled with the stained paper and dirt. When he was finished, the backpack bulged, like a corpse bloated with gas. The final wad of bills went into his coat pocket.

"Here," Ray held the backpack out to her.

"Ray, I can't––"

"Nothing good has come of this. You can make sure something does. Take it."

Ray placed the papers back into the suitcase and zipped it shut.

The two of them didn't speak as they dug into the loose desert soil. The bright moon illuminated their silhouettes against the oak tree as they filled in the dirt over the body of Crispy Morgan.

"Thank you," Ray said, shaking her hand, "Your Highness."

"My name is––"

"I don't wanna know."

He grabbed his cane and the suitcase and began the arduous journey back downhill toward Mulholland Drive, leaving her up on the hill, staring out over the valley.

With a twenty from his pocket held high above his head, he fished for headlights. The flash of bait enticed a cab to stop for him at the corner of Mulholland and Laurel Canyon.

"Chinatown," was all he said to the driver as they headed back to civilization.

40

De kept her word and hadn't sold the eyes Ray had entrusted to her. In fact, it looked like they had brought her a little luck. He found her behind the counter in her father's shop when he arrived, rather than on her knees in the alley. Layers of dust had been removed from the shelves at the front of the store and the piles of junk stacked neatly on small tables made the shop take on the look of a legitimate business. They didn't exchange many words when Ray placed the bundle of bills from his pocket onto the counter.

"It should be enough."

De took the powder down from the shelf without speaking, setting it down on the counter in front of him.

"Did you know?" he asked, his eyes piercing through her, "About the drugs?"

"Yeah," she said, her eyes lowered, "but that's done now."

"Sure," Ray said, not believing her, "the eyes, too."

De ducked under the counter and set the small jar next to the powder.

"It ever gets bad again, De, head down to Lindberg Park before you head back into the alley."

"What's there?"

"You'll see," he said, shoving the remainder of Ernie Politics into the suitcase, "Mention Ray Cobb, you'll be treated right."

He lugged the paper-filled suitcase back onto the street. The glow of neon orange street lamps lit his way as he searched for another cabby's pockets to line with dirty money.

41

Pink and rust set the sky ablaze as dawn enveloped the coast-
line. Beached jellyfish and strings of washed up seaweed, nests
for breeding sand fleas, speckled the dull gray of the wet beach
in the early morning. The sounds of the city had yet to begin
anew, the atmosphere filled with the sound of the tide sliding toward land, occasionally building enough momentum to
crash against the rocks.

Ray walked past several bodies huddled in the patches of
Santa Monica grass, passed out on park benches, and leaning
against the bases of palm trees. L.A.'s true beach communities; loosely organized in squalor like the associations of
riches among the gated homesteads of Malibu. Kicking white
sand into his pants cuffs as he walked, the resistance of the
soft foundation sending pain into his hill-strained calves, Ray
found a spot to rest.

As he dug a hole in the wet beach, the gulls circled over
him, picking the evening's garbage out of the sand and sea.
He placed the suitcase into the sandy grave and opened the
flap. The healing white powder had dumped out onto the
rant-filled papers. He set the small jar on the dusted stack of

words, and channeling all his rage, smashed the glass with the blade of his digging tool. The formaldehyde mixed with the powder to create a thick paste, Ernie's eyes staring at him from atop the pile, perched like a couple of cherries on a chocolate sundae.

"You son of a bitch," Ray whispered to himself, glaring back at the devilish red irises, "Had us all fooled, didn't you?"

Ray pulled a single match from his pocket and struck the side of the box. The head flared and the singe of sulfur mixed with the sea air. He tossed it onto the suitcase and the formaldehyde caught quickly, sending flames into the dawn, fire licking the sky as it mingled with the morning to light up the world.

Ray sat on the beach, watching the white-capped waves crash onto the sand.

Once the fire had died down, all remnants of Ernie Politics and his cursed manifesto finally gone, Ray kicked dry sand over the funeral pyre, extinguishing the smoldering ashes.

Walking back toward the city, Ray thought about how annoying it was going to be to get the sand out of his clothes.

Join my mailing list to find out about new releases at strange scribe.com

I appreciate you taking the time to read my work. Please consider leaving a review wherever you bought the book. Also, tell your friends about **The Last Will and Testament of Ernie Politics** to help spread the word.

There are so many amazing writers out there trying to get noticed, reviews are one of the only ways for indie writers to break free from the pack. It makes a **HUGE DIFFERENCE**. It doesn't have to be long, just honest. Three sentences are a big deal.

If you liked
The Last Will and Testament of Ernie Politics,
you'll love Nick Archer and Ray Cobb's next case,
The Last Dance of Low Seward.
Here's a preview...

Cold January rain spit into Ray's straining face. A mix of sweat and dirt dripped from his greasy hair. Polluted water filled the deep lines in his weathered skin as he cursed into the offending sky. It trickled out of the gloom in a misting stream, as though the clouds were trying to pass a kidney stone and piss was spraying out around the obstruction.

Soaked through, wishing to pass into the hereafter, the details of Ray's diet from the past day ran through his head. A tight fist squeezed his intestines as potential culinary culprits flashed across his memory.

He was usually careful about his pickings before he indulged in a meal. Fast food was the choice of most homeless people. The constant piles of garbage and open dumpsters made it a simple solution for a grumbling stomach. But Ray couldn't eat that crap any more.

A couple of years ago, he'd opened a door to a world he shouldn't have and got a bullet in his guts for the trouble. He thought having his digestive system blown to bits would've kept him from living a normal life, but his scar tissue had healed enough he didn't even limp when he walked. The biggest challenge became what he ate. Processed junk didn't agree with him and he couldn't exactly do his shopping in the organic section of Whole Foods. Good thing Ray Cobb was a resourceful guy.

The restaurants of celebrity chefs had grown in number as more cooking challenge shows were splayed across the cable networks. A couple choice visits to the public library showed him who the best restaurateurs were; who used the best ingredients, who didn't favor art over portion size, and most important, which chefs were perfectionists. High-end restaurants focused on small, flavorful portions, leaving the dumpsters filled with nothing more than carrot peelings and shrimp husks. However, perfectionist chefs would rather have their eyelids branded shut than serve anything that didn't meet their exacting standards. The result was a lot of dumped plates of great food. Delicious to the palates of the unrefined, garbage to the chef who detected a dash too much fennel.

These goodies were kept under tight security, the dumpsters locked to prevent wandering street scroungers from digging through the upscale leavings. Another short visit to the library taught Ray how to make a simple locksmith's bump key. A less intelligent guy would take this information and delve straight into a life of crime, then earn a stint in county lockup after a botched attempt at breaking and entering, but Ray had spent enough time in holding cells to know he didn't want to upgrade to an orange jumpsuit.

As far as he knew, there wasn't a garbage theft division of the LAPD. There were plenty of people arrested for trying to break into scrap yards, but not too many people busted for breaking the lock off a dumpster. Besides, Ray never damaged the lock. He just opened it, took what he needed, and sealed it back up, allowing him multiple hits on the same location with no one the wiser. Unfortunately, Ray must have made the mistake of digging up the wrong plate of grilled quail with plum char-siu.

And the problems kept piling on. Aside from the pissing rain and the knots in his stomach, Kelvin the Chatter had latched onto him.

Fucking Kelvin.

Plenty of homeless wandered the streets talking to themselves, having conversations with no one. Angry rants, hair pulling, heads beaten raw against brick walls—these were the people who scared the normal citizenry, prompting city council meetings about cleaning up the streets. But as long as ranters were engaged in an uninterrupted debate with an imaginary friend, they were content in their own little worlds.

Chatters were a different breed. They lacked the common courtesy to keep their conversations private. Lampreys of the homeless world.

"So you see, that's why... that's why, man, you gotta avoid anybody with contact lenses. That's where they put the cameras. Get off the grid to avoid them man, cuz—"

"Get the fuck away from me," Ray strained.

Ray had screamed, thrown stones, and even beaten Kelvin with a fallen branch. Every attempt to get rid of the dirty son of a bitch had failed. When he thought Kelvin was gone for good, a needle of pain would stab at him and he'd have to stop. And when he stopped, it was always long enough for Kelvin to either build up enough courage to approach him again, or forget Ray was the man who'd beat him with sticks.

Another powerful ripple sent an aftershock through his abdomen and Ray doubled over.

"No, you gotta listen, man, this shit here is important, lemme tell you—"

Ray sprang from his squat, rage taking over. He pressed his elbow down onto The Chatter's sternum, hoping he could snap one of his ribs and puncture one of his lungs, silencing the stream of bullshit. The Chatter flailed beneath him, eyes bulged, face red.

"Shut. The. Fuck. U—"

Ray's bowels trumpeted, filling his pants with warm wetness.

"Ah, fuck me," Ray cursed to himself.

He let go of The Chatter's neck and rolled off of him. Shitting his pants had sobered Ray out of his fury and relieved much of the tension in his GI tract.

He sat in his own filth and smiled with strange gratitude as he looked at the limp body beside him. He checked Kelvin's pulse and sighed in relief when he found a heartbeat, shallow but present. Ray had killed before, but had never murdered anybody. He wasn't about to start a life of homicide because some asshole wouldn't shut up.

Ray kicked his shoes off, along with his soiled pants and underwear, using the cleanest parts to wipe away the residue dripping into his socks. He tossed his dungarees into the bushes and yanked off Kelvin's pants from the ankles. Stealing a man's pants went against Ray's code of ethics, but the chatty fuck had caused him to lose control of his temper and his sphincter. Ray considered it a win he hadn't choked the life out of the talkative bastard.

He slipped on his victim's pants and found them too tight to button. He didn't mind. His gut needed as much room as he could give it.

The Chatter was beginning to groan back to life as Ray made his way down the hill through the trees. He transferred his small collection of possessions into his pockets and found five bucks in the jeans. It was the first good thing to happen to him in the last twenty-four hours.

The pharmacy on Hill Street was still open, one of the few glowing lights in Chinatown. As Ray stepped through the automatic doors, he passed by another skinny homeless man writing on a stolen sales flyer with a broken pencil, the paper close to his face.

"Hey, Notebook," Ray said. Garrett "Notebook" Wilson, didn't bother to grunt in reply.

"Fourteen different kinds of gum, nine types of mints, one cunt-sucking prick face," Notebook said to himself. He walked through the parking lot up toward the highway.

"Good to see you too, Notebook," Ray called to the skinny man's back, not expecting an answer.

He took a glance down the aisles, looking for a restroom sign. Nothing.

"You got a bathroom in here?" he asked the clerk running the only open register.

"You guys part of a club or something? Employees only."

"Make an exception?"

He presented his newly acquired five bucks.

The clerk gave him a look before sighing into, "You gonna buy something?"

Ray figured the clerk must have been the "cunt-sucking prick face" Notebook catalogued. He shoved the worn bill back into his pocket and headed into the store, tempted to drop his pants in the aisle next to the Ruffles and Oreos, leaving the smug dickhead behind the counter to clean up after him.

He grabbed a Snickers and shook it in the security mirror the clerk was using to keep an eye on him. Another lap of the store brought him to the stomach aides and he was able to swipe a box of chewable Pepto-Bismol off the shelf and shove it into his pocket when the clerk decided to answer an incoming text message.

Ray plunked the candy bar and a bottle of water down on the counter and flicked the crumpled five-dollar bill at the clerk.

"Now can I use your toilet?"

"Employees only," the clerk said.

Ray's anger bubbled just below the surface, but he'd already expended enough adrenaline taking out Kelvin.

"Keep the change," Ray grumbled.

The clerk scoffed at him, picked the cash up off the floor, and shoved it into the register. He made a point to squeeze out a handful of anti-bacterial gel. As the doors slid open, Ray heard the clerk mumble under his breath, "Fuck you, you filthy hobo." It gave him pause, but Ray decided it wasn't worth getting into another scrum. He stepped back into the rain.

With half the box of Pepto chewed and washed down, even the waft of pink wintergreen wasn't strong enough to get the residual smell of his accident out of his nose.

He sighed and rubbed the familiar scars under his shirt. The cramps were still present, but dulled. He'd feel better once he had a chance to lie down.

The neon lights of the Foo-Chow Restaurant were a beacon in the distance. Home sweet home.

While most of the city was trying to decide whether it was worth their rental dollars to get a one bedroom with a bigger living room in exchange for access to a washer and dryer, Ray had a smaller list of amenity requests. Warm and dry were at the top of the list. It was also nice to find a place where he wouldn't be ass-raped by a broken bottle in his sleep. If Ray managed to find a special corner of Los Angeles he could make his own, soon there was going to be somebody ready to fight him for it. He tended to avoid altercations, but it was part of life on the streets. He'd won just as many fights as he'd lost, and found even when he'd won a claim, it never seemed worth the cracked tooth or bruised ribs.

The 1974 Chevy Impala abandoned in the Foo-Chow parking lot looked like it had been sitting there for decades. The hood was almost completely rusted through. Small patches of dull yellow paint along the door panels were the only things betraying the car's original color. The tires had probably been flat when the car was left for dead, all of them rotted off the frames, strings of rubber melted into the pavement, the rims scraping the blacktop. Most of the interior had been chewed through, tufts of soiled cotton-poly filling spilling out among the rusty springs and rat droppings. Some other resident had layered the inside in newspaper, old enough to be cracking with age. When Ray found it, there didn't appear to be anyone living in it. His claim to the warm place to sleep had gone unchallenged for a week. Ever since his bowels had rebelled, he'd dreamt of curling up in a fetal position in the back seat.

The Foo-Chow valet lit a cigarette in the doorway of the restaurant and headed down the street, popping the collar of his windbreaker against the damp. The cherry of his cigarette struggled to glow in the rain. Based on the Impala's fixture in the lot, Ray doubted the valet gave a shit whether or not anybody lived in it, but with his intestinal difficulties, he didn't want to run the risk of being found out. He waited until the lights inside the restaurant went dark, leaving only the humming glow of neon.

His hand was on the door handle before he saw the form of a body in the backseat through the dust-layered window.

"Are you fucking kidding me?"

Ray was in no physical condition to get into another fight. Even if he got a drop on the car's new resident, there was no guarantee he would have the upper hand.

Ready to put a fist through the window, Ray took a deep breath and two steps back. Remembering the candy bar he'd bought, he unwrapped it with shaking hands and dug into it, the first food he'd had since that morning. It wasn't going to be good for his sensitive stomach, but he hoped the sugar rush would provide him with enough energy to send the squatter packing. He was so pissed off, he needed to find comfort in anything that might turn the day in his favor.

He sucked at the caramel stuck to his teeth as he made his way into the alley behind the restaurant. The residents of the surrounding apartments treated the alley like they'd never left the Shanghai slums. There was rotting detritus strewn about everywhere. Stained clothes and stinking trash overflowed in small narrows where garbage trucks didn't fit and sanitation workers didn't investigate. Ray pried an old two-by-four off the pile of a half-built shed, complete with a snarl of rusty nails. If he couldn't best his new nemesis, at least he could give the fucker tetanus.

Ray whipped open the door of the Impala, the two-by-four raised over his head.

"Hey fuckface. Find some other place to sleep."

The figure didn't stir.

"Hey!" He kicked the sole of the man's dirty bare foot.

Nothing.

Ray smiled. The drunk asshole fell asleep in the wrong spot, now he would wake up on the wet pavement.

He placed the two-by-four at his feet, careful to keep it within range if the guy came to, grabbed the drunk's ankles, and yanked. The weight didn't move easily and a load of old newspaper came along with him out onto the blacktop. The drunk's bare feet slammed into the pavement with a force Ray was sure would rouse him awake, but no dice. Wanting to get more leverage, he grabbed the guy by the collar of his jacket and pulled, hoping to get him as far away from the car as possible. After a couple steps, his feet slipped from underneath him and he fell on his ass, the drunk's head resting in his lap. It wasn't until that moment that Ray noticed how loose the drunk's neck was.

The blinking neon sign highlighted the man's face with a glow of pink and green. It didn't matter how blitzed Ray got, he never passed out with his eyes open. And the red lines ringing the man's throat were a sure sign he hadn't died of natural causes.

"Fuck."

Eye witnesses tended to misremember things, but if he was lucky enough to get someone who saw him drag the body out of the car instead of being the one who put it there, there'd be a reason his fingerprints were all over the victim's jacket.

He pushed the body off his lap and got back to his feet. He looked around to see if there was anyone in the area. The street was empty.

If he left the body out in the rain, it would be discovered right away. If not that night, then first thing in the morning. By that time, the rain would've washed away most of the evidence of Ray's tampering, but it would also wash away any evidence of whoever had actually killed the guy.

He decided his best bet would be to get the body back into the car, preserving anything that hadn't already been washed away, then he'd call it in. He'd spent enough time trying to avoid police interference to know calling them wasn't always the best course of action. Then again, he was more likely to get a fair shake if he called in the body. The murderer only called the police in the plots of those cheap novels shelved across from the toilet paper in the supermarket.

Ray put his hands under the man's armpits. He noticed the suit coat was well-tailored, raindrops beading on the shiny wool. If the guy had been breathing, Ray might've thought to take it as a toll for occupying his squat, a warm coat to match his new pants. The sleeves bunched up as he dragged the heavy corpse and he caught the faint outline of a tattoo on the dead man's forearm. Whoever this guy was, he wasn't in Ray's social circle.

A flash of rotating red and blue halted his movement. He dropped the body and placed his hands over his head.

There was a new sinking feeling in his stomach and it had nothing to do with what he'd eaten.

To buy
The Last Dance of Low Seward
Visit Strangescribe.com/books

Brad Grusnick graduated from Northwestern University with a Bachelor's Degree in Theatre. He also studied Comedy Writing at The Second City Chicago. He is originally from Wausau, WI and lives in Los Angeles. This is his first novel.

The characters in this novel sometimes make light of their situation on the streets, but homelessness is a real problem in the world. For more information on how you can help in the fight against the homelessness epidemic in the United States and throughout the world, please visit:

Nationalhomeless.org

ighomelessness.org